C000055663

Published by Acoustical Books, LLC

KenLozito.com

Cover design by Tom Edwards

IF YOU WOULD LIKE TO BE NOTIFIED WHEN MY NEXT BOOK IS RELEASED VISIT


WWW.KENLOZITO.COM

Paperback ISBN: 978-1-945223-64-8

Hardback ISBN: 978-1-945223-65-5

e. He believes he's the remnant consciousness of a
ose body died long ago. It was all a lie, but I couldn't
Kierenbot of that.

ought it would be much easier to catch up to Serena
n, but that all changed when I received *that* message.
ays Raylin had instructed us to reach them had gone
ed, which made me believe they were in serious trouble.
is an alien—a shapeshifter with a mysterious past. I
could handle herself; it was Serena I was concerned
e's Human, and when we were on the ship together, the
ed after each other. It had been less than a year since
abducted from Earth and all our lives changed, and I
elp the certainty in my gut that Serena was in way over

ald've been easy to catch up to them.

wrong.

I just didn't want to be too late. The man who'd saved
d asked me to keep his daughter safe. It was his dying
I was failing to live up to it.

ened my jaw, teeth clenching a little as I stared at the
a on the main holoscreen.

*s for saddling me with that, Flynn.*

ed heavily. I'd asked her not to go, but she wouldn't
'd been on the trail of the Asherah, a civilization that
all others in our galaxy, and it turned out that they
en *from* our galaxy. I thought we were making the find
ne, and we were, but we didn't have much to show for
lot of injuries and a whole lot of terrifying memories.

bed my arm where the metallic tattoo had been from
ah artifact. It was gone, along with Larry—the being
d us find the Asherah ruins. Sometimes my arm itched
rtifact was still there.

# SPACE RAIDERS

## DARK MENACE

## KEN LOZITO

ACOUSTICAL BOOKS LLC

intellige
being w
convinc
   I'd t
and Ra
All  the
unansw
   Ray
knew s
about.
crew lo
we'd be
couldn'
her hea
   It s
   I w
   No
my life
wish, a
   I ti
star sys
   *Th*
   I s
listen.
predat
weren'
of a li
it—ju
   I
the A
that h
as if t

# CHAPT

stared as the ship's scanners re
with the shattered remains of st
luck to become entangled. No
rocky remnants strewn out from the
as if the bones of the planets were
together to restore the magnificence

   I'd seen worse places, a lot wors
tion looked to have happened quite a

   The edges of my lips lifted a little
travels, assessing star systems had bec
occurrence. What I once would've st
much more familiar. I still appreciat
bring myself to care about it all that n

   I heaved a sigh and looked at Kier

   "Negative, Captain. Still no res
Serena."

   Kierenbot is a humanoid robot

If Serena had just waited instead of going off to search for the origins of the Human abductions, I wouldn't be here right now, searching for her. She'd be safe. Instead, something was wrong. I knew it in my bones, and I had a pretty good guess as to who was responsible.

I've made some enemies. People like Flynn, my old mentor and friend, would say I have a talent for it.

"What about the other scan?" I asked.

Kierenbot turned toward me, and the red orb that tracked across a sensor bar on his face stopped while he considered. "Negative, Captain. No trace of Kael Torsin, either, or any other Mesakloren military presence."

I lowered my chin once.

The door of the bridge opened, and Ben and Lanaya walked in. Ben is about an inch taller than me, and the thin frame of his twenty-year-old body has been replaced by a layer of athletic muscle and a confident gleam in his eyes. He'd come a long way.

Lanaya is something different. She'd been abducted from Earth as a little girl and was part of a secret operation that we were still trying to piece together. She looked to be about Ben's age, with Nordic blonde hair, the kind that appears almost white, and deep blue eyes the color of ice that forms beneath the surface of the ocean. She had only vague memories of what happened to her, and it had been determined that her memories had been blocked somehow.

The different alien species I'd encountered could do some amazing things, but that also included things that were just wrong. Lanaya was clear evidence that the galaxy wasn't representative of the golden age of civilization, despite the unbelievable technology the different species had developed.

Lanaya looked at me. "Is that it? Is this where the signal came from?"

I nodded.

Her eyes flicked back toward the holoscreen intently, and she pursed her lips. A few months ago, she'd received an anonymous message that triggered something in her brain. The message was just a few strange images, but then she spoke, and it appeared the message was for me.

*Nathan Briggs, I have them. If you want them back, you'll need to do something for me.*

I don't normally receive messages like that, and on that day, I'd gotten two of them. This was by far the more important of the two.

Ben stood next to Lanaya, displaying the young couple's unspoken deference for each other. Since the three of us were the only Humans on the ship, that made me the odd man out in the love department. Not that I was searching for it or anything like that, but sometimes it just hit me between the eyes like the proverbial bullet to the head.

Ben wrapped his arm around her and rubbed her shoulder. "We'll find who sent it."

Lanaya nodded. She had no memory of the message. Luckily, the cameras on the bridge had recorded the event, and I showed Lanaya the recording. Since then, she'd been determined to recover her memories and had become much more independent.

Ben looked at me with his eyebrows raised.

I shook my head. "No sign of them here."

We looked up as Kaz and T'Chura joined us.

Kaz glanced at the screen. "That makes sense. There are places like this all over."

"What are they?" I asked.

"It's an info-hub. It probably started out as a deep space outpost, but once the resources started being mined, it grew to what we see here."

# SPACE RAIDERS

## DARK MENACE

### KEN LOZITO

ACOUSTICAL BOOKS LLC

# CHAPTER 1

stared as the ship's scanners revealed a binary star system with the shattered remains of stars that had the unfortunate luck to become entangled. No planets orbited the stars, just rocky remnants strewn out from the center in clustered masses, as if the bones of the planets were trying to stitch themselves together to restore the magnificence of their former selves.

I'd seen worse places, a lot worse, and this celestial destruction looked to have happened quite a long time ago.

The edges of my lips lifted a little. At some point during my travels, assessing star systems had become something of a regular occurrence. What I once would've stared at in awe had become much more familiar. I still appreciated the view, but I couldn't bring myself to care about it all that much.

I heaved a sigh and looked at Kierenbot. "Anything?"

"Negative, Captain. Still no response by either Raylin or Serena."

Kierenbot is a humanoid robot that's home to an artificial

intelligence. He believes he's the remnant consciousness of a being whose body died long ago. It was all a lie, but I couldn't convince Kierenbot of that.

I'd thought it would be much easier to catch up to Serena and Raylin, but that all changed when I received *that* message. All the ways Raylin had instructed us to reach them had gone unanswered, which made me believe they were in serious trouble.

Raylin is an alien—a shapeshifter with a mysterious past. I knew she could handle herself; it was Serena I was concerned about. She's Human, and when we were on the ship together, the crew looked after each other. It had been less than a year since we'd been abducted from Earth and all our lives changed, and I couldn't help the certainty in my gut that Serena was in way over her head.

It should've been easy to catch up to them.

I was wrong.

Now, I just didn't want to be too late. The man who'd saved my life had asked me to keep his daughter safe. It was his dying wish, and I was failing to live up to it.

I tightened my jaw, teeth clenching a little as I stared at the star system on the main holoscreen.

*Thanks for saddling me with that, Flynn.*

I sighed heavily. I'd asked her not to go, but she wouldn't listen. We'd been on the trail of the Asherah, a civilization that predated all others in our galaxy, and it turned out that they weren't even *from* our galaxy. I thought we were making the find of a lifetime, and we were, but we didn't have much to show for it—just a lot of injuries and a whole lot of terrifying memories.

I rubbed my arm where the metallic tattoo had been from the Asherah artifact. It was gone, along with Larry—the being that helped us find the Asherah ruins. Sometimes my arm itched as if the artifact was still there.

If Serena had just waited instead of going off to search for the origins of the Human abductions, I wouldn't be here right now, searching for her. She'd be safe. Instead, something was wrong. I knew it in my bones, and I had a pretty good guess as to who was responsible.

I've made some enemies. People like Flynn, my old mentor and friend, would say I have a talent for it.

"What about the other scan?" I asked.

Kierenbot turned toward me, and the red orb that tracked across a sensor bar on his face stopped while he considered. "Negative, Captain. No trace of Kael Torsin, either, or any other Mesakloren military presence."

I lowered my chin once.

The door of the bridge opened, and Ben and Lanaya walked in. Ben is about an inch taller than me, and the thin frame of his twenty-year-old body has been replaced by a layer of athletic muscle and a confident gleam in his eyes. He'd come a long way.

Lanaya is something different. She'd been abducted from Earth as a little girl and was part of a secret operation that we were still trying to piece together. She looked to be about Ben's age, with Nordic blonde hair, the kind that appears almost white, and deep blue eyes the color of ice that forms beneath the surface of the ocean. She had only vague memories of what happened to her, and it had been determined that her memories had been blocked somehow.

The different alien species I'd encountered could do some amazing things, but that also included things that were just wrong. Lanaya was clear evidence that the galaxy wasn't representative of the golden age of civilization, despite the unbelievable technology the different species had developed.

Lanaya looked at me. "Is that it? Is this where the signal came from?"

I nodded.

Her eyes flicked back toward the holoscreen intently, and she pursed her lips. A few months ago, she'd received an anonymous message that triggered something in her brain. The message was just a few strange images, but then she spoke, and it appeared the message was for me.

*Nathan Briggs, I have them. If you want them back, you'll need to do something for me.*

I don't normally receive messages like that, and on that day, I'd gotten two of them. This was by far the more important of the two.

Ben stood next to Lanaya, displaying the young couple's unspoken deference for each other. Since the three of us were the only Humans on the ship, that made me the odd man out in the love department. Not that I was searching for it or anything like that, but sometimes it just hit me between the eyes like the proverbial bullet to the head.

Ben wrapped his arm around her and rubbed her shoulder. "We'll find who sent it."

Lanaya nodded. She had no memory of the message. Luckily, the cameras on the bridge had recorded the event, and I showed Lanaya the recording. Since then, she'd been determined to recover her memories and had become much more independent.

Ben looked at me with his eyebrows raised.

I shook my head. "No sign of them here."

We looked up as Kaz and T'Chura joined us.

Kaz glanced at the screen. "That makes sense. There are places like this all over."

"What are they?" I asked.

"It's an info-hub. It probably started out as a deep space outpost, but once the resources started being mined, it grew to what we see here."

"Deep space, far from any enforcement agency but itself," I said.

Ben frowned. "So, what does that mean?"

"It could be dangerous in there. Local authorities only."

"Not to worry, Captain," Kierenbot said. "I'm aware of the local customs, so we'll be able to avoid most of the danger."

Kaz chuckled and I raised an eyebrow toward him. He shrugged. "Somehow he always underestimates the trouble you manage to get yourself into."

"What can I say? He's got a blind spot for me."

"Should I take us in, Captain?" Kierenbot asked.

"One minute, Kierenbot. Are you able to isolate where the signal is coming from?"

"I cannot access the info-hub's internal communication systems from here. We'll need to do that once we're inside. I've installed a new application to your combat suit that will allow your suit computer to scan for it while we're there."

I tilted my head to the side and frowned. "Uh, combat suit? Won't that make us stick out?"

"I hadn't considered that," Kierenbot said.

Sometimes the robot could account for every tiny detail, and other times he missed the forest for the trees.

I looked up at T'Chura, which was to say that my neck ached sometimes when the giant alien, somewhat akin to a Sasquatch, stood nearby. He has a broad forehead, high cheek-bones, and skin with a slight dark-mustard tinge to it. His large brown eyes regarded me calmly as the thick, ropy layers of muscles strained against his black shirt. His long brown hair hung past his tree-trunk-sized neck. At first glance he appeared brutish, but he was among the most honorable beings I'd ever encountered—definitely someone I could count on to watch my back.

"What do you think?" I asked the nine-foot-tall Noorkonian brute.

"Small armament is acceptable at places like these. I'm afraid combat suits would just draw attention to us," T'Chura replied.

"Agreed," Kaz said.

Small armament was a relative term when it came from aliens. Size normally mattered when it came to these things, but not all the time.

"All right," I said. "Kierenbot, send your tracking application to our omnitools."

"Done," he replied.

I glanced down at my omnitool and saw the small notification that indicated a new application had arrived.

"Since we have no idea where the message actually came from, we'll need to split up," I said.

Aliens and people had a lot in common, kinda like opinions. Most of them started to speak at once, except T'Chura. At least *he* knew I was right about this.

I raised my hands. "Look, you can pair off if you want," I said, and looked pointedly at Ben, "but we need to cover as much ground as possible as quickly as possible. We can't afford another dead end. This is our only lead to finding them."

Kaz exhaled through his nostrils. "Nate, Raylin knows how to take care of herself. Serena couldn't have a better traveling companion."

I felt the weight of the others on the bridge watching me as I looked at Kaz. "Then why haven't they contacted us? They left, expecting that we'd quickly regroup with them. It's been months, and not a word has been sent. The only thing we have is the message that came to Lanaya."

There was an edge to my voice, and I didn't care.

"You don't know what Raylin is capable of. Believe me when

I tell you that she is the most dangerous person on the ship, and that's saying something given the crewmembers."

I looked at T'Chura and the Sasquatch nodded once. I shook my head. "Anyone can be overwhelmed. Anyone. Even Raylin."

I looked away from the others. "I shouldn't have let them go. They could've waited a few days and then we could've searched for the people who had Lanaya."

I lifted my gaze toward Kaz and he looked away. That small bit of acknowledgement was all I needed to see.

"Well, what are we waiting for then?" Kaz said.

"Kierenbot, take us in," I said.

The ship flew toward the deep space outpost. Large, rust-colored swaths of gaseous clouds reflected the starlight. They were remnants of the large gas planets I imagined were much like Jupiter. They made the star system appear almost ethereal. It was remarkable, but all I focused my attention on was the outpost.

Ben frowned. "For being such an out-of-the-way place, there are certainly a lot of ships traveling to it."

"It's like finding the only rest area on a long stretch of road. Everyone stops here because who knows how far the next place will be," I said.

Ben snorted a little and shook his head.

"What?" I asked.

"Nothing. You just have this way of putting things in the simplest of terms. It's like the fact that we're so far away from anything remotely like civilization has no effect on you," he replied.

I shrugged. "I left the city a long time ago, kid. You hadn't until recently."

Ben glanced at Kaz for a second. "Yeah, I'd planned to leave, but I never planned on traveling through space."

Kaz rolled his eyes. "Seriously, you guys need to get over this.

We've been through it so many times, and look at how things turned out," he said, gesturing around the bridge.

Ben, Serena, and I share ownership of the *Spacehog*. Kaz lost the ship because of the substantial debt he'd incurred.

I arched an eyebrow and looked at Ben. "He's right. We should probably let it go."

Ben looked at me, slightly amused.

"But then again, where's the fun in that?" I said and looked at Kaz. "You know what? I don't think I *will* let it go."

Kaz sighed. "Are you done yet?"

"I think I made my position on this quite clear. I'm not done. I might never be done, Kaz."

"I don't have to take this from you," Kaz warned.

"Is that right?"

Kaz nodded. "Yeah, that's right. I don't have to stay on the ship anymore. Do you want me to go?"

I regarded him for a few seconds. "Poor baby is upset. It'll be a good six months or more before the overhaul is done on Griff's ship. Even then, they'll only release it after they've been paid. So, unless you plan on staying out here for a very long time, I suggest you just go with it."

Kaz owned the salvage claim on his former mentor's ship. It was supposed to be repaired by the maintenance bots while we searched for the Asherah homeworld, but something must have gone wrong. When we came back for the ship, the maintenance bots were gone, and someone had pilfered several critical systems from the ship. Kaz then asked me to bring that ship to a repair dock he knew about. Since I was first and foremost a capitalist, I negotiated a fair price for this service. Kaz didn't think it was fair, but that's because he wanted me to do it out of the kindness of my heart, to which I replied that it was *that* attitude that had landed him in debt in the first place. You don't get something for nothing. The *Spacehog* required fuel and provisions. That was the reality of the situation.

"I thought we were friends," Kaz said.

"We are. This is what being friends on Earth is like."

Kaz glanced at Ben for a moment to see if I was lying to him. Ben nodded.

"I thought Humans were better than this."

"Says the guy who abducts people from planets," I said.

Kaz glanced at Lanaya, looking a little guilty. "Not like that, I assure you."

"I know what happened," Lanaya replied. "You were searching for someone else and that's when you had to take them off the planet. You probably saved their lives."

I felt my mouth slacken, betrayed. "Whose side are you on?"

She frowned at me.

"You heard her," Kaz said, not missing a beat. "I saved your lives. If I hadn't plucked you off Earth, chances are that Kael Torsin would've found you instead. Tell me, who do you think you were better off with, him or me?"

"Yeah, you're a real saint."

I turned back to the screen, thinking about the outpost again and that it must have some kind of name, or at the very least a unique identifier, but I didn't know what it was.

Kierenbot flew the ship to a docking port.

A message appeared on my omnitool. It was the docking authority wanting to be paid for the privilege of coming to the outpost. I glanced at the payment request and authorized that amount. It wasn't much, which surprised me a little bit since there weren't other options in the area for provisions, but they'd likely get their pound of flesh some other way.

I looked at the others. "We're going to need all hands for this. Ben, you and Lanaya go get Crim and meet me at the airlock."

They left the bridge.

T'Chura looked at me. "How do you want to divide up the outpost?"

I considered it for a few seconds. "Whoever sent the message used the communications systems."

"They could be anywhere," Kaz said.

"Yes, and that's why we need to split up. Use the tracker Kierenbot gave us and see where it leads. As long as we have regular check-ins, we'll be fine," I said.

"Captain," Kierenbot said, "I'd like to use my other chassis for this. You know, just in case."

Kierenbot's other chassis was a modified battlebot that he could offload his consciousness into. It was quick and powerful and had no shortage of tricks available.

"Okay, but remember, we don't want to draw attention to ourselves. We get in, find out who sent the message, and then get some answers. Once we find them, let the others know and wait for backup."

The others nodded and Kaz regarded me for a few moments.

"What is it?"

"These places can be dangerous. Are you sure you won't pair off with T'Chura or Kierenbot?"

I shook my head. "No, we need to move quickly. Splitting up is the best way."

Kaz inclined his head in acknowledgement.

"But if anyone gets into trouble, alert the others and wait for help," I said.

Kaz grinned toward T'Chura. "It's like he thinks we haven't done anything like this before."

T'Chura waved off the comment with one of his giant hands. "He's very agitated lately. Best that we go quickly. The sooner we find the others, the better we'll all feel."

We left the bridge, and after a quick stop at the armory, we met the others at the airlock.

# CHAPTER 2

'd never been in the military, but I'd met plenty of veterans
during my travels. They always had a different bearing about
them that I liked—a no-nonsense attitude when there was
work to be done. Right then, I was appreciating—more envying
—the chain of command and the ability to pull rank over others
in various situations. We'd just left the ship behind, and everyone
had to have their say about what we were about to do. I'm all for
working as a group and getting input from the others, but there
usually comes a time when we simply need to move forward.

We'd been to enough outposts, space stations, and various
types of other installations and facilities, including a few cities, to
get around well enough, but something about this outpost
agitated both Kaz and Crim. The outpost was out in the middle
of nowhere. Technically, most things in the galaxy were quite a
distance from each other. One thing I'd learned from traveling to
remote places back home was that they all had a set of rules, and
if you paid attention, you'd get along just fine with the locals.
The Wild West wasn't as wild as some of the stories said they

were, but they *were* on the frontier, and this outpost was no different. It was just a different sort of frontier that hosted multiple species of aliens doing who knows what.

If the *Spacehog* had been a military ship, the crew would have to do what I said. I was the captain, but we weren't in the military. Our relationship, aside from being friends, was also contractual, so it was a business arrangement. They were free to object to what I wanted to do, but they couldn't interfere. Despite my longing for more concrete leadership, I had a strong aversion to being told what to do. I was never a *follow orders* kind of guy.

I shook my head as I strode through the outpost. We'd finally split up and I was alone. Sometimes it was just better that way. I wasn't opposed to the occasional help, but sometimes I just preferred to be alone. There would be no one looking over my shoulder, commenting about how I was doing something. I shook my head again. Why was it that when I got annoyed my thoughts became irritatingly juvenile? Anger made fools of us all, but it was more than that.

I inhaled a deep breath and blew it out. I was worried about Serena, and I was angry with myself for letting her go in the first place. Maybe if I just acknowledged that, I could focus on what I needed to do.

Sounded good in my head, but it didn't work.

I should have tried harder to convince her to wait, but she was so damn stubborn. I snorted a little at the irony because I knew she pretty much said the same thing about me.

Several Akacians glanced at me. Like Kaz, they had highly sensitive hearing. I'd probably just thrown some kind of challenge toward them and hadn't even realized it.

I gave them a wave and just strode right along, which confirmed a truth that had become universal to me. If you acted like you knew where you were going, no one else seemed to pay any particular attention. But if you acted lost, you made yourself a target.

I wore an earpiece that Crim had made for me. I could hear the others if they used the comlink, but it also put a HUD in front of my eyes that was visible only to me. The little earpiece was standard tech that most species used. The variations depended on the physical characteristics of the species. T'Chura, whose head was almost as large as my chest, would need a different-size earpiece, but all that hair he had would make it easier to hide.

Beyond the docking platform, I took an elevator to one of the lower levels. It was all relative since the outpost rotated on its axis. I thought that was strange. There was some kind of artificial gravity field, and Ben had said that the rotation was more for aesthetics than an actual need to create a field through centrifugal force.

I glanced toward one of the wallscreens that showed a view outside the outpost, and some kind of nebula came into view. The various shades of blues made for quite a sight, and I slowed my pace to admire the view for a few seconds.

The outpost was mostly hollowed out in the central area and curved around on the other side. Ben enjoyed learning about this stuff; I just cared whether I was about to wander into an area that didn't have life-support systems compatible with Humans. Everyone carried individual life-support systems. It was part of the quick helmet that came out of the neck of my black jacket. My clothes were made from some kind of smart fabric that could alter itself to protect me from a vacuum. It wasn't nearly as effective as my combat suit with all its abilities, but I hadn't gone there looking for a fight. Judging by the other species who'd come to this outpost, they weren't dressed for battle either, but that didn't mean they were unarmed. Far from it. The aliens I'd met had taught me a few things about concealment of personal-protection weapons.

The hours went by as I roamed the outpost, exploring different levels and trying to get Kierenbot's tracker to detect a signal.

I received a comlink request from Ben.

"Hey, kid, find something?"

"Not yet. How long do you want to keep at it?"

"As long as it takes."

"Nate, come on. This way is going to take forever, and I think we're being followed."

I climbed onto an elevator and selected another level. I'd been staggering my routes across the outpost to cast the widest net possible for detecting that damn signal.

"Stay calm. Don't give it away that you're aware of them," I said.

I conferenced in the others to the comlink and quickly brought them up to speed. Kaz had to mute his link because the area he was in was so loud.

I moved toward the edge of the walkway and made a show of watching the aircar traffic speed by.

I brought up my omnitool and looked up everyone's location. "T'Chura, it looks like you're closest. Can you start making your way to them?"

"At once," he replied.

"Ben, were you able to get a good look at them?" I asked.

"We're in a crowded area. I haven't been able to get a good look. There are a lot of different species here."

"I've seen them," Lanaya said. "Two Akacians, four Mesaklorens, and even a Noorkon, but I'm not sure if the Noorkon is interested in us as much as the Mesaklorens."

T'Chura was a Noorkon. He was some kind of soldier or

protector. There were other Noorkons who hired themselves out as mercenaries and assassins. They were extremely vicious and deadly.

"Stay away from the Noorkon for sure," Kaz said.

"You don't need to tell me twice," Ben said, sounding as if he was looking over his shoulder.

I'd fought a Noorkon before—been chased by one. The only way to really fight a psychotic Sasquatch was either with the most powerful gun you could find or having a good friend like T'Chura watching your back.

Crim cleared his throat, which sounded like a sack of rocks jumbling around. "It's probably multiple groups following each other. Wouldn't be surprised. Try to stay in populated areas."

Crim's voice sounded strained, as if he'd suddenly caught a cold.

"Are you all right, Crim? You sound like you're sick."

"I'm fine. It's just...what's the word... an allergy."

I frowned, amused. "Allergies? Are you serious? Do you need a tissue?"

"It's not funny, Nate."

I chuckled. "Come on, Crim. It's a little funny. You should hear yourself."

Crim didn't reply. I imagined his craggy old face was glowering at some stranger who happened to be in his line of sight.

"Go back to the ship if you're sick. I'm going to keep looking."

After a pregnant pause, Crim finally said. "I'm fine. I'm going to keep searching. Crim, out."

He disconnected his comlink from the group.

"Give us a status, Ben," I said.

"Uh, no, don't go over there," Ben said, speaking to someone else. I waited for him to continue. "Uh," he said, sounding like he was moving quickly.

"Why are you following us?" Lanaya asked.

I heard her shrill voice from Ben's comlink.

"Yes, you were. What do you want?" she demanded.

"I hope you've got your weapons ready, kid," I said to Ben.

He gave a slightly nervous chuckle. "Sorry," Ben said. "She's just a little agitated. We'll be on our way."

I heard him try to urge Lanaya away.

"Don't let me catch you following me again!"

I couldn't hear the reply, but I did hear Ben continuing to urge her along. "You're crazy," he said, sounding excited.

I blinked.

*Excited?*

I frowned.

"It worked," Lanaya replied gleefully. "You played your part masterfully."

Suddenly, I felt like I was listening to a couple of newlyweds who managed to jam romance into every conceivable moment.

"I guess you guys don't need any help then," I said.

"She bluffed them?" Kaz asked.

"Sounds that way," I said.

"They weren't expecting it," Lanaya replied. "They were trying to be sneaky, and sometimes the best way to handle that is to shine a giant spotlight on it."

My mouth slackened a little. Lanaya used to be a little timid, but that mouse of a girl was nowhere to be found.

"How did you know that would work?" Ben asked.

"It was a calculated risk."

"Yes, but a little warning would've been nice."

"Next time."

I could hear her smiling. Her tone was light, and I knew they were doing that lost-in-each-other's-eyes moment.

"Pay attention guys," I said.

"Nate's right," Lanaya said.

"Stop saying that. It'll go to his head," Ben replied.

I shook my head.

"I see T'Chura. We'll continue our search with him," Ben said.

Both he and Lanaya left the group comlink.

Kaz cleared his throat. "She's become quite a bit more confident."

"It's her training," Kierenbot said.

I'd almost forgotten he was on the group comlink.

"The question is whether she even realizes it or not," I said.

"How could she not?" Kaz asked.

"Well, her memories were suppressed. She's been getting better, but this is new even for her."

"I've observed Lanaya's behavior quite extensively since she first arrived," Kierenbot said. "There is a significant increase in assertive and determined behavior."

I grinned. "She's becoming more independent. It's a good thing. It means she's healing."

"Aren't you worried about what else she'll remember?" Kaz asked.

I frowned. "What do you mean?"

"Has it never occurred to you that she's just one of those hidden messages away from assassinating someone?"

"Whoa, there. Jumping the gun a little bit, aren't you?"

"She is or was a sleeper agent of some kind. That's what she was being trained for. It's obvious," Kaz replied.

I considered that for a few moments and began walking again, weaving my way past a group of Ustrals. Each of them had six legs, and when they walked, it sounded like a parade of clackety clicks on the metallic floor.

"A message is one thing. She didn't lose her free will."

"That we know of. All I'm saying is that it could happen."

"I'm going to keep looking. And just for the record, no, I don't believe Lanaya is going to suddenly kill us for no reason."

"I didn't say for no reason. I said because she was ordered to do it."

"Goodbye, Kaz. Happy hunting, you two," I said and dropped from the group comlink.

I wandered through a habitation section. There was less foot traffic there than in the other districts. I glanced at the tracker application on my HUD and it was still flatlined, meaning there'd been no detection. I stared at it for a few moments with a thoughtful frown.

Why was Kaz suddenly concerned that Lanaya was some kind of sleeper assassin? She hadn't received any other messages specifically for her, and the message had been quite specific. Whoever sent it wanted something from me. How'd they even know who I was? Until I'd met Lanaya, I thought there were no other Humans roaming the galaxy. Aliens that frequented outposts and other space stations tended not to overreact to a species they hadn't encountered before. I might get a few passing glances as I walked by but nothing like actual scrutiny.

Ben was right, this was taking forever. We hadn't covered half the outpost. I could keep exploring and hope that I somehow stumbled onto the same signal that had sent the initial message, or I could try something different.

I exhaled a long breath and brought up my omnitool. I opened the tracker application and looked at the options Kierenbot included. It was in listening mode so that if a similar signal was used, presumably I'd detect it.

"Let's try this," I said as I selected a different option.

I initiated a broadcast using the same signature pattern that had been used in Lanaya's message and kept walking while the broadcast refreshed after a minute.

"One ping only, please," I said, quoting an older movie about a Russian submarine captain who wanted to defect to the United States. God, I missed the nineties.

Technically, I was using multiple pings, but I thought it was for the best. Who knew if anyone was even listening for it?

I allowed the broadcast to work for a short time and then ended it.

The habitat area looked a bit worn out, and I guessed this was the rough side of the outpost. The different types of aliens here didn't make eye contact, but not all of them had eyes, so some of them wouldn't anyway. They kept to themselves, which was fine with me.

I was only too happy when I finally left the area and returned to a more commercial district. Specialized shops lined the wide-open terrace. I didn't understand what those shops were offering, which was a giant indicator that I wasn't their target customer. I quickly moved on.

A detection signal alerted on my HUD. Someone had responded to my broadcast.

"Gotcha," I said.

Kierenbot's application began tracing the signal, and a path highlighted on my HUD. It led me into the commercial district among the shops and what passed for alien entertainment. Above me was an aquatic entertainment module where several different types of aliens watched the foot traffic intently.

I walked along, trying to blend in as much as I could. The commercial district was more akin to a flea market where, in addition to the shops, there were outdoor tables with different species offering their products. Most glanced at me for barely more than a second and moved on, looking for someone else.

The path that had highlighted on my HUD led me right toward a very low-key entertainment module, which was the alien equivalent of a pub or small restaurant. I walked inside and spotted different groups of aliens sitting at workstations along the wall. The holoscreens were operating in privacy mode, so I couldn't see what they were doing, just that they were in use.

Several Noorkons stood over to my left in a wall of long hair and muscle. I heard a subsonic rumble from one of them. My heart rate spiked, and I quickened my pace, which was a natural response to the warning growl of something dangerous. Lucky for me, the Sasquatches were focused on their own workstations, but I noticed that several other patrons moved away from them.

Their holoscreen wasn't using privacy mode, and I saw the face of an Ustral. He didn't look happy.

"The signal was active just a little while ago," the Ustral said.

"We've searched this area already, Menka. There's nothing here."

Menka glowered. "Look again. You missed something."

I slowed down when they mentioned the signal and moved over toward an open table, initiating a session. A holoscreen appeared with the outpost's public info-hub. I glanced at the two Noorkons and saw that they had thick bracers on. The dull glint of metal was exposed from their long, dark coats.

I closed the session and moved on. I wasn't the only one tracking the signal. I glanced around the large room and saw more than a few groups surveying the area.

I blinked as the realization that I might be in a room full of people after the same thing hit me. What the heck had I done this time? The only thing I could do now was beat everyone to the source.

I walked over to a robotic server at the far side of the room. The robot had a round body of dark metal with a small dome atop, where twin glowing green orbs zeroed in on me as I approached.

I regarded it for a second and then used my omnitool to initiate a data session. I stood off to the side, and the robot went back to watching the other patrons in the room.

There were several corridors that led out of the main area. Kierenbot had made several sniffer applications available to my omnitool that were purpose-built for gleaning information from local networks.

I started the tracker application, which began a scan of the area. The signal had come from a service hub, and the scanner took a few seconds to isolate the network session. It came from one of the rooms above.

I walked down the nearest corridor and went toward an elevator at the end. After palming the controls to summon the elevator, I glanced back down the corridor to the main room. The bustle had become somewhat muffled in the distance. The elevator doors opened, and the large opening surprised me. Something twice as tall as I was could easily walk through them. Not wanting to share the elevator with anyone else, I hastened aboard and selected my destination.

Less than a minute later, the doors opened and I entered a service area. A narrow corridor curved away, and I followed it at a jog.

I tried sending a message to the others, but it wouldn't go through. Frowning, I tried again, pressing my lips together and glowering at my omnitool when the message failed to send. I wasn't the only person searching for the source of the signal, and that made my mind race with the possibilities of not only the danger I was in but who else had received a message. The message that had come through Lanaya was for me, but how many others had been sent? What if the abductions weren't limited to just Humans? Lanaya's memories were spotty at best, but she had recognized Raylin, or a species like Raylin.

I shook my head. This was my only lead for finding Serena and Raylin. I didn't have time to go back outside and summon the others. Whoever had sent the messages might be gone by then, or worse.

The tracker on my HUD led me through a service area where there were different species of aliens, as well as robots, performing any number of tasks. A few glanced in my direction, but I just kept moving. Hopefully, none of them would raise an alarm.

I headed toward a room at the end of the hall and palmed the door controls. A small holoscreen appeared above it, and the wide, wedge-shaped head of a Nasarian peered at me.

"Service requests come through the main entrance," he said.

"Is that so? But this is where I was told to go by the guys in the front."

The Nasarian frowned and narrowed his gaze suspiciously. "Who told you that?"

I heard someone speak from farther in the room. I couldn't understand them, but they sounded more than a little agitated.

I smiled and leaned toward the camera. "It's just me. No one else is here. Why don't you let me in so we can talk?"

The Nasarian regarded me for a few moments.

I shook my head and grinned. "Look, I saw three big brutes downstairs that I suspect are looking for you," I said and paused for a second. The Nasarian simply stared at me. "I bet there are a lot of people down there wondering about you guys."

"You don't know what you're talking about. Get out of here."

I sighed and shook my right hand a little. "If I have to break through that door, I will. The bad thing about that is that it'll bring unwanted attention. What's it going to be?"

I heard the other person in the room race toward the door and peer into the camera. He was another Nasarian, but he looked shorter and a bit bedraggled.

I smiled and waved.

The short Nasarian turned toward his partner. "He's not one of them, Darek."

Darek rolled his eyes. He was probably annoyed that his little sidekick had just used his real name.

Amateurs.

I regarded Darek with a wide grin.

"That's another one tripping the alert," the little sidekick said.

I banged my fist on the door. I really didn't want to blow a hole in it, but I did let my hand blaster clang against the door.

Darek narrowed his gaze and leaned toward his sidekick. There was a quick argument between the two, and then the door dematerialized.

The two Nasarians backed farther into the room.

I'd encountered this species before. The ones I'd encountered were quite tall, lithe, and well mannered. The two Nasarians in front of me weren't anywhere near as graceful or as confident as Delos or Quickening.

Darek was the taller of the two. His shoulders were slumped and he was crouching a little, which immediately made me suspicious. Darek looked as if he was hiding something.

The shorter Nasarian looked as if he was half starved. His head only came up to my chest and he reminded me of some kind of alien scathing harpy. His skin was wrinkled, and I wondered if he was an experiment gone wrong.

"We let you in, now tell us what you want," said the smaller Nasarian.

I palmed the controls to shut the doors and smiled. "I think introductions are in order. I'd rather keep this as civilized as possible. Who are you?" I asked, raising my chin toward the short Nasarian.

He waved a finger at me. "I don't think so. You came in here first. *You* tell us who *you* are."

"Fine, I'm Nate."

"Nate? What the heck does that mean? What's a Nate?"

"Jeshi, come on. There's no reason we can't be civilized."

Jeshi scowled at me with tiny fury. "He's a Human. What do they know about being civilized?"

I knew a stalling tactic when I saw one. I thrust my hand blasters out in front of me, and they immediately became active. I had one pointed at each of them.

"Someone sent a message from this room. I'm here to find out who sent it. The next word that comes out of your mouths better tell me what I want to know, or I'll get nasty."

Darek twitched a little and then stopped.

Jeshi's hands shot up. "Don't shoot! Don't shoot! I'll tell you anything you want to know."

"Don't," Darek began to say and stopped as I raised my hand blaster so it pointed at his face.

"Good choice," I said to him and looked at Jeshi. "Start talking."

Jeshi's hands lowered a little, but his eyes were wide with fear. "It's a game. It's all just a stupid game," he said and glared at Darek. "We couldn't have picked a worse place to hide."

I shook my hand. "Hey, focus, Jeshi. Right here." I stepped closer to him. "What do you mean this is a game?"

Jeshi's narrow shoulders slumped, and he looked at me guiltily.

An alert chirped from one of the nearby holoscreens, and a video feed of the corridors where the elevators were came to prominence.

Jeshi cried out as if he'd been struck, and I watched his arms flail as he ran around in a circle. "I told you. I told you. I told you. Knew they were coming. They're coming for me. I gave away my location and now they've found me. They're coming. They're coming to kill me."

I glanced at Darek, and he looked surprised by Jeshi's behavior. Maybe the two of them weren't partners.

"Who's coming?" I asked.

Jeshi looked at me incredulously and gestured toward the holoscreen. "They are."

"Who are they?"

Jeshi backed toward the far side of the room, muttering about having stayed there too long and they'd finally caught up to him.

I thought Jeshi wasn't playing with a full deck.

"Is it Menka? Is that who's coming?" I asked.

Jeshi froze and looked at me.

"Where did you hear that name?" Darek asked.

"Downstairs when I came in. Someone named Menka was speaking to a trio of Noorkons."

"See!" Jeshi shrieked. "Menka Tamplin is here. Those are his thugs. I knew the game was dangerous, but I played it anyway. I had to play. Detected the signal and I had to play. Sent the messages, I did."

Darek lowered his hands, and I narrowed my gaze. "I don't think you want to shoot us."

"I'd rather not."

"Good, but this complicates things. Jeshi is a little challenged."

Jeshi was in the middle of a panic attack.

"Is there a backdoor out of this place?" I asked.

Darek shook his head while Jeshi darted toward the back room.

We followed and I gestured for Darek to go first.

"Can't have you at my back," I said.

Darek quickly went through the door and found Jeshi in a back corner. He was yanking hard on a storage container, but it was only inching away from the wall.

"Weak point. Weak point. Escape through here," Jeshi said.

I gestured toward the storage container. "Help him."

I upped the power output of my hand cannon while Darek pulled the large container away from the wall. It moved easily enough for him.

Jeshi stood by the wall and gestured toward it. "Blast it."

"Get out of the way first," I replied.

Jeshi hopped to the side as if the thought of getting caught in the blast hadn't occurred to him until that moment.

I aimed my hand cannons at the wall as I heard the door chime from the outer room. I squeezed the triggers, and twin molten plasma bolts blew a sizable hole in the wall. There was a dark corridor beyond.

Jeshi darted forward, but Darek grabbed him.

"Maintenance tunnel. Only means of escape," Jeshi said.

Darek looked at me. "See if the way is clear."

I narrowed my gaze suspiciously for a second, and then moved toward the makeshift doorway. I glanced out into the dark corridor.

"Clear," I said over my shoulder and stepped through.

They followed me out.

"Do you know where this leads?" I asked.

"No," Darek said while Jeshi said, "Yes."

I sighed. "Which one is it, guys?"

Jeshi gestured emphatically ahead. "Down there, and then take the shaft on the left. It'll get narrower as we go."

I gestured for them to go first. "Lead the way."

Jeshi darted ahead.

"Not too far, unless you want to be target practice," I called after him.

Jeshi slowed down.

Darek moved ahead of me, and I was right behind him.

Jeshi raced down the corridor and went down one of the connecting tunnels. I heard a loud burst from behind us. Someone had blown out the door to Jeshi's hideout.

"What were you going to do if I hadn't shown up?" I asked.

Darek was quiet for a few seconds. "We were preparing to leave."

"Yes," Jeshi said. "Had to clear out my toolbox first."

I frowned. Neither of them were carrying anything, so I doubted Jeshi meant an actual toolbox. He must've meant something else.

"Menka Tamplin sounds dangerous," I said.

"Very dangerous," Jeshi replied.

Darek didn't respond and kept his gaze ahead.

"How does he know you?"

Jeshi shuddered. "Dangerous game. Dangerous. I shouldn't have done it."

"Why did you send out the messages? What game?"

Jeshi began muttering to himself.

"You're not going to get any answers from him now," Darek said.

The tunnel straightened and we quickened our pace. I was even with Darek, and Jeshi was just ahead of me.

I peered ahead and saw a control panel. Jeshi raced toward it at a trot, and I quickly caught up to him as he reached for the door controls. Grabbing his hand, I slapped the panel.

Jeshi tried to pull away from me, but I wouldn't let go. "You didn't think that was going to work, did you?"

Jeshi yanked and glowered at me. "Let me go. Don't touch me!"

He gritted his teeth as he tried to overpower me, which would've been amusing if he hadn't been so serious.

The door opened to a well-lit corridor and I walked out, taking Jeshi with me.

I lifted him into the air. "Stop squirming," I said through clenched teeth. "Tell me where they are and I'll let you go." I jerked my head toward Darek. "One step closer and your head is gone."

Darek backed away.

That was twice he'd tried to get the drop on me.

Jeshi looked away from me, staring at the ground. "It's the game. It's all a game. That's all it is."

He seemed to be having some kind of breakdown, and I swore. I lowered him to the ground but didn't let go.

We went down the corridor back toward the commercial sector. We'd emerged into a connecting tunnel between districts. As soon as we left the tunnel, Jeshi shrieked. It was so loud that it startled me, and he nearly tore my arm off as he slipped out of my grasp.

Jeshi tumbled backward, rolling to a stop a short distance away.

We were surrounded by a large group of menacing-looking Ustrals—six-legged aliens wearing armor that covered their torsos. Most of them carried some kind of weapon. Rifles, hand cannons, and other weapons I didn't recognize were all leveled at us. One of the Ustrals moved toward us. He was the only one I recognized.

"Delivered right to me," Menka Tamplin said. "Kill the others. Bring me the little one."

The breath caught in my throat as the Ustrals brought up their weapons, ready to fire.

# CHAPTER 3

laughed. "Thank you for finally getting here. I could only stall him for so long. Delivered to you as promised."

Ustrals have craggy faces with dark eyes. Their skin is a dirty tan color and their legs made effective weapons. The lot of them looked like Crim's evil cousins. Crim was a veteran soldier, but these Ustrals looked to be in their prime. They were muscular and menacing, and I was about ten seconds from being fired upon.

Why hadn't I worn my combat suit again?

Oh, that's right, I was supposed to blend in. If only the spider-hybrid aliens believed the same. Sure, we both had weapons; it was just that they had more of them. I wasn't beyond seeing the irony of my current predicament. Having T'Chura, Kierenbot, or Kaz would've helped a little. It was one of those defining moments that I waved at as it sailed on by.

I gestured toward Jeshi, who regarded me with a bit of betrayal.

Menka Tamplin frowned. "I don't recognize you."

I nodded. "I know. This is a disguise. But trust me, I work for you."

He didn't look convinced, but there was a little doubt there so my ruse wasn't a total loss.

"You really don't remember? I mean, we've never met before," I said gesturing toward him. Several of the armed Ustrals tensed. "Sheesh, calm down. I know I'm new to the team and all, but what kind of welcome is this? Haven't I delivered what you wanted right here?"

I gestured toward Jeshi and then included Darek with a lazy gesture. Both of them stared at me as if I'd grown another head.

Perfect.

Menka Tamplin gave me a once-over. "Who is your contact?"

I blinked. Menka Tamplin was testing me, and my answer would determine the level of pain I was about to experience. "Oh right, the contact. He had something for me to give you so you knew I was authentic." I lowered my hands a little and the mercenaries pushed their weapons a little farther toward me. I stopped. "But we've got Jeshi. I was trying to get him to talk—you know, give up what he knows—but he's stubborn. Keeps going on about a game. I think he's a little crazy. Something definitely not right with him."

I glanced at Jeshi, and he sneered at me with furious hate.

"I mean, look at him. He's about to go for my jugular. You know what I mean?" I said and laughed at Jeshi.

Jeshi snarled and leaped toward me, moving faster than I was expecting. His long fingers gripped my neck, and the little Nasarian began to choke me.

Jeshi screamed as I swung him around, trying to loosen his grip enough to get a breath in. The Ustral thugs hesitated, and some even lowered their weapons.

I backed away from them, thrust out my hand cannons, and fired my weapons.

Plasma bolts belched out, but my aim was terrible because the deranged Nasarian kept trying to choke me. However, the great thing about fighting Ustrals was that they never wore armor on their legs, and since they had six of them each, it was like I couldn't miss.

All right, I missed a little, but they did hop into the air. They jumped high, and their claws penetrated the metallic walls of the outposts.

Jeshi was still ringing my neck, and I glared at him.

"Dammit! I'm trying to help you," I gasped.

I think I might've pushed Jeshi too far because he ignored me. That furious little Nasarian was really trying to kill me, and my neck was starting to hurt.

Gritting my teeth, and with my vision starting to narrow into a long tunnel, I punched the little shit, hoping his kidneys were near the same place as an ordinary Human's were. This only infuriated him further, so I stopped firing my hand cannons and slammed both my fists into Jeshi's side. His grip on my neck loosened as he cried out in pain.

I heaved in a deep, precious breath of air.

Something moved in front of me, and I saw Menka Tamplin raise his rifle and fire. There was a burst of light as I fell and lost consciousness at the same time.

I'd been stunned before, courtesy of Crim. He'd wanted to acquaint me with the different non-lethal weapons that were sometimes used. It reminded me of playing with pepper spray with my friends in high school. No one did that twice. Feeling like your eyes were being melted out of your skull was enough to never want to repeat the experience.

Getting stunned was very much the same feeling, except it

wasn't just your eyes. It was a whole-body experience of debilitating pain. God, it really sucked.

I slowly regained consciousness. My muscles were sore, which tended to happen when enough energy was forced through them to make them rigid. It wouldn't hurt for long, but my throat was already sore from Jeshi choking me.

I decided to forego pretending to be asleep because no one would've fallen for it anyway. I sat up and looked around. I was on the ground in some kind of warehouse. Drones flew by, guiding grav pallets stacked with storage crates, and the rocky wall of the asteroid was behind me. I really hoped we weren't at the outer wall. There was something unnerving about having an unknown but undoubtedly insufficient amount of rock separating me from the vacuum of space.

Jeshi lay unconscious next to me, and Darek was on my other side. He was awake, but the fact that he sat on the ground made me think he'd also been stunned.

I sighed and regarded Menka Tamplin with the hint of a smirk. "I guess a thanks for not killing me is in order."

Menka moved toward me. When a large alien with six naturally armored legs came toward you, your instinct was to flinch and move back. I was used to Crim, but sometimes the creepy-crawly legs triggered some vestige of my brain that said this thing wasn't right and it was going to kill me.

I shouldn't show weakness to a predator, so I looked Menka Tamplin in the eye and slowly got to my feet.

The other mercenaries regarded me hatefully. More than a few of them had healing packs on their legs, or what was left of their legs. I wouldn't like it either if someone had shot off one of my legs. But at least they had others to compensate whereas I didn't, so they should count themselves lucky.

They didn't think they were lucky. They looked like they really wanted to get some payback, which I guess was fair.

I turned toward Menka Tamplin. "I guess I should level with you. I don't work for you."

Menka Tamplin glared at me for a few seconds and then raised his rifle and shot a plasma bolt over my head. I ducked, squeezing my eyes shut. Superheated rock landed near me, with a few small pieces bouncing off my head. I lurched forward and glared at my captor while swiping the hot pebbles off my head.

"What do you want to know?" I asked.

Menka Tamplin leveled his rifle toward a spot just over my shoulder again. I glanced behind me and saw a good-sized crater in the rock.

I raised my hand in a placating gesture. "Communication is a two-way street—"

He fired again.

I ducked but didn't move forward because Menka Tamplin aimed his rifle at my face next.

I saw Darek shelter Jeshi from the debris. Jeshi was starting to wake up a little.

"Fine," I said. "I came here looking for him." I gestured toward Jeshi. "I've been tracking a hidden message that came over public transit. That's why I'm here."

Menka Tamplin tilted his head to the side, frowning as if deciding whether he believed me or not.

"Is that why *you're* here? Jeshi kept saying it was part of a game."

"A game?" Menka Tamplin said. He lifted his gaze toward Darek. "What's this about a game?"

Darek whispered something to Jeshi. I think he was trying to comfort him. Then he stood. "Jeshi is a tinkerer. He works with patterns. He said they were games to him."

Menka Tamplin's gaze slid toward Jeshi with a menacing glare.

"Hey, come on. This might all be just a simple misunderstanding," I said.

He shook his head. "You have no idea what this has cost me or the impact of what he's done. He's going to pay for that."

I moved to the side, edging to block the path to Jeshi. That little shit was my only link to finding Serena and Raylin, and I wasn't going to let him get shot.

"I get it," I said, and Menka Tamplin stared at me coldly. "He messed up your operations and you probably thought there was some kind of breach, but there wasn't. Let him go. I'll make sure he doesn't do it again."

"Why should I do that?"

I blinked. "Because I asked you to. Maybe there's some kind of arrangement we can reach."

Menka Tamplin considered that for a few seconds. "What are you offering?"

# CHAPTER 4

Menka Tamplin's question confirmed a couple of things. First, he wasn't beyond making a deal if it was worth it. Second, while he was dangerous and could just as easily kill me, he was willing to indulge me for a moment. The way I saw it was that I was just buying time to level the playing field a little while I figured out a way to escape.

"I could just start naming things, but that would be counter-productive. I'll tell you what I want, and you tell me what it'll cost me." I gestured toward Jeshi. "You want this particular problem to go away and never come back. I can make that happen. If you let me take Jeshi…" I said and paused for a second. Darek stared at me intently, and I sighed a little. "And Darek, I will ensure they never become a thorn in your side again."

Menka Tamplin frowned. "No thorn can pierce my skin."

I nearly rolled my eyes but stopped myself. "It's just an expression, a figure of speech. I'm just saying the problem goes away, never to come back again."

"No, it doesn't. You're proposing to take them with you. The only assurance I have that the problem is dealt with is if I eliminate all of you. That way the problem is taken care of with zero chance of recurring."

I gave him a dispassionate once-over. "I thought we were making a deal. If you eliminated everyone who had the potential to cause a problem, there wouldn't be anyone left to deal with. It's a bit short-sighted, and that doesn't fit with the Ustrals I've worked with before."

Menka Tamplin frowned, and his eyes blinked a few times while he considered what I'd said. "Why do you want them? What are they to you?"

I considered lying to him or being vague, but he'd see right through it. "I need them to find some friends of mine."

Something switched in Menka Tamplin's demeanor—something cold and deadly.

"Hold on, I thought we were negotiating. I told you why I needed them. Now, name your price."

Menka Tamplin raised his rifle, as did the other mercenaries. "Negotiations are over."

A loud screech from above caused us all to flinch as something large and metallic slammed onto the ground. Within a second, the battlebot unfurled its limbs in a singular twisting motion as it attacked Menka Tamplin and his mercenaries.

I didn't waste any time. I activated my hand cannons and fired my weapons at the mercenaries.

"Time to go," I called over my shoulder.

Darek helped Jeshi stand.

I provided covering fire as Kierenbot took on the mercs. I saw Menka Tamplin using storage containers for cover, and I fired a few bolts in his direction so he knew he hadn't escaped just yet.

"Friend of yours?" Darek asked.

He'd hoisted Jeshi over his shoulder.

I nodded.

The surviving mercs scattered, and Kierenbot moved toward the nearest target.

Battlebots were fearsome fighters, and I knew all the upgrades that had been added to the chassis Kierenbot was using. He had the speed, power, and training to rival any highly skilled soldier. He was also an artificial intelligence that was convinced his consciousness had been transferred from his dying body into a robot. It was a lie but try telling him that.

"Hey, showoff! Time to go!" I shouted.

Kierenbot dispatched the closest merc, making even that look like he was showing off. Then he spun around and began running toward me.

"They have reinforcements! Run!" Kierenbot said.

We ran the length of the warehouse and went through a door into a corridor.

"Where's the ship?" I asked.

"Nearby," Kierenbot said. "An effective test, wouldn't you say, Captain?"

Kierenbot very much wanted my approval.

"It was beautiful. I look forward to hearing your report as soon as we get out of here. Where are the others?" I asked.

Kierenbot began to answer, but the corridor lit up from a hailstorm of plasma bolts being fired at us.

We flattened against the wall, and I returned fire. Kierenbot did the same.

Darek continued onward, carrying Jeshi over his shoulder.

"I'll cover you, Captain," Kierenbot said.

The battlebot moved away from the wall, filling up the corridor as much as he could and returning fire. His armored plating would give him protection, but everything gave out sooner or later.

I ran down the corridor and closed in on Darek. He looked at me. "Wouldn't want you to go anywhere."

He didn't say anything.

"I need Jeshi to come with me. You can join us until we get out of here and sort some of this out."

Darek nodded. "Fair enough."

"Run faster!" Kierenbot shouted.

I glanced over my shoulder, looking past him.

Three armored Noorkons—Sasquatches, and not the good kind—ran toward us full tilt. Each of them carried a shield that Kierenbot's plasma bolts couldn't penetrate.

I could run fast. Speed was something you were either born with or you weren't. Lucky for me, I was born with it. I raced forward, going as fast as I could, and Darek was able to keep pace with me even though he was carrying Jeshi. Darek was a lot stronger than he appeared.

Kierenbot was right on our heels.

We reached the end of the corridor and entered a public promenade that led to the spaceport. I started to go the wrong way, and Kierenbot grabbed my shoulder and shoved me onto the correct path. Darek followed.

The other aliens in the area watched us as we ran, and several scrambled out of our way. I saw flashing lights in the distance, making their way toward us as the outpost's enforcers finally joined the chase. We needed to outrun them both. I'd had a few encounters with local authorities, and while incarceration was always a possibility, the more likely outcome was heavy fines. It was best if we just got away.

A comlink came from the ship.

"Take your time, Nate. We'll wait for you," Kaz said.

"You'd better be ready to leave," I said.

"Three Noorkons! When you go looking for trouble, you never disappoint," Kaz said, and then sounded like he was leaning away from the microphone. "Yes, three of them. You better head down there." Kaz returned to the microphone and said, "Help is coming."

"Send a message to the local authorities and report that we've been attacked by a mercenary named Menka Tamplin. He tried to kill us, and we need help."

"I told you help was coming. T'Chura is—"

"Do what I say, Kaz. Just send them the damn message," I said.

There was a pause before Kaz replied. "Sending message as requested."

I ignored his sullen tone. "About time."

The *Spacehog* was located ahead of us. The docking-tube door opened and T'Chura burst through, carrying a very large and deadly rifle.

"That's our ride," I said to Darek.

He looked ahead and stumbled. Jeshi slipped off his shoulders and rolled onto the ground, so I grabbed Jeshi and slung him over my shoulder. Jeshi began to struggle a little. He was only partially awake.

I heard a loud, sizzling *thwap* sound and saw that T'Chura had fired his weapon. Despite what some people might say, size definitely mattered, especially where firearms were concerned.

A searing red bolt bigger than my whole body raced overhead. I risked a glance behind me and saw that one of the Noorkons had been knocked back. The upper half of his shield was missing, and the merc lay sprawled on the ground.

Kierenbot ran toward me, gesturing for me to get moving. I turned toward the docking corridor and ran toward it.

Jeshi being so short didn't mean he was a lightweight. Carrying someone else's deadweight was a good test of anyone's fitness level. I was gasping, but I still had strength left. I pumped my legs, forcing them to carry me forward. My thighs were burning, and my shoulders ached from the additional weight.

T'Chura swung his weapon toward Darek.

"He's with us," I said.

T'Chura quickly aimed back toward the mercenaries with a determined and almost serene expression.

The mercs staggered their approach and were using cover to close the distance. Normal outpost patrons had scattered and were leaving the area, and local authorities were on their way.

"Watch out!" Kierenbot said.

Something clanged next to me, and some unseen force knocked me to the side. Jeshi cried out in pain and almost slipped off my shoulders.

Darek helped to steady me, and we raced toward the docking bay doors.

I went through first and then Darek. Both T'Chura and Kierenbot guarded the entrance to the ship, using suppressing fire to slow the mercs down for a few seconds, and then followed us in.

The airlock doors sealed, and the indicator lights switched to red. I glanced at the video feed of the area just outside the doors. The viewpoint shifted as the *Spacehog* sped away from the docking port of the outpost. Less than a minute later, we were clear and the outpost was left behind.

"He's hurt," Darek said.

I lowered Jeshi to the ground and Darek helped.

Jeshi had several metallic shafts sticking out of his side going from his leg to his back. I blinked in surprise. The little Nasarian was bleeding.

Ben and Lanaya stood just inside the airlock.

"We need to get him to the autodoc," Ben said.

"Get the grav pallet," I said.

Ben backed away from the airlock doors and raced down the corridor. He was soon back with a long grav pallet. I'd had them stored near all the entrances for just such an occasion.

We carefully lifted Jeshi onto the pallet. I could hear Serena in my mind, warning me to keep him stable or it could make the wounds worse. She'd been an inner-city ER nurse before trekking across the galaxy.

Darek began to follow him, but I held him back.

Ben and Lanaya pushed the grav pallet down the corridor.

"They'll get him to the autodoc," I said.

Darek considered this for a second, and after a quick glance at T'Chura and Kierenbot, he didn't offer any protest.

I gave him a once-over. "Are you hurt?"

Darek thought for a second. "No."

I wasn't wounded, and that was only because Jeshi's body had shielded me from the metallic shafts that were sticking out of his body.

I leveled my gaze at Darek. "Jeshi's not your partner, is he?"

"Yes, he is. We've worked together for quite some time now."

I grinned a little and then raised my chin toward Kierenbot with a head tilt toward Darek. "Tear his arm off."

Kierenbot's crimson orb flashed and then swung toward Darek.

The Nasarian's eyes widened, and he stepped back against the wall.

"Wait a minute. You told me we could sort this out when we got on the ship."

I smiled. "This *is* me sorting it out. I don't have time for bullshit right now. Friends of ours are missing, and Jeshi is our only link to finding them. Assuming the outpost's authorities believe it was Menka Tamplin who caused all that destruction, we should be able to escape without issue."

Kierenbot slowly moved toward Darek.

Darek held up his hands. "I can help you with that. I have contacts with the outpost's authorities."

I shrugged. "They're an irritation and would saddle us with fees rather than expending resources to haul us all back there. Start talking."

Kierenbot closed in on Darek.

"I'm… I'm investigating the abduction of juvenile aliens. That's it. I'm conducting an investigation."

Kierenbot grabbed Darek's hand and pulled him away from the wall, lifting him off the ground.

"Investigating for whom? And explain the bodies that were in the hideout. Talk fast because my friend here cannot wait to show off just how strong the battlebot really is," I said and glanced at Kierenbot. "The actuators in the arms are from that new composite alloy, right? The new stuff from the Mesakloren military?"

Kierenbot grinned. "Indeed they are, Captain."

Darek was a Nasarian. Their skin was already pale as moonlight, but I think whatever color he had was gone.

"All right. Stop. I'm a Tamiran Consortium intelligence agent. I'm investigating the abductions of juvenile species," Darek said.

"Nate," T'Chura said quietly. I looked up at him, and he gave me a firm nod. "Truth."

I nodded. T'Chura had the kind of empathic abilities that gave him keen insight into people.

"All right, Kierenbot. No feats of strength today. Let him go, please," I said.

Kierenbot looked at me. "Are you sure, Captain? He did hesitate before coming clean. There should be consequences for that. What if I removed just his hand?"

Darek's mouth hung open.

"No, that won't be necessary."

"How about a finger? He's got three others. He won't miss it. It'll just pop off, easy-peasy. I bet the autodoc could reattach it. In fact, it's been a while since we've used the Nasarian healing libraries for the autodoc. This would be a prime opportunity to test their limits. It's only a finger, after all."

I grinned and shook my head. Sometimes Kierenbot's sense of humor was quite scary. Even I couldn't tell whether he was serious or not.

"Let him go," I said.

Kierenbot vocalized a sigh and released Darek.

The Nasarian clutched his hand to his chest and glared at the battlebot.

"Go put the battlebot back in the cradle. I'll meet you on the bridge. Outstanding job today. Thanks for coming for me," I said.

"Happy to serve, Captain," he said and regarded me for a moment. "I couldn't be more pleased with its performance. Did you see me take on those Ustrals? Flinging them into the air was just so satisfying."

"I bet it was," I said.

Kierenbot walked down the corridor, and I thought I saw a spring in his step.

I turned back toward Darek and regarded him thoughtfully. "An intelligence agent. A spy, and you give up your identity just like that?"

"I'm very attached to my limbs, and…" he replied, glancing

at Kierenbot's back as he walked down the corridor, "I have a serious aversion to pain."

I grinned. "Fair enough, but still."

"There are times when only the truth will provide the best way forward. I judged that now was such a time," Darek said.

I placed my hand on my chest. "How poetic of you. I can feel the 'trust me' vibes pouring right off you." I stepped closer to him. "If you give me a reason to be any more suspicious of you than I already am, I'm going to invite Kierenbot to spend some quality time with you. I'll even tell him to impress me with his creativity. Is that clear?"

Darek blinked a few times and nodded wordlessly.

"T'Chura." Kaz's voice came from a nearby hidden speaker.

"I'm here."

"You have a comms session request with a Noorkonian ambassador," Kaz said.

I frowned and looked at T'Chura. He looked troubled, almost like someone who'd been caught doing something they shouldn't have.

"Very well, I'll be right there," T'Chura replied.

I cleared my throat. "Is everything all right?"

T'Chura shook his head. "No, it's not."

# CHAPTER 5

T'Chura was quiet as we walked to the bridge, but that wasn't completely out of the ordinary. Sometimes he just preferred it that way, but there was a brooding quality to his walk.

"If you need some privacy for this, we can clear the bridge for you," I offered.

T'Chura shook his head. "That won't be necessary. This will likely affect you as well."

I frowned and Darek looked at me, considering.

I licked my lips for a second, stalling for time while I tried to think of something intelligent to say. "Okay look, whatever it is, I've got your back. You've saved my ass a bunch of times. I owe you."

T'Chura looked at me and smiled a little. "I am proud to have your friendship, Nathan Briggs."

Such a formal address usually conveyed the seriousness of a situation. I'd tried not to worry about this, but T'Chura's vibe was seriously damaging my calm.

I nodded toward Darek. "What about him? Do you want me to make him wait somewhere else?"

"I appreciate the thought, but it would be unwise to set him loose on the ship. I have no secrets that I wish to keep from him," T'Chura said.

Sometimes the huge alien Sasquatch had a mysterious way about him, like he was some kind of roaming warrior monk. It was insightful at times, but right now it was unsettling. When the calmest person I knew got alarmed, I'd be a fool not to pay attention to that.

We entered the bridge and Kaz stood up.

"Who's our guest?"

"He claims to be a spy from the Tamiran Consortium," I replied.

"Actually, I told you I was an intelligence agent," Darek said.

"Like there's a difference," I said.

Darek's gaze narrowed a little and I shrugged.

"T'Chura," Kaz said, "the messenger claims to be a Noorkon Ambassador with diplomatic credentials. Are you in trouble?"

"I'm about to find out," T'Chura replied.

Kaz regarded him for a long moment and then nodded. He looked at me. "I'll take our guest to see Crim. He can scan him for any hidden devices."

"You don't want to stick around?" I asked.

Kaz glanced at T'Chura and then at me. "Not for this. You should be here, though, because you're the captain of the ship. Ben should be here, too, since he's also the only other owner present."

"Ben's at the autodoc. Let him know to come up here for me, please," I said.

Kaz nodded and gestured Darek toward the door. They left.

I looked at T'Chura. "Is there anything I need to know?

Believe it or not, I'd rather not cause an incident if it can be avoided."

T'Chura snorted a little. "Not to worry. I will advocate for you."

"Okay, I guess we should get this party started then."

T'Chura walked to the nearest workstation, and a few moments later the main holoscreen powered on. A communication session was being established. About a minute later, a Noorkon's head and shoulders appeared on the screen. He was officious looking, with long gray hair, aged skin, and intelligent, alert eyes.

T'Chura and the ambassador regarded each other quietly for a few moments.

After what I thought was enough time, I cleared my throat. "Hello, Ambassador, I'm Nathan Briggs, Captain of the *Spacehog*."

The older Noorkon looked at me. "Greetings to you, Captain Nathan Briggs of the *Spacehog*. I am Telon Oldin, Ambassador of the Noorkonian Star Alliance."

I bowed my head a little in acknowledgement. It just felt like the right thing to do.

T'Chura followed my lead. "Ambassador Oldin, I hear and acknowledge this summons."

"Rarely does something like this come to my attention. I wait for your explanation before I proceed," Telon Oldin said.

"Forgive me," I said. "I'm at a loss as to what's happening here. Has T'Chura done something wrong?"

Telon Oldin regarded me for a few moments. There was nothing hateful or angry in his gaze, just genuine curiosity. "I do not recognize your species."

I smiled. "I'm Human, from a planet called Earth."

Telon Oldin blinked a few times. I don't think he understood me.

"Nathan Briggs is from a juvenile world that has yet to ascend to the galactic community," T'Chura said.

Telon Oldin considered this for a few moments, regarding each of us before settling on me. "And yet, you're the captain of a ship. I assume you hold T'Chura's service contract."

"It's quite a story," I began and noticed a slight shake of T'Chura's head. I took the hint. "For another time. I hold T'Chura's service contract, along with two others."

"They should be present here. I request that they join us at once," Telon Oldin said.

I frowned. "One is on his way here, but the other isn't on the ship at this time."

Telon Oldin nodded. "That is acceptable. A majority is available."

The door to the bridge opened and Ben walked in. He looked up at the main holoscreen.

"Ambassador Oldin, this is Benjamin Stone," I said.

Ben looked at me with a frown, and I tipped my head toward the screen.

"Hello," Ben said.

Telon Oldin nodded his head once. "Thank you for joining us. I must request that you release T'Chura from his service contract so he can return to Napus."

Ben frowned and looked at me.

I gestured for Ben to wait, and I looked at T'Chura, who wouldn't meet my gaze. I looked at the holoscreen. "I don't understand. Why does T'Chura need to return home?"

Telon Oldin's gaze slid toward T'Chura. "You haven't told them? This is highly irregular. They should've been told of your obligations."

I looked at T'Chura and he slowly raised his gaze toward mine. "What's going on here, T'Chura?"

"There are different sects within our society who serve in promoting harmony across the galaxy. We're allowed... encouraged... to travel and live among the other galactic species for a time. Then, it is expected that we return so that our experiences can be chronicled."

"Doesn't sound so bad. What? Do you just send them your video logs or something like that?"

"Recounting experiences is part of it, but I must also teach the younger generation so that our society may grow and expand beyond what we were before," T'Chura replied.

I blinked several times. "You have to leave?"

"He does," Telon Oldin said. "He is duty-bound to return, share his knowledge, and procreate so that our species continues to flourish."

I watched Telon Oldin for a few seconds. "I've never known T'Chura to renege on any of his obligations. I trust him."

"I appreciate your opinion of T'Chura's character, but your judgement is clouded in this matter. T'Chura was honor-bound to return over a year ago. Multiple summons have been sent."

"I've replied to all summons and requested an extension," T'Chura said.

"Indeed, you have, and they have been granted until your most recent summons. That request was denied," Telon Oldin replied.

T'Chura's gaze sank.

I swallowed hard and Ben looked at me.

"I don't understand," Ben said.

"When did the last summons come?" I asked.

"Six months ago," Telon Oldin said.

I looked at T'Chura. It was six months ago that Serena, Ben, and I became owners of the *Spacehog*.

"This seems like a misunderstanding," I said.

"There is no misunderstanding," Telon Oldin insisted. "T'Chura's request has been denied. He must return home without delay."

"But he has a service contract with us," I replied.

"Yeah, but we could just—" Ben started to say, but I interrupted.

"What do *you* want to do, T'Chura?" I asked.

Ben's heart was in the right place. He just wanted to appease the old ambassador, but this was T'Chura's decision.

"I have no choice, Nate. I must go back, but I'm also obligated to you," T'Chura said.

Telon Oldin cleared his throat. "This is why I ask you to release T'Chura from his contract. I will see that you are adequately compensated."

He was trying to buy out T'Chura's contract, but there was a tone about it that I didn't care for. I didn't think T'Chura wanted to leave, regardless of what his obligations were.

"There's more to this than compensation. If T'Chura wishes to return, he will have my full support." I regarded the ambassador for a second. "He'll also have my full support if he wants to stay on the ship."

Telon Oldin's gaze hardened. "Juvenile species sometimes lack the capacity for understanding and respecting other cultural obligations, so in this one instance I will forgive this slight."

I stared at him, putting a bit of firm resolve behind my own gaze. "Well then, let me reiterate my point so you understand. If T'Chura doesn't want to leave, no force in this galaxy is going to make me force him to go, and that includes self-important government officials such as yourself. However, I will forgive this slight against me one time as well in the interest of fairness."

Telon Oldin inhaled a breath and I continued. "Make no mistake. T'Chura is my friend. I don't know what that means to you, but to us on Earth it means a great deal. It means we never turn our backs on them when they need us. It also means we don't sell them out for any amount of compensation. Am I clear, Ambassador Oldin?"

I could feel Ben's wide-eyed gaze on me. He really shouldn't have been surprised by this, not after all the time we'd spent traveling together.

I heard a subsonic growl coming from Telon Oldin. Despite his advanced age, there was something dangerous in his expression that almost made me step back a little.

T'Chura looked at me for a few moments, and I thought I saw a certain amount of pride in his gaze. He turned toward the holoscreen.

"Ambassador Oldin, honor is as important to Humans as it is to us. Two members of the crew are missing, and we are trying to find them. We believe they are in grave danger. I would be remiss in my duties if I forsook them now. However, I promise to return home once we've either found our lost companions or brought those responsible for harming them to justice," T'Chura said.

Telon Oldin inhaled a slow, steadying breath, and then looked at T'Chura. His gaze softened when he did.

"Very well, T'Chura. You have been granted a very short extension to resolve this problem to which you've committed yourself. If you fail to return home after that, I'm afraid the enforcers will be dispatched to collect you," Telon Oldin said.

"I understand," T'Chura replied.

Telon Oldin turned toward me. "Captain Briggs, you profess to be loyal to T'Chura. I urge you to see that he fulfills his obligations because the price if he fails will be quite severe. This may appear harsh to someone who isn't familiar with our laws, but I implore you to do this for me. For T'Chura's sake."

He seemed sincere, and despite the seriousness of his tone, I couldn't sense any of his previous anger. "I will. You have my word."

Telon Oldin regarded me for a long moment and then severed the comlink.

I frowned in thought for a few moments.

"What was that about?" Ben asked.

"I'm not exactly sure," I said and looked at T'Chura. He appeared as if he were expecting something from me. "What was that at the end? This is personal. Telon Oldin isn't just some government official."

"He's not," T'Chura said. "He's my father."

I winced a little. "Maybe we should sit down."

We each sat.

"I'm guessing this is pretty serious if...Your father is an ambassador?"

T'Chura looked more than a little distracted.

"You should meet *my* father sometime. Then we could compare notes."

Ben stared at me. "Your father is an ambassador, too?"

I shook my head. "No, but he did work in government. Really not that important right now."

T'Chura lifted his gaze and seemed to have snapped out of his breakdown. "Thank you for standing by me."

"What are friends for?"

"I was aware of the risks associated with my requests for an extension."

"It sounds like there are serious consequences if you run."

"I would never run. That was never my intent."

"Then where does that leave us?"

"I will remain with you until Serena and Raylin are found," T'Chura said.

I sighed and took a few moments to figure out what I wanted to say. "I don't know all the details, but when government officials—even ones we're related to—begin to use language like 'severe consequences,' it's usually pretty serious."

"I made a promise to protect the crew. If I leave before my task is finished, it will hinder everything I do for the rest of my life. It will cast a shadow over everything I would teach. I will not abandon the crew no matter how many enforcers are sent to collect me."

"It's just a contract. Things happen," Ben said.

"It might appear that way to you, but when we enter into a binding agreement, we cannot simply walk away from it," T'Chura said.

"Well, we both know that's not true," I said.

Ben's eyes widened a little and T'Chura regarded me.

"Your father wanted you to leave and pay us off, so there is some wiggle room."

"I will not walk away."

I shrugged. "Fine, but you don't need to be so dramatic about it."

I grinned, and after a second, T'Chura joined in with a deep basso laugh.

Ben slumped in his chair, looking confused. "Why do I feel like you guys are having a different conversation that I'm not part of?"

"Bah," I said, waving away the comment. "This is what it feels like when you and Crim talk the mysteries of the universe and stuff."

Ben frowned. "You mean physics?"

I mimed a shiver, and Ben rolled his eyes.

I turned toward T'Chura with a solemn expression. "So, this is it?"

He bobbed his large head. "When we are done with this, I must make arrangements to return home."

I hadn't expected T'Chura to ever leave the ship, and certainly not because of some kind of obligation that compelled him to. "For what it's worth, you're welcome on the *Spacehog* anytime you want. Especially if you need a little vacation from all that procreating."

T'Chura laughed, but there was something that seemed to weigh it down a little.

Normally, I would have extended my hand for a good manly handshake and a nod, but since T'Chura's hands were so much bigger than mine, I couldn't bring myself to do it. "When we find Serena and Raylin, I promise to take you wherever you need to go."

T'Chura smiled a little. "I appreciate it."

"Oh, and I won't charge you for it. Free ride. A bit of a sever-ance package. Also, I'm really curious to see where your home world is. Would I be allowed to explore it a bit?"

"Of course. You would just need to apply for visitation, and after a review period, they would allow you to visit the planet," T'Chura replied.

"Somehow, since I'm bringing you home, I figured they'd fast track that whole review process."

"Indeed."

I blew out a long sigh and stood. Our traveling days were numbered. I couldn't imagine not seeing T'Chura's quiet, powerful presence here on the ship. I wasn't going to enjoy that, but I understood a thing or two about obligations. I just tried to avoid them as much as possible.

"Time to interview our new guests," I said.

# CHAPTER 6

We left the bridge and walked toward the elevator.

Ben looked up at T'Chura.

"Yes, Ben?" T'Chura asked.

Ben bit his lower lip for a few seconds, considering. "They want you to go home to chronicle your journey. Does that include the people you've met?"

The elevator doors dematerialized, and we walked in.

"Indeed, it does," T'Chura replied and arched a sizable eyebrow toward Ben. "You're wondering if you'll have an entry in what I'll write."

Ben's cheeks reddened a little and he nodded. "You don't have to. I was just wondering."

"No need to wonder. All meaningful encounters have a place in my chronicle that will be preserved for all time."

Ben smiled a little. "Really? What will you say about me?"

I sighed and gave him a pointed look. "Pry much? It could be private."

Ben grimaced, and he looked at T'Chura. "I'm so sorry. If it's private, then never mind. I was just curious."

The elevator doors opened to H-Deck.

T'Chura shrugged. "There is no need to apologize. All of you have entries in my journal."

I arched an eyebrow up at the big guy. "Now *I'm* curious."

"There's nothing wrong with curiosity," T'Chura replied.

They walked down the corridor, heading toward the medbay.

After a few moments, I grinned.

Ben frowned. "What?"

"He's messing with us. Getting us curious and then not elaborating."

Ben shook his head. "I don't think he'd do that…" his voice trailed off as T'Chura gave him a guilty smile.

"It's fine," I said. "I don't want to know."

T'Chura's face became a stoic mask of serenity. "Then I shall respect your wishes," he said and was silent for a few moments. "Ben, there is nothing I've added to my journal that I haven't already conveyed to you. These aren't secret things. Noorkons don't behave that way."

I chuckled. "That's true. Remember N'Jaka? He hated me from the start and didn't even try to hide it."

T'Chura pressed his lips together, grimacing as if he'd bitten into something bitter. N'Jaka was also a Noorkon, but he was the antithesis of the ideals of Noorkonian society. N'Jaka was far from the only member of the species to reject the traditions of their elders, but what was both interesting and scary was the physical manifestation those differences presented as they aged. It was like encountering someone with a persistent glower; they were never going to be the life of the party. But in the case of N'Jaka, he'd likely slaughter the party because he didn't like the way they looked.

Ben stared at me for a moment and I shrugged. "There are assholes in every species. Why would aliens be any different?"

"I guess. I just would've hoped they were better at working out their differences," Ben replied.

"It's hard, but there also comes a point where people are just delusional. Pandering to those delusions is a disservice to those individuals and bad all around."

Ben smiled a little. "Here we go again."

I frowned and looked at them both. "What?"

Ben shrugged. "You just assert your opinions in a consistent manner."

"That's because they're right. As a kid I wanted to be Superman—fly, be super strong, and all that. No matter how much I pretended, I was never going to be Superman. It would be wrong for me to expect everyone else to cater to my own pretend world."

Ben nodded. "I get it, and I agree. It's silly."

I looked up at T'Chura. "You're awfully quiet."

"You'd be surprised at how much you learn by simply listening."

"So, what have you learned?"

"That complex problems rarely have simple solutions. In our history, we've been extremely violent and have grown to be more compassionate," T'Chura said.

"Are you saying I need to be more tolerant?"

"Only to a point. What you've described is anarchy, which only ends in death and destruction. The trials of your species will be ongoing for a while."

Ben's face paled a little in alarm.

"However," T'Chura continued, "it is within your capacity to overcome these issues, and when you do, you'll be better off for it."

I smiled and tipped my head toward Ben. "See, T'Chura has faith in us, kid. Don't be so worried all the time."

"I'm not. At least, not as much."

"Good, now we've got a couple of newcomers who will hopefully have information that will lead us to the others," I said.

We walked into the medbay. Kaz stood inside the lounge near a small hallway that led to several examination rooms. Kierenbot was there and back inside his normal humanoid robot body of dark metal.

"They're almost done," Kaz said. "The autodoc was able to heal Jeshi's injuries, but he'll be a bit sore for a while."

I remembered seeing the broken metallic shafts sticking out of his small body. "He looked pretty bad off before."

"The autodoc is quite familiar with Nasarian physiology. The reason your visits took longer is because it hadn't encountered Humans before." He sighed. "I can barely remember what that was like," he said wistfully.

I snorted and he grinned. "Darek says he's an intelligence agent. You just left him alone in the autodoc?"

"Negative, Captain. I've been monitoring his activity. His scans are complete and he's heading for the door now," Kierenbot said.

True to Kierenbot's word, the door to one of the exam rooms opened and Darek walked out.

"Any injuries?" I asked.

"Not anymore. The autodoc series is quite impressive," Darek replied.

"Oh?"

"The multi-species libraries are quite extensive, and the data libraries are kept up to date. That's something that gets neglected all too often."

I glanced at Kierenbot for a second. "Well, we try to keep the ship in tiptop shape."

The far door opened and Jeshi walked out. He spotted Darek and then the rest of us.

I waved him over. "How are you feeling?"

Sometimes people just jumped right into the thing they wanted most, but if there was time, I usually got a much better response by easing into it.

"I sustained no less than eight deep puncture wounds—two in my leg, two in my side, and four across my back."

"And yet here you are."

"You almost killed me."

I shook my head and frowned. "Actually, I saved your life."

"Well, you did a poor job of it," Jeshi replied in a matter-of-fact tone. "I'd like to return to my quarters. There are things there I must retrieve."

"That's not going to be a good idea. Did you forget the friendly Ustrals that were trying to kill us?"

Jeshi frowned and glanced at Darek. "You said you'd protect me."

"I did protect you. You're still alive," Darek replied.

"But all my things are gone. Where are we? I don't think I've been to this part of the outpost."

I was beginning to wonder if Jeshi had taken a blow to the head. "You're on my ship."

Jeshi's eyes lit up. "A ship! Really? Truly? You have a ship?"

I nodded. "Want to see the bridge?"

"Yes!" Jeshi replied, nodding vehemently.

"Well, come on then. I'll show it to you. We'll all go," I said.

We left the medbay and went back to the bridge.

"This is the cleanest ship I've ever seen," Jeshi said.

Kierenbot preened at the compliment. He organized the cleaning bots that took care of everyday things like that.

Ben leaned toward me. "Is this really who sent the message?"

I nodded. "Yes, and there were people willing to kill him for it."

We entered the bridge and Jeshi's eyes widened as he took in the sight. I waited a few moments for him to look around.

"I need your help, Jeshi. I came to find you because of the message you sent."

Jeshi looked up at me. "I send lots of messages. The outpost is the communications hub for the sector. So many signals to play with."

"Yes, and you mentioned a game."

Jeshi nodded. "Yes, secret messages. Very old."

"Do you remember the message you sent me?"

Jeshi shook his head. "I don't know the individual messages. I sample the network traffic and use automated parsers to put out a new message. Sometimes I just alter what's there."

I brought up the main holoscreen. "This is the message we received. It was addressed to Lanaya."

A series of images and flashes of color appeared.

"When Lanaya watched the message, this is what happened."

I brought up the recording of Lanaya on the bridge.

*"Nathan Briggs, I have them. If you want them back, you'll need to do something for me."*

Jeshi watched it intently. "Message protocols hidden in the images and colors was interpreted by a conditioned agent."

I nodded. "But you addressed it to me."

Jeshi shook his head. "No, I didn't. The message construction was such that it was addressed to the captain. This is how the game is played and the pieces are moved."

I looked at the others. "What do you guys think of this?"

Ben shrugged. "Conceptually, it makes sense."

"I would also agree," Kierenbot replied.

Both Kaz and T'Chura nodded.

I tried to hide my disappointment. I'd hoped I missed something important that the others had picked up on. I looked at Jeshi. "Why do you do this? Why play the game?"

"They try to hide the messages. Finding them is fun. It's a challenge," Jeshi said.

"He's telling the truth," Darek said.

"Why do it, though?" I asked.

"He can't stop himself," Darek said.

"What do you mean?"

"It's how his brain works. It looks for puzzles and patterns."

"And that's why you were looking for him for that agency you said you worked for?"

Darek nodded. "Tamiran Consortium."

I glanced at Kaz, who gave me a slight shake of his head.

"That's interesting," I said, moving toward Darek. "The Tamiran Consortium is a military contractor."

Darek nodded. "They are. I'm in the intelligence division. I have credentials if you'd like to verify them."

I eyed him for a second. "I bet they'd look authentic, but I really wouldn't know how to determine if they're fake."

T'Chura moved to stand behind Darek.

I leveled my gaze at Darek. We were about the same height. "So I guess I'm going to have to trust my gut, and it's telling me you're lying."

"I assure you that I'm not being dishonest," Darek said.

He'd stepped back from me and bumped against T'Chura's muscled body.

I gave him a once-over and then inclined my chin toward

T'Chura. He grabbed Darek's arms, easily pinning them to his side.

"What's the meaning of this? I already told you who I was. I told you everything," Darek said.

I stepped across the bridge and palmed the controls for the escape pod, making a sweeping gesture. "In you go."

T'Chura pushed Darek into the escape pod and I palmed the controls to jettison it.

"What have you done!" Jeshi shouted. "Why did you do that? He was going to help me."

"Yeah, he promised to help me, too, but he's lying. It's time he learned that this is unacceptable," I said and looked at Kierenbot.

"Tracking the escape pod," Kierenbot said.

I nodded. "Good," I said and looked at Kaz. He raised his eyebrows. "I have to say, it's much better being on this side of that whole thing." I gestured toward the escape pod doors.

Kaz grinned. "It's effective."

"It certainly is," I replied.

Jeshi stared at the holoscreen, which showed the location of the escape pod. "There is no help for him within range. But the emergency broadcast beacon should work fine."

"You're assuming the beacon works," I said.

Jeshi's eyes widened and he stared at the holoscreen.

"Tell me more about this game," I said to him.

I had a few minutes to kill while Darek contemplated the futility of his situation.

Jeshi blinked and looked around the bridge. "It's secret messages. They try to hide them from me, but I also find them. Then I change them up and send them on their way."

I shook my head. "And you never thought someone would come looking for you?"

Jeshi shrugged narrow shoulders. "It's a game. They're playing a game, too."

I gave Jeshi a long look. "I don't think it's a game."

"What else could it be?"

"Someone's operations."

"Yes, their secret, clandestine operations."

I wasn't sure how much help Jeshi was going to be. Serena and Raylin's lives hung in the balance.

"Kierenbot, give me a channel to the escape pod," I said.

"Ready, Captain."

A smaller window appeared on the main holoscreen.

"Hello, Darek, if that's your real name," I said.

Darek swung his head around, trying to find the source. I hadn't activated the video on his end, so he could only hear me.

"Let me explain the futility of your situation. Right now, you're in a modified escape pod. Life support is only going to work for a few hours. Emergency broadcast beacons are disabled, and we're out in the middle of nowhere. I doubt anyone knows you're here, but regardless, we'll be long gone before anyone comes to collect you."

I watched as Darek looked around the escape pod. Some of the panels had been opened, but he was smart enough not to try to do anything with them.

"Okay, I admit that I'm completely at your mercy," Darek said.

"What's your real name?"

"Darek Senesca."

I glanced at Kierenbot, who gave me a nod.

"Kierenbot says you're being truthful. That's a good start. Who do you work for?"

"I already told you. I'm an intelligence agent with the Tamiran Consortium."

Kierenbot put up an analysis of Darek's speech patterns on the window next to the video feed from the escape pod. I brought up the life-support configuration for the escape pod, and a small holoscreen appeared in front of Darek.

"This is your current life-support capacity. Watch as I now cut it in half."

The meter went down by half. Darek now only had ninety minutes of artificial atmosphere left.

"If you continue insisting on these lies, I'm going to keep reducing your life support until there is none left. By the way, I cannot put it back."

"Why can't you put it back?" Darek asked.

"I mean that once it's gone, there's none left. I'm venting it into space. Feel like telling me the truth now?"

"I am an intelligence agent—"

"I already know that part. You know what? I'm taking another half away just because you're irritating me," I said.

The escape pod's life support was reduced to forty-five minutes.

"Nate, are you really going to kill him?" Ben asked, his voice sounding uncertain.

"I will if he doesn't cooperate," I said.

Ben looked at the others and I ignored him.

"I'm waiting for an answer, Darek. Better answer quickly. Ben's getting uncomfortable," I said and waited a few seconds. "Whoops, there go the heaters. It's going to get quite cold in there now."

Darek clutched his arms around his body and shivered. I was actually surprised it happened so fast.

"I'm an agent with the CGH," Darek said.

"I love a good acronym. Can you guys confirm what the CGH is?" I asked.

"CGH is the Council for Galactic Harmony," Kierenbot said. "It's a multi-species initiative that works to ensure stability across the galaxy."

"And do they use intelligence agents?"

"Yes, dammit. They do!" Darek shouted. "But they don't advertise the fact that they have agents out in the field. Now turn the heat back on."

I enabled the camera near me so Darek could see my face. "I'm afraid it's not possible."

Darek sneered at me. "Listen to me. I was investigating the abductions of juvenile species. I wasn't lying about that. Recently, there has been a resurgence of clandestine programs. I'm part of a task force that was formed to figure out who's involved."

"That's it? You figure out who's doing it, and then what? They just go on with business as usual?"

Darek shivered, and I could see a puff of steam leave his mouth. "No, don't be obtuse. My mission serves a greater purpose. Intelligence must be gathered before the groups involved can be neutralized."

I regarded him for a few seconds. "Obtuse? Is that some kind of fancy way of calling me stupid? I don't appreciate that kind of talk. I mean, I'm a member of a juvenile species. I'm probably prone to all kinds of primitive behaviors. You know, like just killing people who lie to me or are a problem. Nah, that was Menka Tamplin. You remember the Ustral that tried to kill both of us? He's one of the enlightened ones. No, I don't like being called obtuse. Not at all."

The life-support meter went down by half and then half again. "You're down to eleven minutes now. It's not looking good for you, Darek."

"Stop it! I'm cooperating. You're just…"

I tilted my head so my ear was closer to the camera. "I'm just what? What were you going to say? I'm just what, Darek?"

Darek just glared into the camera.

"What about Kael Torsin?"

Darek frowned. "What about him?"

"I think he's involved in this. I think he captured my friends and is going to hurt them to get back at me. Do you know where Kael Torsin is?"

Darek shook his head. "He's dead."

I blinked and then glanced at Kierenbot. He gave me a nod. Darek was telling the truth.

"I don't believe you," I said and began reaching toward the escape pod controls.

"Wait. Wait! We investigated Kael Torsin. There were some raids and military equipment was stolen. We thought he was part of the group that was resurrecting the programs that were doing the abductions, but I swear to you that he is dead. I saw the operation that killed him. No one could've walked away from that. No one, not even Kael Torsin."

I looked at the alien lie detector and it showed that Darek Senesca, agent for the CGH, was telling me the truth.

I narrowed my gaze and reached toward the holo-interface. "See, Darek, I can be reasonable. With the right motivation, even someone like yourself can be made into a cooperative guest. Not bad for someone considered to be your junior."

Darek swallowed hard. "What happens now?"

He looked cold, and his shivering affected how his words sounded.

I looked up at Kierenbot. "Okay, bring him back."

"At once, Captain."

# CHAPTER 7

The escape pod retrieval had really come down to the wire for Darek's life support. The pod had been recovered and was now in Crim's workshop. While Kierenbot used retrieval drones to guide the escape pod into the small hangar bay, we arrived in time for Crim to open the pod.

Ben kept giving me sidelong glances. He was worried that I would've killed Darek if he hadn't cooperated.

I arched an eyebrow toward him. "What's on your mind, kid?"

"Nothing."

I rolled my eyes. "I wasn't going to kill him."

"You could've fooled me."

I smiled. "That's the point. Darek needed to believe that I would do it. *That's* what was important."

Ben stared at me for a second. "And if he'd kept lying?"

"Then he'd have no further use. He'd be a ticking time bomb just waiting to go off at the worst time."

Ben shook his head. "So you'd just leave him?"

"I already said I wouldn't. I'd knock him out and he'd wake up on whatever space station I decided to dump him on."

Ben heaved a sigh. "God Nate, sometimes I can't tell what you'll do."

"I'm not about to go on a killing spree, if that's what you're worried about."

He looked down at the floor. "I know you wouldn't. Well, I guess I had doubts about that, and that's what concerns me. I know there are some unresolved things between you and Serena. That's gotta be gnawing away at you."

I quickened my pace to join the others inside, and Ben sprinted to catch up with me.

"That's it? You're just going to ignore me?"

I sighed. "I didn't think you needed a reply. Was there a question buried in all those weepy-eyed statements?"

That came out a lot harsher than it was supposed to, and I regretted it a little.

"I'm just trying to help," Ben said.

It was my turn to look away. Ben was good people. He didn't deserve to be snapped at, and I wasn't mad at him. "Flynn wanted me to make sure she was safe. It was his dying wish, and I screwed it up."

His eyes widened. "I didn't know that."

"Yeah, well now you do."

"You couldn't have known what was going to happen. She chose to leave," Ben said.

I gritted my teeth for a second. "Doesn't matter."

Crim called out to me. He stood near the escape pod. "You two want to hurry up and get over here, or should I just let him die in there?"

I spared Ben a quick glance and tipped my head toward the pod. Then we jogged over to it.

"I'm here. Don't get all uppity about it," I said.

Crim flung an arm off to the side. "You!" he shouted. Jeshi had been walking toward the battlewagon, one of Crim's most prized possessions. "Get away from there if you know what's good for you. There, that's it. Get back over here where I can see you."

Sometimes Crim reminded me of a crotchety old mechanic. He had a no-nonsense attitude, and his workshop was his domain that just happened to be on my ship.

Crim popped the hatch and I heard Darek suck in a deep breath. He quickly climbed out and stood on the ground, bent over and gasping for breath. After a few moments he glared up at me and scowled. When he saw that I didn't care about his distress, he stood up.

"I'm glad we could get that cleared up," I said.

Darek growled and lunged at me. I'd been expecting it.

I stepped to the side, grabbed his arm as he went by, and flipped him onto his back. Darek stared up at the ceiling as I loomed over him.

"You can do better than that, but you might want to think about where you are," I said.

Darek looked around at the rest of the crew and sighed.

I backed up, giving him room to get to his feet.

"Do we have an understanding?" I asked.

Darek bobbed his head.

"I don't want to have a repeat of this conversation."

"You tossed me in an escape pod, drained my life support, and cut off the heat."

I looked at him for a few moments. "I know. Sucks, doesn't

it?" I said and glanced at Kaz. "But effective. The way I see it is that we can work together, but only if you stop jerking me around."

Darek glanced at Kaz and then looked at me. "Fine. I'd like to use your communications systems to report back—"

I laughed and shook my head. "You've got to crawl before you walk. I'm going to check your credentials."

"You won't find anything. I have a contact I can give you. You can be there the whole time and monitor it."

He was persistent, but I wasn't about to trust him. "You'd be surprised. I know influential people too."

Darek looked at me and his shoulders slumped.

"Put yourself in my shoes for a minute—Never mind. I've made the decision, and that's it. Prove yourself to be an asset and you'll live longer. Don't, and the next time you leave this ship will be through the airlock *without* an escape pod."

Darek bridged his hands in front of his chest. "Very well."

I pursed my lips for a few seconds. "Moving on, are you sure about Kael Torsin?"

Darek frowned in genuine surprise. "The reports indicate that he died while leading a raid on a Mesakloren military compound."

"How do they know he died?"

Darek glanced at the others before answering. "Because of the explosion. No one survived. I'd thought he was involved with the abductions."

"That can't be right," Lanaya said. "I was just a little girl when I was taken."

I nodded. "She's right, the timeline doesn't add up. Are you saying that Kael Torsin was involved in the old programs then?"

"We're not sure."

"Why not?"

"It was before my time at the agency. I reviewed the investigations from when the old program that was performing the abductions was stopped. Survivors were returned to their home worlds," Darek said, and looked at Lanaya. "The agents involved did everything they could."

"They hid us. My memories of it are distorted," she said.

"So someone restarted the old programs," I said, "and retrieved the hidden pieces like where Lanaya was held captive? It's unclear whether Kael Torsin was involved, and you believe he's dead. Do you have any other information about who's involved?"

Darek shook his head. "Like you, I was tracing the encrypted messages to their source. That's when I found Jeshi. He was being tortured when I arrived. Those were the bodies you saw in his hideout."

I looked at Jeshi. "Is that true?"

"Yes, they hurt me. They didn't believe me about the game."

I looked up at the ceiling and sighed. "So we're back to square one without much to go on."

"Nate," Lanaya said, "I've tried to remember more about the facility where I was kept. Raylin gave me exercises to perform that would help unlock the memories, but I can't make it work. I'm sorry."

"Don't be sorry. It's not your fault," Ben said.

She smiled regretfully, looking ashamed.

"He's right, Lanaya. I know you'd help if you could," I said.

She lifted her gaze to me, her eyes misty. "It is my fault. They went searching for the facility because of me." She balled her hands into fists. "I've tried so hard to remember."

"It's not your fault. You hear me? You didn't ask for this. They did this to you," I said, feeling my own anger and frustration rising.

Jeshi cleared his throat and looked as if he was about to say something.

I raised my eyebrows. "You look like you've got something to say. Don't be shy now. Say it."

Jeshi's eyes darted to Lanaya and then back at me. "There might be a way to unlock her memories."

I looked at Lanaya and frowned. "How?"

"The secret message protocols. They're designed to be used by trained agents."

"And you know the protocol that will unlock her memories?"

Jeshi shook his head. "I've used the protocols, but there's nothing about memory recall per se."

I frowned. "I'm confused."

Lanaya stared at Jeshi. "What do you think you can do with the protocols?"

"I might be able to trick the blocks that are in place to reveal themselves and help you remember. I think this will be a most challenging game," Jeshi said.

"It's not a game," Ben said. "Lanaya, this sounds dangerous. He doesn't know what he's doing. He's just grasping in the dark, hoping to get lucky."

Jeshi nodded thoughtfully. "Luck does play a part in the game. Must be accounted for, but—no, it can work. I just need access to—"

"I'm not letting you anywhere near her!" Ben shouted.

Lanaya moved in front of him, and he stared into her large blue eyes. "Ben, I want to do this. It might be the only way we can find Serena and Raylin."

He swallowed hard. "It's not safe. It could damage your brain. You have no idea what's been locked away, what's been done to you. There has to be another way."

Lanaya leaned toward him until their foreheads touched.

They grasped each other's hands, and then she pulled back a little. "It's my risk to take. I want to do this," she said. Ben shook his head. "Look at me. No matter what happens, I know you'll be there for me. How can I stand by and do nothing? I can't. I want you to be with me. Help them. Make sure they do it right. Will you do that for me?"

Ben squeezed his eyes shut for a few seconds. "I don't know if I can do this."

"You can. There's no one else I trust more than you. You must do this for me."

Ben inhaled a deep breath and nodded.

I watched them and found myself agreeing with Ben, but I wasn't immune to the risks that Lanaya was willing to accept, and I also had to agree with her. Unlocking those memories could be the only way to find Serena.

I turned toward Kierenbot. "Can you help with this?"

"With what, Captain?"

"Jeshi's proposal. Using the protocols to trick the blocks in Lanaya's brain to reveal where she was being held captive."

Kierenbot's red orb swung toward Lanaya and then Jeshi, considering.

"I can't say whether or not this is possible without learning the details of what Jeshi has done."

Jeshi rubbed his hands and stared at Kierenbot. "A worthy adversary."

I shook my head. "Uh, no. Not an adversary. I want you to work *with* Kierenbot. You're on the same team."

Jeshi frowned while he considered it for a few moments. "Do you mean a collaboration?"

"Yes, with Ben, too. Lanaya as well. She might have insight into it, too," I said. Ben frowned. "Go with it, kid. Something might kick over a rock and a lightbulb will come on."

"Okay," Ben said.

"There are standard messages we can try," Jeshi said, and then he became quiet, but his head still bobbed as if he was having some kind of inner dialogue.

I snapped my fingers and he looked at me. "You guys need to work together. Come up with a plan. Then before you do anything, you tell us what the plan is. Understood?"

Jeshi nodded. "A plan of attack to be reviewed by the general," he said and offered some kind of salute.

I shared a look with Ben for a second and then looked at Crim. "Can you help them?"

"This is beyond my capabilities," Crim said.

I rolled my eyes. "Don't give me that. You're an engineer. See if you follow their logic and help them stay on task."

Crim frowned thoughtfully and eyed me for a second. "Okay."

I looked at Ben. "If things start unraveling, I expect you to let me know. Same with you, Lanaya. I know you want to help us find Serena and Raylin, but weigh the risk appropriately."

"I will," Lanaya said.

"Where are you going to work?" I asked.

"Here," Crim said. "We have space over there."

He gestured toward a workbench by the wall, and they walked over to it. That left me with Kaz, T'Chura, and Darek.

I looked at Kaz. "Take Darek, get him some food, and let him get cleaned up. T'Chura, why don't you go with them."

Darek looked at them and didn't say anything.

"What are you going to do?" Kaz asked.

I shrugged. "Oh, you know, take a nap or something. I mean… I'm the captain. I delegate." I pretended to yawn, then I stretched my arms over my head. "Yup, a nap is just the thing. I'll be on the bridge," I said and headed for the door.

I paused and turned back toward them. "Oh, and if Darek gives you any trouble, let Kierenbot know. He wanted to demonstrate what the battlebot can do. Feats of strength and all that."

Darek glanced at Kierenbot, looking worried.

"Understood," Kaz said. "Go enjoy your nap, Captain."

# CHAPTER 8

A nap was the furthest thing from my mind when I stopped at the commons area to make a cup of coffee. The food processor chimed, indicating that the hot water was ready. I scooped a couple of spoonfuls of coffee grounds into the French Press and poured the hot water into it, inhaling the soothing aromatic air with hints of milk chocolate, cherries, and caramel. I set a brew timer and opened the cabinet door where we kept the coffee mugs. There was a set of them that had a cartoon version of the sun and moon on them. Serena liked them, and they'd grown on me. I found that I'd absently grab one of them instead of the plain white ones I'd created using the fabricator. They seemed so ordinary now. I picked up one of the white mugs and held it in my hand.

Kael Torsin was dead, and Jeshi played some kind of game with the messages he'd intercepted. But who'd sent the message in the first place?

I stared intently at the plain white mug in my hand for a

minute, then put it back on the shelf and grabbed one of Serena's mugs.

The countdown timer chimed, and I poured my coffee. After adding cream and sugar, I took a sip. It was sweet, a little bitter, and delicious. I looked at the nearby table, remembering all the meals I'd shared with the crew. Sometimes we were all together but also in ones and twos. It just depended. Ever since they'd left, it felt like something was missing on the ship.

I sipped my coffee and shook my head, trying not to think about my promise to Flynn. It did motivate me, but Serena was worth more to me than that. As the months went by, I'd become more and more desperate to find her. I wanted to find Raylin too, but I couldn't help feeling that I'd failed Serena somehow. The stupid arguments we'd had seemed to swirl around me and just fall away, daring me to admit they didn't matter. She was in trouble, and I needed to find her. It was as simple as that.

I'd scared Ben. He thought I was going to kill Darek, and he might not have been wrong about that. After I'd gotten what I needed, I could easily say I wasn't going to kill him, but when I put myself back in the moment, I couldn't be sure about that. Ever since I'd gotten that message, I'd thought Kael Torsin had taken them prisoner. If there was someone in the galaxy who wanted to get revenge on me, it was him. I was even willing to let Lanaya risk her life for this. Sure, I'd tried to minimize the risk, but I was more than willing to let her try.

I set the cup down on the counter and gritted my teeth.

"Time to do something useful," I said and walked toward the door.

Eager to place some distance between myself and my memories, I hastened to the bridge. Sometimes I really hated downtime. At least while I was working I could keep my mind occupied with the task at hand, but it was only a temporary reprieve from imagining what was happening to Serena. What little Lanaya could remember was terrifying enough. She had been powerless against her captors.

By the time I reached the bridge I was ready to kick the damn door in. I didn't because I knew it was futile, but that didn't mean I didn't want to hurt something.

I went to the nearest workstation and brought up the communications interface. I had a limited number of contacts, but the ones I did have were quite resourceful and had access to things I just didn't have.

I initiated a comlink and waited for it to connect. A few minutes later, the connection was established, and a video call became active.

"Hello, Delos," I said.

"Nate, this is unexpected."

"I appreciate your taking this call."

Delos was a Nasarian VIP on the Zerian Board of Directors, a very powerful and influential mega-corporation in the galaxy.

"Always, Nate. What can I do for you?"

"I need information. We encountered a Nasarian who claims to be part of the Council of Galactic Harmony. His name is Darek Senesca. Are you able to validate that he is who he says he is?"

"I'll look into it."

I frowned. Delos had high levels of clearance. "You can't just pull up a data session on your holoscreen and find out?"

Delos grinned and shook his head. "Not for the CGH."

"Oh," I said dejectedly.

"It won't take long. I have a few contacts at the CGH that I can ask. Is the agent with you?"

I nodded. "Yeah, he's on the ship," I said and told him how I traced the message.

Delos regarded me for a second. "CGH agents are very good. You must have done a convincing job to get him to cooperate."

"I can be persuasive, Delos. Never underestimate my ability to get people motivated to cooperate."

Delos leaned away from the camera. "I probably don't want to know."

"Agreed. There's something else I'd like to ask you."

"What is it?"

"Kael Torsin. According to Darek, he was killed in a raid for some military equipment. Can you confirm that?"

"It's true."

"When did it happen?"

"It's quite recent. About a week ago."

"Okay, do you know anything about this program Darek was investigating?"

"I've been digging into this for months, ever since Serena first told me about it. There were abduction programs being run by various rogue groups and some intelligence agencies who work for influential corporations and governments."

"Zerian?"

Delos shook his head. "No, my aunt would never have allowed it. But the Tamiran Consortium had been implicated in those operations. They were shuttered and disbanded."

"Well, someone's been starting it up again. Lanaya proves it."

"I'll do all I can to help you, Nate. But without more to go on I'm not sure what else I can do."

"Thanks anyway, Delos."

"What are you going to do now?"

"I'm going to keep searching. I have a few things to check out. If I learn something, I'll let you know."

I severed the comlink and stood on the bridge.

"Kierenbot, are you there?" I asked.

A small window with Kierenbot's face appeared on my holoscreen.

"I'm always available, Captain."

Kierenbot could multitask with the best of them.

"I need you to do something for me."

"Of course. What is it you need?"

I just looked at him for a second, trying to figure out how I wanted to put this. "Well, it's not so much you as it is who's monitoring you."

Kierenbot frowned. "Monitoring me? I'm afraid that's impossible."

He had no memory of what had happened.

"You'll have to take my word for it."

"I trust you, Captain. But I must insist that if there was someone monitoring me, I'd know about it. I would initiate protection protocols, and if that didn't work, a reset of storage matrix. We took every precaution when we migrated our minds to their current forms."

Kierenbot was an artificial intelligence and believed it was actually part of a living species that created technology to allow their minds to be transferred into a robot.

"I realize all that, but you're going to have to have a little faith no matter how strange it might sound. Can you do that for me?"

"Yes, Captain. What exactly do you want me to do?"

I looked around the bridge. I was alone. I leaned toward the camera. "I'm going to say some things and I don't want you to respond. Just listen and wait."

He frowned. "Are you sure you're feeling okay, Captain? I know you don't like the autodoc, but it might be able to help."

I shook my head. "No. Just go with it. I'm going to start."

Kierenbot stared at me.

"I know you're listening. You're monitoring everything. I need your help to locate Serena and Raylin. They've been missing for months."

Kierenbot continued to stare at me.

"I need the Collective to help me. Remember that Kierenbot was cleared for level three regarding Human interaction. I didn't forget. You must be able to help me."

Kierenbot didn't say anything.

"Is Kael Torsin alive?"

Nothing.

"Can you at least acknowledge that you've received this message?" I asked, beginning to feel foolish.

No response.

I slammed my fists on the workstation. "Dammit! I know you're there. I know you can hear me. Answer me."

"Captain, I'm not sure what you expect from me. Perhaps I should inform the others. Maybe they—"

"No!" I said harshly, then grinned a little. "It's fine, Kierenbot. No need to involve them."

Kierenbot regarded me for a few moments. "If you say so."

I sighed. "Never mind. Go back to what you were doing."

"Are you sure?"

"Yes," I said.

The comlink severed, and I leaned forward, resting my face in my palms. I knew the Collective was out there, some kind of AI group that monitored everything through who knew how many robots and perhaps even other kinds of computer systems. They'd spoken to me once. Why wouldn't they do it again?

I blew out a breath. Now I really wanted to punch something.

# CHAPTER 9

It was sometimes shocking to me how much time could be spent searching for the wrong things, hoping it would lead to the right ones. I knew better than that, but I felt like I had to do something. It wasn't enough, and I had to admit that I'd run out of options—at least the options I'd come up with.

Kaz had told me that sometimes Raylin would leave the ship to do something on her own. They had protocols to contact one another by way of coded messages delivered through some kind of public transit. It had worked reliably before, but now nothing worked. All attempts at communication had failed. There wasn't even so much as a status update, which I couldn't imagine Serena going along with. She knew I'd come searching for her. Therefore, something had to have happened early on that prevented them from contacting us. The problem was that I couldn't imagine what that could be.

I stood up and dismissed the multiple holoscreens I'd been working on. I wasn't getting anywhere doing this.

I left the bridge and went to the commons area where Kaz and Darek were.

I looked for T'Chura, but he wasn't there.

"He's organizing his log entries," Kaz said.

The two were sitting at a table. There were empty bowls that had held some kind of soup, only it wasn't soup. They called it something else, but I couldn't remember what. Kaz was particular about his meals. Sometimes they had a distinctly unpleasant smell that reminded me of the pungent body odor that builds after days without a shower.

I wrinkled my nose and Darek frowned.

"They don't like the smell of our food," Kaz said.

"As long as it doesn't affect your breath, I'm fine with it," I said, sitting down at the table. I looked at Darek. "Refreshed?"

"I'm warm now."

I nodded and looked at Kaz. "I've been trying to think of reasons Raylin would've stayed out of contact, outside of them being hurt, that is."

"She's never done it before, but I wouldn't put it past her. She's always been independent. She knows how to blend in, so I doubt they were captured. At least, not at the onset."

I looked at Darek. "What do you think?"

"Me?"

I nodded. "You're an intelligence agent. Didn't you ever go undercover?"

He frowned. "Only if someone was shooting at me."

I rolled my eyes. "I meant a disguise. You know, for infiltrating somewhere."

Darek glanced at Kaz for a second. "I see what you mean."

I divided my glower between both of them.

Kaz shrugged. "It's just a joke, Nate."

"I'm not in the mood for it."

Darek leaned back, looking worried. "I meant no offense. Yes, I've participated in many infiltration assignments. I've even worked with Tamerrons who are adept at changing their appearance. Bottom line is that if they didn't want to be discovered, they wouldn't be. I'm sorry I can't say the same for your friend."

"I'm aware of the reality of the situation," I replied. The others maintained a pitying silence that I hated. "They could be dead. All right, I said it, but I'm not going to stop until I find out if they are. So, stop tiptoeing around. Raylin is skilled. She's a former intelligence agent."

"She never confirmed that," Kaz said.

I shrugged. "So what? She was. If I'm wrong, she can tell me herself."

Darek watched me for a few moments. "It's a difficult profession to leave behind."

"But not impossible."

Darek didn't look as if he agreed, but he hadn't met Raylin.

"I think they went undercover to find out Lanaya's origins. When we first found her, she had the strongest reaction to Raylin. She was afraid of her, remember?" I asked Kaz.

"Yes, and this made Raylin believe it had to do with the abductions."

"Yes!" I said. "She was aware of these programs and was maybe involved in shutting some of them down." Darek frowned at me. "You think there was only one of them? Big galaxy, multiple species, a good amount of competition, each group looking to give themselves an edge."

"This is what the CGH strives to prevent," Darek said.

We were all quiet for a minute.

"I don't think they're dead," I said.

"That doesn't explain why they haven't contacted us," Kaz replied.

"If I knew that, I'd know where they are."

Darek leaned toward me. "The more time that passes, the less likely this will have the outcome you want."

I felt my face become hot, and I gritted my teeth. "Then I'll hunt down every last one of them who's responsible. Every. Single. One."

"So the plan is to wage your own personal war?" Darek asked.

"Don't doubt him," Kaz warned. "And he wouldn't be alone."

Darek eyed us, considering. "Understood."

A message buzzed on my omnitool. I stood. "Come on. Crim says they're ready."

We headed for the door.

"Ready for what?" Darek asked.

"To help Lanaya access her memories. Try and keep up," I said.

"I didn't think they'd be done so quickly."

"Funny, I was thinking it was taking them too long."

Between the quick pace and the silent anticipation, we soon entered Crim's workshop.

I led the others over to the workbench where Crim and Jeshi were speaking. There was a metal chair with smart-fabric cushions. It looked like something stored in Crim's spare-parts stockpile. There were dark scorch marks on the side, and I stared at it for a few seconds, frowning.

Crim gestured toward the chair. "Recognize it?"

I nodded. "Looks familiar. Is that from the old battlewagon?"

Crim smiled. "Indeed, I salvaged what I could from it."

Crim was a pack rat, always reluctant to discard anything that could be used, even if he couldn't think of a use for that thing at the time. I'd been on him a few times about getting rid of some of the junk he'd collected.

He gave me a knowing look, and I rolled my eyes. "One chair doesn't make up for using nearly half the ship's storage capacity for your junk."

Crim's eyes widened. "Not junk!"

He always took everything personally. I raised both my hands in a placating gesture. "I don't want to get into it now. What have you got?"

Crim narrowed his gaze for a few seconds, and Jeshi shifted next to him. He glanced at him, and Jeshi raised his eyebrows and tilted his head toward me. "Jeshi has taken me through some of the protocols for the encrypted messages he intercepts."

Ben came over. He and Lanaya had been in the nearby storage room.

"Did he tell you it's a jumbled mess? Jeshi doesn't know what he's doing," Ben said.

Jeshi's mouth hung open with indignation. "I am the Master of Games. I decipher their secret protocols. I rearrange their messages and measure the reaction. Do not presume to lecture me on the extent of my knowledge."

Ben glared at him. "I will absolutely question your so-called expertise. Especially with what's at risk."

I walked over to Ben. "What's the matter?"

"They don't know what they're doing," Ben said. He looked at Crim guiltily. "I'm sorry, Crim, but you don't."

"Ben," I said, "talk to me. Tell me what you're worried about."

He sighed and stared at me intently. He'd become even more upset since I'd left them to work on this.

Lanaya stood at his side. "It's me. He's worried that the memory locks in place will hurt me."

"How?"

Ben looked at her. "You can't do this, not after coming so far." He turned toward me. "Nate, please. They're just guessing."

"Educated guessing," Lanaya said.

Ben inhaled deeply. "The locks might have fail-safes to prevent tampering. You could die."

My eyes widened a little. "How could she die?"

Lanaya's gaze sank to the ground. "We don't know for sure."

I turned toward Darek and Kaz and waved them over. "If there's some kind of brainwashing or repressed set of instructions and they're activated incorrectly, could there be safeguards in place that will hurt her?"

"It's possible," Darek said. "Depends on the kind of training Lanaya received. Did your autodoc detect any devices inside her body?"

I shook my head. "No. That was one of the first things we checked for. This seems to be conditional."

Ben cleared his throat. "Yes, conditional with repressed memories you'll force her to take on all at once. We don't know what they did to her, and we don't know how. You're asking her to face all those horrors at the same time." He turned toward Lanaya. "You're better off not remembering."

Lanaya met his gaze calmly, almost serene, with unshakable resolve and determination. "But I wouldn't be whole."

Ben's chin quivered a little and he looked away from her.

She leaned toward him. "How can we be together if I'm only half of what I could be?"

He lifted his gaze to hers. "It doesn't matter, Naya. You are enough."

Naya? They were using nicknames now. I really was the third wheel here.

"Oh, Ben," she said and hugged him, "I can't live with myself if I don't try. I still feel their call—the ones who called themselves the masters. I'll never be free of them, but maybe if I do this, if I help you find Serena and Raylin, maybe I can be whole and truly break free of them." She paused for a few seconds and Ben looked at her. "I'm going to do this, and I want you to stay with me."

His chin lowered toward his chest, and he sighed. Then he gave her a small nod.

"Thank you," she said.

"You don't have to thank me."

I wasn't beyond taking a risk, and despite popular opinion, I did try to minimize it. I also tended to speak before my brain offered an opinion on what I was going to say. It's gotten me into trouble, but I remained quiet. Waiting for them to work through this was the smartest thing I could do.

I frowned. Perhaps if I'd been—

"I'm ready, Nate," Lanaya said, interrupting my thoughts.

I looked into her eyes for a long moment. "I wish you didn't have to."

She smiled at me. She was a stunningly beautiful girl, and Ben was a lucky man.

"I do. I really do. I will not allow what was done to me to hinder the rest of my life."

I'd seen some awful things during my travels, things I wished I could forget. Lanaya didn't know what was going to happen to her, and I hoped she didn't regret it. I could tell her not to. Maybe this really was going too far. She must have sensed my thoughts and placed her hand on my arm, giving me a knowing look. Then she walked away.

I looked at Ben. "I'm sorry," I said quietly.

He regarded me for a second and gave a slight nod as he went to stand next to Lanaya. She climbed into the large seat and Ben helped strap her in.

I frowned and looked at Crim. "What's with the straps?"

Crim minimized the data window on his holoscreen. "It's to protect her. We're not sure if we'll trigger some kind of latent protocol."

I shook my head. "You make it sound like she's a ticking time bomb."

He regarded me solemnly. "She might be, Nate."

He was right. She'd been abducted as a little girl and spent a little more than a decade in training. At least that's what we thought. Lanaya didn't know. I wondered if the aliens had the technology to speed up her development to condense the time. What if they'd only taken her five years ago, but her body had aged more than ten years? I dismissed the thought. Lanaya didn't act like a young girl. It could be her training, but I had to draw the line somewhere.

"Okay, take me through what you're doing," I said.

Jeshi turned from his data window. "I've constructed—"

"*We've* constructed," Crim interjected.

Jeshi frowned in disdain for a moment. "I've allowed Crim Cormin to watch how I work, but I'm the expert in the secret messages." He paused for a moment, and much to my surprise, Crim didn't protest the point. He did roll his eyes though. "The messages are successive in design. They're to trick the sleeping protocols to remove their blocks on the host."

"How do you—" I began and Jeshi hissed for me to be quiet. I was so surprised by his assertion that I actually did it.

"It's better if you don't interrupt. Using the sleeping protocols to insert a message is easy. I can demonstrate this if you want."

I shook my head. "That won't be necessary. I'll take your word for it," I said quickly before Ben started yelling at him.

Jeshi looked a little disappointed. I knew the type. He was so focused on function and capabilities that he forgot the Human aspect to what he was doing. If he strayed too far, I'd have to remind him.

"I cannot program a question that will ask Lanaya where she was being held," Jeshi said.

"Why not?"

"Because she might not know."

I frowned. "What? How could she not know? How would she ever get back once her mission was completed?"

Jeshi winced and glanced at the holoscreen. "I might've used the wrong words. She knows. I think she does, but she might not be able to speak it."

Crim cleared his throat. "This is why we'll allow her to use a holoscreen with a navigation-training interface. We're hoping to trick her into inputting the star system coordinates that will take us back to the Academy."

"That doesn't sound so bad," I said.

"Just wait," Ben replied.

I looked at Jeshi with raised eyebrows.

"I'm not exactly sure which protocol will initiate the return-to-base instructions."

"So, you're guessing?"

"I prefer to think of it as a calculated risk. I've had great results with these protocols in the past," Jeshi said.

I looked at Crim.

"It's not exact."

"You think? Come on, Crim, I expect more from you."

"We didn't do this kind of thing. It's risky inputting latent protocols into any life-form. Jeshi has taken me through what he intends, and I can follow the logic of it. I'm afraid that's the best I can do."

I considered it thoughtfully for a few seconds. "Can you just remove all the blocks?"

Jeshi tilted his head to the side a few times, muttering to himself. "I thought you were concerned about her mental wellbeing. It is impossible for me to know how many secret protocols are active."

"Also," Crim said, "there isn't an all-powerful on and off switch. We do one thing at a time and see what happens."

Ben gave me a pointed look, and I understood why he was so upset.

"This is the only way," Lanaya said and held an open hand toward Ben. He took it, giving it a gentle squeeze.

T'Chura entered the workshop and walked over to them. Kaz quickly brought him up to speed.

I finally noticed that Kierenbot had been unusually quiet this whole time. "Well?"

"The data provided is insufficient to make an informed decision, Captain," Kierenbot said.

"No kidding."

"I wasn't attempting humor, Captain," Kierenbot said.

"I know."

"Oh, I see. Based on the information provided, I believe this is our best option," Kierenbot said.

"All right, let's get started," I said.

Jeshi moved toward Crim's holoscreen, and his small hands deftly navigated multiple interfaces. After a few minutes, he nodded toward Crim.

A holoscreen appeared in front of Lanaya and she focused on it. A series of colors appeared in rapid succession. Lanaya stared at the screen intently, as if she were entranced. There was an odd sort of detachment in her gaze, but at the same time she was attentive.

Then the image of a star appeared. It remained on the screen for a few seconds and then it went dark.

Ben began to speak, but Jeshi shook his head, gesturing for him to wait.

Lanaya closed her eyes and became still. I couldn't tell if she was breathing. A minute passed. Then the muscles in her neck became rigid, as if she was clenching her teeth. She suddenly yanked her arms up, pulling against the restraints, making us all jump. Then she exhaled explosively and began to gasp.

She blinked rapidly and looked around, suddenly confused. She jerked her hand away from Ben and leaned away as if she didn't recognize him.

"It's me. Lanaya, it's Ben."

She swung her head toward me, narrowing her gaze. "I shouldn't be here. This is not right. I must report in. I must report to the masters. It has to be quick. It must be quick. Release my restraints. You must—"

She abruptly stopped speaking as another message came to prominence on the holoscreen in front of her. In addition to the series of colors, Jeshi added various types of images that flashed by so fast they blurred together.

Lanaya stared helplessly at the message, her mouth agape and her eyes wide. Her breath came in gasps, as if she was only just remembering to breathe. Tears began streaming down her face and her shoulders trembled.

"Stop it!" Ben shouted. "That's enough. You need to stop this now. It's not working."

He lunged toward Jeshi, but I grabbed him.

"Hold on, Ben," I said.

He struggled against me. He was strong, but I managed to maneuver him toward the others. Kaz and Darek helped restrain him.

"Look," Crim said.

We all stopped moving and turned toward Lanaya.

She'd quietly used the navigation interface, peering at the list of galactic sectors. She scanned the long list and then brought up a search bar and entered a set of coordinates. Star system data came to prominence, and she selected a destination. The interface was a training simulator and only showed a successful acknowledgement of the coordinates. Then the screen turned off.

Lanaya sagged back against the seat.

Ben was next to her in seconds. "Lanaya, are you all right?"

She stared at him for a few moments and then seemed to recognize him. Her eyes were a little haunted, as if she'd just witnessed something horrible. She reached toward Ben, but the restraints restricted her movements. Ben quickly removed them and held her in his arms, rocking her a little bit.

"I saw it. I saw the Academy where we were taken. Oh Ben, they hurt us for so long. They trained us mercilessly. Nothing was given and everything had a cost. There was never enough for all of us."

"It's okay. You're safe now."

I walked over to her. "Do you remember who took you away from there?"

Lanaya frowned and squeezed her eyes shut. Her expression became serene. "I remember waking. Breathing is hard. My eyes are covered with something sticky. It covers my entire body. They lift me out of…it's like the medical capsule in the autodoc. I can't move. I don't know why. They won't talk to me. I have questions, but I can't speak."

The others came over.

"Captain, I believe Lanaya was in a stasis pod," Kierenbot said.

I looked at Lanaya, but she looked as if she was trying to sort out her memories.

"It makes sense," Darek said. "The operations were stopped, but they could've put their prisoners into storage with plans to resume the project at a later date."

"For how long?"

"Stasis environments can last for decades. There really isn't a limit if the pod has power. It would explain her disorientation. It would be hard for anyone to remember much from that."

I considered this for a few moments and looked at Lanaya.

She slowly shook her head. "I'm sorry, Nate. I'm trying to remember all I can."

"Hey," I said gently, "you did great. We've got another lead now. We're one step closer to finding them, and that's all thanks to you." She looked away from me and shivered. "How are you feeling?"

Her bottom lip trembled and her face crumpled. "I don't know," she said with a soft moan and leaned toward Ben.

I bit my lower lip, wishing I could help her. I looked at Crim. "Isn't there anything you can do for her?"

Crim shook his head. "I'm afraid not. Her mind has to catch up to what's been unlocked."

"Not good enough," I said.

Crim blinked.

"We need a way to protect her."

He frowned. "From what? She's safe on the ship."

I shook my head. "No, I mean from these messages. Someone else could send something like this and do something to her. How do we block it?"

Crim considered that for a few seconds and looked at Jeshi.

"You want us to create a filter so if she encounters another message with the secret protocols, she won't be subjected to their instructions," Jeshi said and paused for a few moments, considering. "A new challenge!"

I stared at him, and he shied away from me. "Can you do it?"

"For every problem there is a solution," Jeshi said and went over to the workbench. He opened three holoscreens and began working.

I looked at Crim.

"I'll keep an eye on him. He's actually quite good at this," Crim said.

I arched an eyebrow. Crim was like the stoic father who was almost impossible to please. "Really?"

He gave me an annoyed look and I shrugged. He wouldn't have said it if he hadn't meant it.

I turned toward the others, and Ben looked at me. "I'm going to bring her back to our room so she can rest."

I nodded and they left.

I looked at the others. "What's located at those coordinates?"

"Datronia Star System, Captain," Kierenbot said.

Kaz frowned and leaned toward the holoscreen. "Are you sure?" he asked and then shook his head. "Never mind."

"Do you know it?" I asked.

Kaz nodded. "Yeah, it's a prime world."

I frowned. "Sounds special."

Darek looked as if he didn't believe it. "What?" I asked him.

"It's one of the central locations for the CGH."

I chuckled a little. "Well, I guess we'll all find out how deep this rabbit hole goes, now won't we."

# CHAPTER 10

Some things were easier said than done—a mantra that had punctuated my existence as a whole. For example, I flew away from a crash site and found an ancient ruin from the oldest civilization in the galaxy. Then, I convinced the others we should search for it. What followed was a long journey and some of the most terrifying events I'd ever experienced, such as star systems that contradicted the accepted laws of the universe. On top of it all was the realization that the Asherah were stumbling in the dark as much as we were but were capable of things we hadn't even dreamed of yet.

Another example: I thought it would only take a few days to catch up with Serena and Raylin. It should've been easy-peasy, but here we were months later and not a word. We only had the slightest of hints as to where they might be. I was beginning to think that most things in life existed by the thinnest of margins. I'd underestimated the little things, and it was kicking me in the ass, over and over again. It felt like a giant version of Biff from

*Back to the Future* was banging his ham-sized fist on my head, demanding that I think.

These were my thoughts as I sat across from Ben in the commons area.

"So, they can't do it?" I asked.

"It's harder than they thought it was."

"What do you think?"

Ben was pushing the last bit of scrambled eggs on his plate with a crust of toast. He frowned and looked at me. "Me?"

I rolled my eyes. Sometimes the kid was on it and other times he completely missed the mark. This time he'd missed the entire target.

Ben seemed to sense my disapproval and blushed a little. "Crim should be able to figure it out. Jeshi has ideas, but some of them are way out there."

I leaned back in my seat and crossed my arms. "They're also not like us."

Ben's eyebrows pushed forward.

"Just hear me out a second," I said, and he nodded. "You're a smart kid. Half the time I see you working with Crim, I can only follow half of what you're saying. So why don't *you* work the problem? Do you really want to sit there and imply that Lanaya would be in better hands if she were left to Crim or Jeshi?"

Ben's gaze hardened, and I could tell the wheels were turning.

"They're brilliant, and I trust them. But they're not you, kid. I'm not saying you're better than them, but you could easily be their equal. How would you protect Lanaya from these hidden messages that she's vulnerable to?"

Ben inhaled and sighed. "Keep her away from those types of messages. It's not practical, I know, but you can't be burned if you stay out of the fire."

I stared at him for a second. "So, throw her in a box and

keep here there." Ben snorted a little and I smiled. "You're right, not practical at all," I said and arched an eyebrow. "And quite barbaric, kid. I'm gonna keep my eye on you."

He grinned and shook his head. "That's not what I meant."

I shrugged.

"I thought about using glasses, something intelligent. It could detect and filter out the messages before they could do any harm."

I pressed my lips together and considered it for a moment. "The thing is we don't know how fast it works. I'm going to venture a guess that it's pretty fast, like speed-of-thought fast."

Ben rubbed his chin. "You're probably right about that since it's been trained into her brain. I'd hoped it would just go away in time." He shook his head. "That's stupid."

"No it's not. You might be right. It's not the most immediate solution, but if it's behavior-based, wouldn't it be like a habit that just needs to be broken?"

Ben looked skeptical. "Somehow, I think it's more complicated than that. The autodoc didn't detect anything in her, but that doesn't mean this isn't something biological. What if they did something to her brain? As in, they conditioned— And now I've come back to brainwashing again. Yeah Nate, I'm not sure I can do this."

"It's complicated, and maybe we need to admit that we can't do anything about it right now," I said.

The door to the corridor opened and Crim walked in. Jeshi followed him.

Since Crim had six legs, he moved differently than the rest of us. He walked, but the cadence was different, and it seemed to register with my brain sometimes.

"Hey Crim, why the long face?" I asked.

This was an ongoing joke between us. Crim's head was elongated, with short, stubby tentacles, eyes that were almost black in color, and skin that was rough like the coarsest sandpaper. Ustrals were at home in deep rocky environments and harsh atmospheres.

Jeshi looked up at Crim. "Why does the Human speak in riddles?"

I cleared my throat and Jeshi looked at me. "Uh, I'm Nate, and it's called a joke. It requires a sense of humor."

Jeshi frowned and shook his head a little. "Peculiar."

Crim waved away the comment and looked at me. "We've considered many options, from advising Lanaya to wear a helmet to replacing her eyes with something artificial."

Ben looked mortified and shook his head.

Crim nodded. "Well, let's just say it became more extreme from there. We could work on conditioning her until she stops responding to the messages, but that takes a lot of time, and I don't think it's wise to do that."

"Yeah, continuing to hurt her to make her better doesn't sound right," I said.

"Don't oversimplify it. I wouldn't knowingly hurt the girl," Crim replied.

I arched an eyebrow. "Do you think that sounds better?"

He sighed heavily. "You were much easier going when you first got here."

I grinned. "What can I say, you've corrupted me."

Ben had been drinking water and nearly spit it out.

Lanaya came out of her room and walked over to us. She looked better than before. Sleep really was the cure we all needed sometimes.

She eyed us for a moment.

"Yes, we were talking about you, but it was in a good way," I said.

She smiled and sat next to Ben. "When will we arrive?"

"It won't be long," I said and glanced at Ben.

She noticed and looked at Ben. "What is it? What aren't you telling me?"

"We were trying to figure out a way to protect you from those hidden messages. Nothing we can come up with is going to work, at least not in the short term."

Lanaya considered this for a few moments and then looked at me. "I can still help."

I smiled. "I know you can," I said, and Ben gave me a warning look. "But it might be better—safer—if you remain on the ship."

She leaned away from Ben and scowled. "I can do this."

I sighed and leaned toward her from across the table. "Hey," I said soothingly, "I know you can. This is what we're going to do. A team is going ashore to look for the Academy."

"How are you even going to find it? You've never been there. I have to come with you to help you find it," she said, looking more like an impatient young girl than how she'd been before. Maybe what Crim and Jeshi did was working, and Lanaya was becoming more like the girl she was rather than the prisoner she had been.

"Here it is," I said. "I'm going to give it to you straight. You, Ben, and probably Crim and Jeshi are going to remain aboard the ship. You'll be able to monitor where we go from the video feed from our suit cams as we explore the area."

"What if something disrupts the signal? I won't be able to help."

"It's possible, but we'll be able to scout the area. Then, we'll take it from there."

Lanaya combed her fingers through her long, Nordic-blonde hair, then crossed her arms and nodded.

"You're going in combat suits?" Ben asked.

I nodded. "Yeah, but we'll cover them up so it won't be so obvious. I'm expecting trouble, kid, so I'm not playing nice this time."

He frowned and I rolled my eyes. Sometimes Ben was entirely too literal. "You know what I mean."

He smiled. "I was going to say that we've never been there before, so…"

I sighed. "You remind me of my older brother sometimes. He has your rigid-framework mentality too. It's got its place, but sometimes…" I raised my fist in the air for a second.

He grinned. "I was just kidding, Nate."

It had been a while since I'd been on the receiving end of the button-pushing.

"I see. You know what, Lanaya—"

"All right," Ben said loudly. "I poked the bear. So how are you going to find the Academy? It's not like they're going to have a sign on the door or anything like that."

"You know it would be much easier if they did," I replied. He frowned for a second. "This is an arrogant group we're dealing with. They're running some kind of secret trafficking operation here on this prime world. It's like they're thumbing their noses at this Council for Galactic Harmony," I said and frowned.

Ben blinked. "You don't think?"

I nodded. "That somehow the CGH is involved? Yeah, why not? I hadn't considered it until just now, but we're dealing with corruption. Are there any organizations that are entirely pure?"

Crim shook his head and glowered. "The implications of this are beyond measure. The CGH is tightly knit into sector governments and mega corporations across the galaxy."

"That just means they have a lot of influence," I replied.

Crim considered it for a few moments. "I've dealt with corruption before. It rears its ugly head from time to time, but it's usually the CGH that exposes it."

I shrugged. "It's probably someone cleaning house." I looked at Lanaya for a moment, sensing a thought that was just out of reach.

A broadcast chimed from overhead and Kierenbot spoke. "We're approaching the Datronia System."

I stood up. "Let's head to the bridge and see what we've got."

We met up with Kaz and Darek on the way to the bridge. T'Chura was already there.

We entered the bridge and saw a distant view of the Datronia Star System. There weren't many planets. There was an Earth-like planet among the inner system and one Jupiter-sized planet in the outer system. In between were large moons.

"Fifteen-hour days and six-hundred-day years," Ben said, reading the summary on the system map.

"Datronia was without an intelligent species and was an early colony world, but because of its location in relation to the senior species, it serves as a defacto meeting area for the sector," Kierenbot said.

I peered at the data on the holoscreen. I didn't relish the thought of exploring an entire planet.

"The planet has five moons," I said.

"Not the barren kind," Kaz said. "They're quite rich in precious mineral deposits."

I looked at Darek. "Where do you think the Academy is?"

The Nasarian considered it for a few moments. "I've seen training facilities before, and they can be scattered throughout a given star system. There are likely a few facilities on the planet, probably one for each district."

I nodded. "So, high traffic areas. That would make stations, shipyards, and any place that supports a workforce a candidate as well."

Darek inclined his head once. "While there is regular traffic between the planet and the various space stations, I think our best option is to search the space stations first. It's very likely that Lanaya was kept there."

I eyed him for a moment, considering. "Are you sure about that?"

"Absolutely. It's easier to hide storage in plain sight. Anyone can purchase warehouse space."

I glanced at Lanaya and felt a flash of irritation, then turned back toward Darek. "How big was this operation before you shut it down?"

"Difficult to say. It was large enough to span multiple star systems, and the victims were spread across a large number of species."

"This is disgusting," Ben said. "Why is this allowed to happen? Aren't you better at stopping things like this?"

"I understand your frustration," Darek replied.

"I don't think you do," Ben said, raising his voice.

I looked at Ben. "He doesn't condone it, Ben. He's giving you the facts. It's probably part of his training. You know, keep the emotion out of it."

Ben looked down for a few seconds and nodded. "They just show up and take whoever they want, and we don't even know they were here. Or worse, we can't do anything to stop them. Where's the justice in that?"

"We're here now, and we're doing something about it. They did something about it before," I said.

Ben shook his head. "It's not good enough—"

"Let's stay focused on the task at hand," I said, interrupting him so he didn't say anything else. Darek was a CGH Agent, and since I had no plans to kill him, I had to assume he would be reporting back to his superiors at some point. Somehow, I doubted they'd be pleased with Ben giving Humanity a leg up on the technological development scale. Conversations about it with Crim were one thing because I trusted Crim, but I hadn't even broached the subject with Delos, who was a highly influential player on the galactic stage.

Ben stared at me for a few seconds but got the hint.

I looked at Lanaya. "Is there anything you can remember? Some detail? Something about the training you received?"

Lanaya frowned while she thought about it. "I'm not sure."

"She wouldn't know," Darek said. "Sometimes they used abductees for experimentation, and others trained in observation and both delivery- and retrieval-type missions."

I stared at him, pursing my lips in thought. Darek was likely sanitizing his response because it was a sensitive subject, but I couldn't keep the scowl from my face. "It's worse than that, isn't it?"

Darek regarded me for a long moment and the others watched in silence. He nodded his head a little.

"What does that mean?" Ben asked.

I turned toward him. "It means that there is a dark under-belly of society that is both abhorrent and disturbing. Sometimes ignorance is better than knowing."

Easy for me to say, but that didn't keep my mind from racing with the dark possibilities that juvenile species were being molested by the dredge of galactic societies. I wondered how many of them knew about it.

I closed my eyes for a moment and cleared my mind. I couldn't stand there and point my finger at any of them. The very same willful ignorance about those dark, awful occurrences existed on Earth, secreted away in places no one liked to talk about, but eventually the glaring truth of it made its way to the public all the same.

"We should focus our search in the entertainment areas, the kinds that provide the services powerful people use. These would be beings who pay a premium for anonymity," I said.

Darek regarded me with a surprised expression. "I'm curious to learn what your occupation was before becoming captain of the ship."

"And ruin the mystique? No way," I said and glanced at Kaz. "Let's just say that my abduction ended on a more positive note than most."

Kaz rolled his eyes. "This again."

I shrugged. "History is history. No use sweeping it under the rug." Kaz grinned, and then I continued. "Given where I think we need to go, it makes the most sense if we stick together in there."

T'Chura nodded enthusiastically. "I'm glad you've finally seen reason on this. I was concerned I would have to convince you."

I smiled up at him. "Just how insistent were you planning to be?"

The edges of T'Chura's thick lips lifted a little and he regarded me for a moment. "Very insistent, Nate."

T'Chura had a dangerous side to him. He'd probably refer to it as his warrior persona, but I preferred to think of it as his beast-mode. He hated the reference because it implied that he was more of an animal than an intelligent being. I don't care who you are, when a nine-foot-tall Sasquatch is offended by something you said, you make every effort not to anger said Sasquatch.

"Well, I'm glad we can agree. See, I can be cooperative—a team player and all that."

Kaz blew out a breath. "Indeed, you're the absolute spirit of harmony."

"I'm glad you've finally seen the light."

Crim cleared his throat. "Nate, there is a problem with your combat suit."

I frowned. "What's the problem? Last I checked it was fully charged and ready for us."

He shook his head. "It's not that. There are restrictions in place that you must abide by. They cannot be bypassed."

"What are they?"

"You're not going to like it. Here, have a look," Crim said.

He made a passing motion and my omnitool buzzed. I opened my personal holoscreen and read through what equated to a visitor's guide for Datronia Prime Space Habitat.

Ben peered at me. "What's the matter? Are firearms restricted or something?"

I shook my head. "No, this isn't New Jersey, but they've limited personal power units to a specific range."

Ben considered this a few moments and then shrugged. "Doesn't sound so bad."

I shook my head. "We can't use our combat suit's flight systems. The power restriction makes it impossible for them to be used effectively," I said and was quiet for a second. "Crim, what if we just dialed down the suit's power unit and give me the capabilities to increase it if I need it?"

Crim stared at me, exasperated. "Just how stupid do you think their security team is?"

"Not as stupid as I would like," I replied glumly.

Kaz stared at me, mouth partially agape. Then his shoulders slumped a little. "You've got to be kidding me. This is about imitating that Iron Man character again."

"Actually, for me it started with Superman. Weren't you ever a young Akacian who dreamed of doing something amazing? An ideal to strive for? For me, it was flying, being impervious to everything, and saving the girl. It's kid stuff, but it's okay to admit it."

Kaz blinked for a second, and then gave me a knowing smirk —the kind of smirk that conveyed he'd had way better toys than I had growing up.

"Don't you worry, we'll catch up," I said to him and looked at Crim. "How are you going to reduce the power core to meet the requirements?"

"I'll have to downgrade the fuel source. Won't take that long," Crim said.

"Okay, let's get in there and start poking around," I said. "Oh, and Kaz, I'm not that worried about transportation. I mean I could always just commandeer an aircar, delivery drone, or something else. Improvise. Adapt. Overcome."

Kaz nodded. "That's the spirit."

Darek looked at Kaz. "Is he serious? Doesn't he realize that those things can be tracked?"

"Don't underestimate him. He knows exactly what he's doing. You should have seen what he did on Vaiost," Kaz said.

# CHAPTER 11

I stood in the armory and watched as my combat suit went from a pulsating block of nanorobotic particles to covering my body with protection that could withstand any type of ammunition from back home. I wasn't sure what the upper limits for explosions were that my suit could protect me from, but I thought it was quite extensive. I looked in the mirror and saw that my body was covered from the neck down in a black, semi-reflective combat suit. It was flexible, but if someone hit me or shot at me, the armor either dispersed the energy or hardened to protect me. Essentially, I was covered in multiple layers of highly intelligent and adaptable tiny robots whose purpose was to protect me and assist me in a variety of situations. I could make a shield or use a glide-suit configuration, which had been life-savingly useful when I'd leaped off one of the tallest buildings I'd ever been on. Aside from deadly Mesakloren soldiers trying to capture me, gliding through the air with my armored wingsuit had been a lot of fun. I usually didn't have trouble looking for the upside of the obstacles that came my way.

The combat suit covered my skin and hugged my muscles. I wasn't bodybuilder huge, but I definitely had an athletic build. I trained for function rather than showing off, but I wasn't above the occasional "show off" if the situation called for it. Given that my preferred audience for such displays wasn't on the ship, I hadn't had the opportunity to use those skills.

Crim stood nearby. He had his omnitool out and was adjusting my combat suit's power level.

I reached inside my locker and grabbed my gray coat, picking up my multipurpose weapon that was able to change shape to form a variety of handheld weapons. It was in a stick configuration that was capable of unleashing a powerful sonic blast from its end. I twirled it around for a few seconds and then put it over my shoulder. My combat suit kept it secured to my back. I checked that my hand cannons were fully charged, which they were. Never hurt to check those things multiple times.

"Are you done preening in front of the mirror?" Crim asked.

I closed my locker and turned toward him. "I've got to look the part. Are you done dialing down the power core?"

"Yes."

I checked the configuration on my HUD. "So, the capacity is still there. You've just drained the battery, so to speak."

Crim narrowed his gaze. "Yes."

"So, what's to stop me from topping off the tank once I get inside?"

Crim rolled his eyes. "They track energy signatures, Nate. They'll detect it. That's when local security enforcers show up. Stop trying to find a way around this. It's not going to work."

I shrugged. "Never know until you try. So, the answer to my question is yes, but it'll draw unwanted attention. Got it," I said and headed for the door.

Crim followed me. "Listen to me," he said. I turned to face

him. "You can get away with things at smaller stations and the like, but that's not going to work here. They have all the advantages. They have better equipment, Nate, better weapons, and superior ways to capture and subdue you, and they will not hesitate to use those advantages."

Crim had been a soldier. He was older and more experienced than I was, so I had to take his warning seriously.

I smiled. "You know I love it when you care."

Crim snarled in frustration and quickly moved around me. The door had barely opened when he stormed outside. For an older Ustral he was still faster than I thought he would be.

"I love you too, buddy!" I shouted after him.

His grumbles echoed down the corridor as he left.

I grinned and went to meet the others at the airlock. When I stepped off the elevator, I heard Lanaya speaking to Ben.

"Stop it! I'm going and that's the end of it," Lanaya said.

I couldn't quite hear Ben's reply. It sounded muffled because he was still inside the room.

"No, he'll never find it if I'm not there," Lanaya said.

They were inside Crim's workshop, and I thought about just walking past, but the decision was taken from me as Lanaya stormed out. She looked at me, startled, but quickly recovered.

She wore a combat suit similar to mine.

I gave her a once-over with pursed lips, considering. "Going somewhere?"

She gave me a determined look and nodded. "I'm coming with you. There are things I'm remembering, but it's better if I'm there with you. I need to see it. It'll help me remember. Please, Nate?"

It was the "please" that got me sometimes, although I wasn't immune to a beautiful woman either. Aside from all that, I wasn't Lanaya's keeper. She looked alert and definitely determined.

"Okay," I said.

Ben stormed through the doorway, his face flushed with anger. "Are you kidding me! What happened to the plan?"

I walked past him and tipped my head for Lanaya to follow.

Ben sprinted in front of us and blocked our way.

I looked at Ben for a long moment. "She's made up her mind, Ben. There's nothing wrong with her. I'm not going to hold her here like some kind of prisoner. And I'm not going to let you do it either. Now, either you come with us or stay here, but you're not going to get in our way."

Ben stared at me, unwilling to concede that he'd already lost this battle. I glanced at Lanaya. If he wasn't careful, he was going to lose more than that.

I placed my hand on his shoulder, giving him a firm but gentle shake. "You'll do the right thing, kid. You always do," I said and moved past him.

Ben blew out a breath. "All right, just don't leave without me," he said, and I heard him speak softly to Lanaya.

Soon, we were assembled near the airlock. Kaz frowned toward Ben and Lanaya, then looked at me.

I shrugged. "What can I say? The thought of me being so far from them was too much for them to bear."

Kaz shook his head. "Yeah, that's what it was."

I looked at the others. We all had standard arms and armament, except for Darek. He watched me, and the unasked question lingered for a few seconds.

"Give him a weapon," I said to Kaz. Then I looked at Darek. "I swear to you that if I get the sense you'll betray us, I'll make sure you don't get away."

A subsonic growl came from T'Chura, and Darek's eyes widened a little.

"I'm not going to betray you, any of you. I promise," Darek said.

Kierenbot's heavy footfalls came down the corridor. He'd transferred himself into the battlebot.

I frowned. "I'm not sure they'll allow you inside."

"That is incorrect, Captain. I've adjusted my power level according to the requirements, and there are no provisions against having a personal protection robot at your side," Kierenbot replied.

I nodded and opened a comlink to the bridge. "All right, Crim, we're heading out. Don't let Jeshi break my ship while we're gone."

"Understood, Nate. We'll monitor from here. Happy hunting," Crim replied.

We entered the airlock and were soon on Datronia Station. I felt my eyes stretch wide as we entered a vast atrium with a stunning view of the bright blue and green planet below. I spotted a steady stream of ships going to and from the planet. Even from where I was, I could make out the vast cities on the planet. It made me wonder how many beings lived there.

"Look at that," Ben said.

I glanced at the others. They were equally impressed with the sight of the prime world. It wasn't just the planet but the enormous space elevators that went right to the surface. Datronia Station was a massive network of stations that were built around the planet's closest moon.

We entered a huge tunnel with a canopy of windows across the entire ceiling. I wasn't sure that calling this place a space station was even appropriate. It was an enormous habitat, and I wouldn't have been surprised if the population there was well into the billions.

I stood there, more than a little awestruck at the sight as my brain tried to catch up to what I was seeing. There were millions of beings in the unbelievably huge atrium, and it didn't feel crowded in the least.

After a few minutes, Kaz looked at me, considering. "I didn't think it was possible, but you're speechless."

I exhaled forcefully. "I mean…Wow. I've seen my share of amazing sites, but this is right up there."

Kaz nodded. "It is impressive. Most prime star systems are like this."

Ben looked around, mouth agape and eyes wide. I could only imagine what he was thinking.

I glanced at Lanaya and she was just as awestruck, which was telling in and of itself.

Ben finally looked at me and shook his head. "I didn't know this was even possible. I mean, look at this place. Look at everyone here. This is our future, Nate. This is where we're heading. This is what's possible."

Amid the wonder, I saw something in him that had been growing since we'd started trekking all over the galaxy—hope and determination. He wanted to show the people back home that they had an unbelievable future ahead of them. The future was definitely bright, but I knew it also came with its own set of unique challenges.

"Remember why we're here. Things are impressive because it's meant to be like that. Someone put their trafficking operation here right in the thick of it. Don't get caught up too much because there is danger here like anywhere else," I said.

Ben and Lanaya shared a meaningful look.

"Now that you've gotten a glimpse as to the scope of this search, where do you want to begin first?" Darek asked.

"Stick with the plan. We need to explore the entertainment modules. It'll be where people let their guard down…" I began to say and then looked at Kierenbot. "Can you initiate a search for other Humans here? That's probably the most obvious. Search for Serena and Raylin, but can you also search for anyone who's Human as well?"

"I can help with this," Darek said.

"How?"

"We're trying to keep a low profile. If Kierenbot attempts to infiltrate restricted systems, it could be detected. I advise using the public system that's available for anyone," Darek said.

I frowned, considering. "You're suggesting we use the public surveillance system to find our friends? That's not going to work."

"Why wouldn't it work?" Ben asked.

"Think about it. This is a well-connected espionage group that knows how to cover their tracks. The data that's likely available to the public is filtered. We need access to data used by the enforcers or an agent with the CGH," I said, looking at Darek. "My guess is that we might have a better shot that way."

"I'll try. Strictly speaking, I'm not authorized to carry out operations here, so my access is limited."

I laughed. "That would make you a poor excuse for an agent."

Darek closed his eyes for a moment. "You don't know as much as you think you do."

"Are you going to help or not?" I asked.

Darek stared at me for a few seconds and then brought up his omnitool, navigating through a whole bunch of options. Kierenbot watched him intently and gave me a slight nod.

"Search initiated," Darek said.

We gathered around him and watched his personal holo-screen. There was a long list of species on Datronia Station but nothing that actually stated Human. I hadn't thought it would be that easy.

"We should probably start moving," Kaz advised.

I looked around and saw that Lanaya and Ben had gone over to an info-terminal that was available for public use.

Lanaya was navigating the interface, hesitantly at first, but gaining confidence as she went. Ben glanced at me, and I nodded.

I always had trouble watching other people use a computer back on Earth, and here on an alien space station was no different. Lanaya blew through the interface, bringing up multiple data windows as if she'd done it thousands of times before. She ignored the rest of us as she worked.

I waved Ben closer to me. "Has she been like this before?" I asked quietly.

Ben shook his head. "I think it's like she said. Some part of her remembers."

Kierenbot loomed over my shoulder. "She's initiated a check-in with someone else. I think it's the only way she can find her way back."

Darek's eyes widened, and he nodded. "Makes sense. They must've kept their operations mobile, so this Academy could be anywhere."

"That's probably why it's so hard for you to find them," I replied.

"She's got it," Kierenbot said at the same time Lanaya stepped away from the terminal.

She blinked several times and looked as if she'd been deeply focused. It reminded me of being connected to the Asherah machine for unlocking the secrets of the universe, or the flow state.

"Are you all right?" I asked her.

She considered it for a few seconds and then nodded. "I just knew what to do once I initiated a session on the terminal."

"What did you learn?"

"I was given a destination to report to," Lanaya replied.

"It's located on a different module than this one. We'll need to use local transport to reach it," Kierenbot said.

I looked up at the battlebot. "Did you watch the entire interaction?"

"Yes, she used a private network for secure communications," Kierenbot said.

I looked at the others. "Anyone know something about this place?"

The location was some kind of consulting firm or training facility but looked to be in the heart of a commercial district.

"Let's get going," I said.

We made our way through the station and hired an aircar to take us to our destination. As we traveled, the enormity of what had been built made me think of how easy it would be for someone to get lost there. How could anyone keep track of anything in this place?

There were more intelligent species than I thought were possible. Intermixed with them were different types of robots, and I couldn't help but wonder if they were monitored by the AI Collective. If I could've gotten them to help, I would've gotten here much sooner.

I looked at the others—seven of us, including Darek. I would never give up on searching for Serena, but given how big this place was, I had a new perspective of what a needle in a haystack truly was.

I tapped the window of the aircar with my right hand just to expend some energy. I no longer had the Asherah artifact infused into my skin, but sometimes I still felt it there. I remembered what it had felt like using the machine, experiencing all those timelines and witnessing the infinite possibilities. The whole experience had brought me to my knees, and I swore to myself that I'd never tempt fate like that again. But sometimes I wondered if I could still do it. Could I use what the Asherah had taught me to find Serena? So far there hadn't been enough information for me to even make the attempt.

I heard Lanaya speak to Ben. She looked as if she was trying to retrieve the memories that had been stolen from her. Everywhere she looked her eyes were intensely focused. I paid attention, too, but gnawing doubts were nipping at my thoughts. What if Serena had been captured and what was done to Lanaya had been done to Serena, or worse? What if she'd been killed and had been dead for months?

I clenched my teeth, trying to ignore those thoughts. I was usually pretty good at it, but they just kept coming back with renewed determination.

The aircar flew us toward a landing platform and we got out. Lanaya started to go ahead, but I stepped in front of her.

"Let some of us go first and you tell us where to go. Also, engage your helmet just in case someone recognizes you," I said.

A few seconds later, Lanaya's head was covered by a helmet. Ben did the same, and after a few moments I did the same as well. Better safe than sorry. We probably should've done it sooner.

I wasn't sure what to expect, but this section of the station, which was really a city unto itself, was different than the others. I thought we'd traveled quite a way to get there and that was after arriving on the *Spacehog*. The area we'd been to before was pristine, bright, and felt almost parklike but filled with things I'd never seen before. There were plants I couldn't identify. The area we were in at the time was more urban in design, with metallic architecture that looked to be formed from one solid piece of metal. Each metallic building had a distinct color across the spectrum that *I* could see, but I knew it might appear differently to other species. Accommodations for different kinds of lifeforms were available in an organized spread that wasn't difficult to understand. One thing I'd noticed, not just there but other places as well, was that similar species of aliens traveled together. There were mixed groups like ours, but I guess the old saying about safety in numbers also held true out in the galaxy. This section of Datronia faced away from the planet and the star, but there was a stunning view of a distant nebula that was the color of my coffee with ribbons of creamy white.

Huge walkways interconnected the different levels. There was so much open space, and I still wondered at how they balanced the atmosphere to service the different species. Half the beings I saw were using their own life support, but others, like Kaz, brazenly walked as if they didn't have a care in the world. T'Chura, Kaz, and Darek had an extremely tolerant capacity to handle multiple kinds of atmospheres. T'Chura had told me that the use of genetic enhancement helped them adapt to different types, especially since atmospheres weren't as widely varied as one might think. Technically, I could breathe the air on the station, but there were higher amounts of helium and nitrogen than I was used to. I was glad I'd decided to use my own life support because it sharpened my mind. I suspected the oxygen levels maintained on the station might be too low—not low enough to trigger a warning but enough to have a subtle effect.

There were pads that extended from the walkways, and the aliens stepped onto them. The pads glowed yellow, and the aliens rose into the air as if they were suddenly weightless. Then, the unseen force also guided them to the level above where a receiving pad waited.

I had just happened to glance down at one of the lower levels when I spotted Serena.

I blinked several times and leaned over the railing, peering into the crowd below. There were other species that had hair like ours, but I knew what I'd seen, and now I couldn't find her.

My helmet provided enhanced vision, so I zoomed into the crowded walkway, trying to spot Serena.

Kaz was by my side. "What is it?"

"I saw her, but now I can't find her."

Kaz leaned over the railing, searching. "I don't see her."

The others came over, but I ignored them.

I closed my eyes, trying to build the memory in my mind. It had been barely a second that I saw the side of Serena's face, her long brown hair hanging neatly past her shoulders. I couldn't get a good look at her face, but it had to be her. She'd been right there.

I grabbed the railing and pulled myself over. Kaz's shouts quickly faded as I fell through the air. The level beneath us was at least fifty yards down. I spread my arms out wide, and my combat suit spread itself thin, becoming a wingsuit that extended beyond my hands. I glided downward. Several aliens shouted a warning to the others and they scrambled out of my way.

The combat suit computer could anticipate what I was doing and knew I was closing in on the ground. The nanorobotic material separated between my legs and I hit the ground running. Flailing my arms, I regained my balance and charged ahead, weaving my way through the crowd.

Since I'd only seen her for a few seconds I couldn't be sure how far ahead she'd gone. I tried to recall all the details, but there wasn't much. I thought she might've been wearing a white shirt. I should have called out to her.

I ran ahead, only slowing down to peer at anyone who looked remotely like a woman. There were many alien species that shared our basic shape.

Someone must have declared that this was the day everyone wore white, which meant it must have been before Labor Day and no one told me. I pushed through a throng of Akacians and some of them pushed back. They might've shouted at me, but I didn't care.

A group of Mesaklorens lumbered in front of me, looking brutish and intimidating in their dark-brown combat suits that were similar to mine and not the heavy kind soldiers wore, but that didn't make them any less imposing. They were a warrior race, and thick, ropy muscles pushed against their armor, but it was the crazy jaw that made me sneer at them. They weren't a pretty race. Their jaws had thick mandibles with large canines that closed over their inner mouth. They looked vicious and aggressive even as they moved on the walkways.

As I went around them, racing ahead toward the travel plat-form, I saw several shorter aliens in white that appeared as if they were in a daze. Some had a semi-translucent holoscreen in front of their eyes. The crowd shifted as more of them climbed aboard the platform. The border flashed a red and yellow warning.

I saw her. Serena stood toward the middle of the platform. Her head was tilted to the side a little, and her lips were pale, but her eyes didn't look as if they registered anything. She looked as if she were sleepwalking.

"Serena!" I shouted, trying to get her to hear me over the bustle of the city.

The group of Mesakloren thugs surrounded me, trying to reach the platform before it left.

I pushed through them, screaming Serena's name.

One of the Mesaklorens grabbed my arm and I yanked it away, charging forward as the platform began to rise into the air.

I leaped, trying to reach the platform, and slammed into an amber shield. I bounced backward into the waiting arms of the Mesakloren thugs.

# CHAPTER 12

Strong hands took hold of my arms and held me. The thugs surrounded me as one of them stared after the departing platform.

"Let go of me!"

The lead thug regarded me for a second and gestured toward the open space over his shoulder. They didn't so much lightly toss me off the walkway as flung me. Mesaklorens were strong, and a group of them could give even T'Chura a challenge.

I tumbled through the air, watching the walkway get farther and farther away. I spread my arms wide, and my wingsuit formed, slowing my descent. My flight system didn't have enough power for sustained flight, but it could push me back toward the walkway.

I arched my body and engaged my combat suit's flight system. A burst of energy shoved me toward the walkway. I had no idea how many levels I'd descended, and I'd also lost sight of Serena.

Something large and metallic flew toward me. I peered at it and a comlink registered with my combat suit.

"Angle toward me, Captain," Kierenbot said.

The battlebot had become an elongated capsule with flight capabilities. I dipped one of my arms downward, twisting my body, and swung toward him.

Kierenbot slowed down just enough so I could grab hold. I clung to the capsule and laughed.

"Oh thank God," I said.

Kierenbot flew toward the nearest walkway.

"No! Go up."

"But Captain, strictly speaking I'm not supposed to be doing this."

"I don't care. I saw her. I saw Serena. She just got on a transport platform. We have to follow her. This place is huge, and we could lose her forever here."

Kierenbot put on a burst of speed so fast that I almost slipped off. The levels of walkways passed by in a blur for a minute and then he slowed down. I peered ahead, trying to find the large transport platform, and finally spotted it in the distance. It was just arriving at its destination and the patrons were already offloading.

"There, right ahead of us. That's it," I said.

Kierenbot flew toward it.

"We need to tell the others," I said.

"Already did, Captain. They're on their way now."

I wanted him to go faster, but I knew he couldn't. I'd slip right off him as soon as he slowed down. There wasn't anything for me to really grab onto.

By the time we reached the transport platform, the patrons were already climbing back aboard. It reminded me of being in a crowded train station right after it arrived at a stop.

Kierenbot flew us just beyond the platform and landed in the middle of the walkway. He then quickly unfolded himself into a tall battlebot. I'd only paused for a second before running ahead, and he quickly caught up to me.

"Can you see her?" I asked.

Kierenbot had highly capable sensors and what Ben referred to as a kind of quantum computing, which meant he could process untold amounts of data inside a second. None of that helped him spot Serena.

A new comlink registered with me.

"Slow down, Nate," Ben said. "Lanaya knows where she's going."

I didn't slow down. Serena couldn't be that far away. I was so damn close. The others could catch up to me.

Lanaya must have joined the comlink. "Nate, please, I know where she's going. The Academy isn't far from here. You can't barge your way inside."

"Watch me," I said.

I strode ahead, careless of whoever got in my way. They'd done something to Serena. She wasn't herself. She wouldn't have ignored me. They'd brainwashed her the same way they had with Lanaya.

Growling with frustration, I pushed my way through a throng of people until someone grabbed me from behind and hauled me off my feet.

"Captain, please, this is undignified. I can see her," Kierenbot said.

I stopped struggling. "Where?"

"She's ahead. I've deployed several small recon drones. I'll patch you into their video feed."

A new window appeared on my HUD, and I saw her. She was among a group of aliens. I had no idea what species they were, and I didn't care. She was there, but she was doing that sleepwalking thing. She moved as if she were being remotely controlled, heading inside a large building. There were crowds of aliens heading inside as well, but they looked more alert.

"Follow her," I said.

"I am, Captain. We won't lose her. They're locked onto her. Trust me. We won't lose her again," Kierenbot promised and set me down.

I stared at the building, trying to assess the danger. Lanaya was right. If I barged in there like a first-rate amateur, I'd most likely fail. Serena could get hurt once whoever had taken her figured out why I was there.

I knew the smartest thing to do was to wait for everyone else to arrive, and we'd get the layout of the place thanks to Kierenbot's drones. I knew it was the right thing to do, at least on the surface, but I also knew that things changed too quickly, and I wasn't going to lose her again.

"I'm going in," I said, and slipped away from Kierenbot.

Once I made a decision like that, I never looked back. Hindsight was for people who stayed on the sidelines, wondering why things never went their way.

The architecture of the large building displayed a swirling technique that made the metallic bronze appear that it was always in motion—a motion that seemed to lure you toward it. I glanced up and took in the dizzying height of the building, which had countless paths leading to it, as well as aircar traffic and what appeared to be automated delivery drones. They flew overhead and circled around among the different spires of the Academy.

The Academy was more than a training ground for alien traffickers; it was an entertainment module with flashing lights and showy effects that drew attention, but it also seemed to be a central point for exports and imports. It was like a major port in a city on Earth but on a scale that made even the largest cities back home seem inconsequential in comparison.

I merged into a group of Ustrals, easily keeping up with them as they headed for one of the large entrances.

"Kierenbot, can you highlight Serena's path for me?" I asked.

I could've done it myself, but it would require me to stop and use my omnitool, and I didn't want to lose whatever ground I was gaining.

A highlighted path flashed to my left away from the Ustrals heading inside. Once through the entrance, the atrium was filled with so many flashing lights and signs that I was blinded for a few seconds. My HUD quickly filtered them out by dimming their vivid display and I focused on Serena's path.

There were small, furry aliens that looked similar to a monkey, but their dome-shaped heads and teacup-sized eyes made them look like out-of-place tourists as they constantly stopped to peer around.

I saw flashes of white-uniformed patrons through the crowd and did a doubletake.

In the upper right corner of my HUD was a live video feed from Kierenbot's drones. As they flew overhead, I could see Serena walking down a long corridor with a dozen other beings.

I didn't know what was causing the crowds to rush out of the various shops, but the thoroughfare ground to a halt, and I was forced to shorten my stride because there was nowhere for the beings in front of me to go.

"I've just entered the complex, Captain," Kierenbot said.

"I'm stuck. Can you access the layout of this place?" I asked.

The path that Serena had taken flashed periodically on my HUD, as if I was going to forget it somehow.

"You're still on the fastest route. Access to the maintenance routes is restricted. I'll keep trying, but their network is very untrusting. My query initiated a very terse reply from the system, which I didn't care for."

In any other situation I would've laughed at the fact that Kierenbot was offended by another computer system, but it was just another obstacle.

"Do what you have to do."

I finally reached the long corridor Serena had taken, and I started running. There weren't many others using it. I glanced at the video feed and saw only a closeup view of the wall. The drone slowly backed up and I realized that it was a door.

"The drones are cut off," I said.

"There was a risk of that happening, Captain. I'm truly sorry I didn't warn you."

I blew out a harsh breath and raced down the corridor. There was a small group of... I had no idea what they were. They had four long arms that were a mustard-yellow color. Two of them dragged behind them like an afterthought. They had a long head that reminded me of a walking banana but not as delicious looking. They gathered in front of the door, and I saw others joining them from adjacent corridors.

I slowed down and watched as one of them used a control panel to open the door. Another panel opened on an inside wall and began scanning them as they went though.

"Damn it," I said and stopped. "They've got a security measure here. Some kind of scanner."

"My advice to you, Captain, is to run very fast. You need to be through the door before it rematerializes!"

"Uh, Nate, Kaz here. Don't do that. You'll never make it. If the door rematerializes, you could get stuck. These aren't the same as the doors on the ship."

I stepped toward the group, waiting to go through the door.

Some kind of counting mechanism allowed two small groups through at a time.

I hesitated. "Well, which is it guys?"

There was only a small group of beings left, waiting to go through. They looked asleep on their feet.

I cursed.

"It's a secure facility. There won't be a safeguard in the entry points—"

"Don't listen to him, Captain. You can make it through."

Kaz scowled. "Stop trying to get him killed."

"I would never do that!"

Kierenbot sometimes didn't think through all the outcomes, despite being a highly evolved AI.

They started arguing and I tuned them out.

I crept closer, staying near the same wall as the scanner. Maybe it wouldn't detect me.

"Nate, don't go any closer. It's suicide. Wait for Kierenbot. He can open the door for you."

The door dematerialized and the group of aliens began to slog through.

Gritting my teeth, I ran toward the door as the last of the group began to step through it.

The combat suit had the capability to enhance my movements so that I was faster and stronger, and if I had a full power core, I could fly. Right then, I'd settle for being fast enough to breach the door before the hazy rematerializing cycle completed.

I dove toward the opening and a warning flashed on my HUD. The door was rematerializing.

I flew through the air, and it felt like I was pushing through a thick, wet curtain. After long seconds of intense resistance, I was through, and I crashed into the hapless, defenseless aliens who were sleepwalking ahead of me.

I went down in a tangled mess amid the long-limbed aliens that looked to be something akin to Cousin It, but with long, thick, fleshy vines for hair. I tried to untangle myself, but it was as if they wanted me in their slippery clutches.

A gooey-brown substance smudged across the cameras on my helmet. I couldn't see, which I wasn't afraid to admit made me panic a little. I crawled blindly, shoving anything that felt foreign away from me while trying to wipe the sludge from my face.

It helped but only a little. I could now see blurry shapes instead of nothing. Growling, I retracted my helmet so I could see.

That was when things got a little weird.

After I extracted myself from the shaggy alien, I went down a short corridor and emerged into an assembly line of long pods that the brainwashed prisoners were climbing into.

I ran toward them, peering inside the window to see the occupants' faces. They floated down a pathway, heading out of the assembly area.

"Shit. Shit. Shit!"

"What do you see, Nate?" Kaz asked.

I scrambled down the pathway, pausing to peer inside each pod. A jade-colored glow came from inside, and the occupants were still, as if in some kind of trance. Serena was in one of these pods and I had to find her.

"Can't you get this door open?" Kaz said. He must've been speaking to Kierenbot.

"There is a lockdown protocol in effect. An alarm must have been triggered when Nate went through," Kierenbot replied.

I looked for a control panel that would stop the automated systems from working, but there wasn't one. The enter system must've been controlled somewhere else.

I raced along the path, searching for Serena's pod. The recon drones flew ahead, flying by each of the pods in rapid succession. They were ahead of me, not far from where the pods were headed toward what looked like a storage container. They were being stacked for shipping. The damn thing was a shipping container!

I raced toward it and jerked to a halt. Serena stood in the pod, and I gasped.

I banged on the pod.

"Wake up!" I shouted.

I called her name several times.

She stared ahead, ignoring me completely.

I tried to push the pod off the pathway, but it wouldn't budge.

"No! no!" I said and pushed harder.

It wouldn't work.

I backed up a few steps and then threw myself at the pod. My only success was that the pod slowly spun in place with me hanging onto it.

Serena blinked and I lowered my face toward hers. We were inches apart with a window between us, and I couldn't get her out of there. She didn't even seem like she was aware I was there. She blinked, and her eyes suddenly locked onto mine. She frowned as if she was trying to remember me.

"It's me. Nate. I'm trying to get you out of there."

Her eyelids drooped and she closed her eyes.

I couldn't get her to wake up by banging my palm on the window, so I activated my hand blaster and aimed it at the bottom of the pod, thinking I might be able to disable it by shooting it.

"Don't shoot it!" Kaz screamed. "She's in stasis. If you break the pod, you could kill her."

"I can't get her out of there! I can't move it. Help me, Kaz. I'm running out of time."

T'Chura raced toward me, easily outpacing all the others, but just as he was about to reach us, the assembly line of pods lurched forward, speeding toward the container.

There was a flash of light as I was shoved away from the pod, and I landed on the ground a short distance away. Filled with trepidation, I watched helplessly as Serena's stasis pod was loaded onto the shipping container.

I shot to my feet and raced toward it. T'Chura burst ahead of me, just about to grab the doors, but the container sped away.

"No, damn it! No!" I screamed.

I'd been so close.

# CHAPTER 13

I screamed in frustration, glaring at the container as it sped away, rising into the air and following an air-track with other vehicles.

I spun toward T'Chura. "Give me access to your power core."

"Nate, we'll catch up to her."

"I don't care!"

I quickly spun around him and opened the power core on his back. T'Chura started to turn, but I stayed at his back. A cable extended from the power core of my combat suit to his, and I began siphoning from T'Chura's core.

The others spoke, moving toward us, but I ignored them. I wasn't going to lose her.

The power meter quickly filled, and a warning flashed about the core stability. I yanked the cable out and activated the flight system of my combat suit. The suit computer did a quick pre-flight check and was ready to be used.

Then, with a running start, I leaped through the opening

where the storage container had been and flew upward like a bat out of hell.

I locked my arms at my sides and maximized the power output beyond safety measures for acceptable use. Warnings flashed on my HUD and I ignored them. I shot upward faster than a bullet. The combat suit computer's collision-avoidance system helped keep me from slamming into anything, but I was pretty sure I was setting off all kinds of alarms.

I spotted the large storage container ahead. It was dark gray with faded yellow stripes along the sides. I locked on, speeding toward it as I weaved my way through the crowded airways of automated drone traffic.

As I closed in on it, I opened a comlink back to the ship.

"Crim, I need your help."

"Nate! What happened? Where are you?"

"I need a way to override the control system for an automated delivery drone on a shipping container."

"What? Are you serious? What do you need a shipping container for?"

A large silver flying bus flew right in front of me. Clenching my teeth, I swung to the side, but I wasn't fast enough. I clipped the edge and somersaulted in the air, out of control. It took me a few seconds to get myself right, and then I sped toward the shipping container I was chasing.

"Crim, it's Serena. They've got her in a stasis pod inside a damn shipping container. I need a way to override the automated drone. There are other prisoners in there. I can't lose them!"

"All right. All right. Let me think a moment," Crim replied, and muttered a few things.

I thought I heard Jeshi in the background. "Isn't Kierenbot with you? He should be able to override the controls."

"I'm flying through the air. Any second now, the local

authorities, security, or whoever is going to join the chase and there isn't much I can do about it. Kierenbot isn't with me. I need your help. If I lose her now, I'm never going to find her again."

I knew I was speaking a mile a minute and my brain was racing with worry. If the shipping container made it to wherever it was going and I couldn't stop it, I'd never see Serena again.

Delivery drones only had a certain authorized range, so it was likely that the container was heading for a ship.

"Are you on the container yet?" Crim asked.

The skies were crowded, and I was doing my best to weave my way through the thick of it.

Some kind of drone about half my size flew alongside me and flashed its lights.

"This is a Datronia Security Enforcement Drone. You're in violation of—"

I shot the drone, and it sank from view with a long line of smoke trailing in its wake. In for a penny, in for a pound.

A warning flashed on my HUD about my quickly draining power core.

I made a beeline for the shipping container. There was a square drone attached to it that had a pair of thrusters on the bottom of it. It controlled several other smaller drone thrusters that were along the sides and the bottom of the container. I considered shooting them off, but then the container would crash. Not a great plan.

I finally caught up to the drone and managed to get hold of it. I swung my feet forward and magnetized my boots. They stuck to the container, but I doubted they'd hold if I let go with my hands.

"I'm on. What do you want me to do?"

"First, activate the video feed so I can see what we're dealing with," Crim said.

I added video to the comlink. The container swung to the side in a surprising lurch, and I clambered to stay on.

"Hold still," Crim said.

I bit off my reply and did as he asked.

"Okay, there is an access panel to the right. Open that up."

I searched for the panel, but the drone was all smooth metallic surfaces. I felt along it and a holo-interface became active.

"Sending a hack interface to you that should give you access to it," Crim said.

A suite of applications appeared on my HUD, and I initiated a connection to the delivery drone.

A list of failures began to appear.

"Uh Crim, it's not working."

"Give it a chance," he said in that I'm-wiser-than-thou tone.

I saw bright flashes of light off to the side. The container was flying near some kind of industrial district.

More flashes of light raced nearby.

"Nate, where are you? That looks like weapons fire."

I watched as a group of dark-armored soldiers fired their weapons at a watchtower with several guards inside. They returned fire and several drones launched from the top of the tower.

The storage container dipped to my left, moving us toward the battle.

"Woah. Woah. Crim, what's happening?"

"You tell me, Nate. You're on the damn thing."

I looked at the holo-interface. "It's resetting...The entire system is cycling!"

There was a bright flash and I saw dozens of other soldiers

moving among a complex of some kind. There were long rows of shuttles parked on the ground, and soldiers were racing toward one of the buildings. Several guards shot their weapons at them using bright green bolts. I had no idea what they were, but when the soldiers fired their weapons back at them, it was easy to see who had the most powerful arms. The guards were outclassed and didn't stand a chance.

"That's good, Nate."

"No it's not, Crim!"

How the heck was he so damn calm. Of course, he was calm. He was on the ship. He *always* waited on the ship because he was too damn smart to be caught out in the thick of it.

The delivery drone was bringing me right toward the battle. Any second now, someone was bound to notice a storage container the size of a bus heading right for them.

"Trust me. Once the system resets, you'll be able to take control of it."

The watchtower exploded, and I felt the force of it shove me against the delivery drone. My grip on the drone slipped and I started to fall. My magnetized boots held me in place for only a few moments and then I fell.

I tried to engage the fight system, but I only got short bursts, which slowed my fall.

Sometimes during a crash there is this odd sort of detachment, as if this were happening to someone else. Your brain decides that it has had enough, and you are just going to ride copilot for your own body. Either way, I was falling through the air, and I made myself into a ball. A second later I hit the line of shuttles.

The combat suit could withstand certain levels of blunt-force trauma, but with enough force I'd more than feel the impact. It was like running into something after misjudging the distance. A shocking jolt rocked my world.

It hurt.

I'm sure I bounced off a shuttle or two, perhaps more? These shuttles didn't have wings or a tail. They were like large metallic footballs. And solid, because slamming my body into them sent shockwaves through my combat suit that I felt.

I was like a smooth stone being skipped across a lake, only not as fun. I eventually rolled across the ground, making manly sounds for each impact until I stopped. I was pretty sure that if I'd been watching that happen to someone like Kaz or Ben I'd be laughing. However, since it was me, it wasn't as funny. Someone just got a great show of Nate the rag doll being tossed about.

I lay on my side, my arms flopped out on either side of me. I tried to sit up, but it took a while. I still felt like I was spinning. I looked for the flying storage container and saw it had landed in an area a few hundred yards from where I was.

For some reason, I suddenly began thinking about Ben trying to get me to switch to the metric system because being on an alien spaceship meant the Imperial system of measurement wasn't good enough. But centimeters were never going to be as cool as inches. It just didn't work that way. I was five feet, eleven inches tall or five-eleven. It was much easier than saying a hundred and something centimeters tall. Sorry world, there were some hills I was willing to die on, and this was one of them. However, I could get behind pints. Good beers come in pints, and what can I say? I'm a man of wealth and taste.

"Nate, are you all right?" Crim asked.

"Won't you guess my name?" I sang as I stood and began jogging toward the storage container.

"Huh? He's not making any sense. Well, he's just crashed."

"Woo, woo," I said, doing my best to back up Mick Jagger's singing in my head.

Crim was silent for a few seconds. "You're singing that song again, aren't you? Don't tell me. Rolling Rocks, right?"

"You got it—no, that's not right. Why is it you can only remember music from the 50s and 60s? What happened to the rest? There was great music after the 60s, Crim. It's not like we suddenly stopped. Anyway, it's the Rolling Stones."

"Ah, I knew there was 'rolling' in there and something about rocks."

"Stones, Crim. *The* Stones," I said and shook my head. "Man, that crash really hurt. The meds are working, though."

I wobbled onto my feet as I tried to run. Maybe the meds that my combat suit computer decided to administer hadn't been formulated correctly because I felt a little woozy.

I stopped. "Crim, I don't feel right. I think the formula is still off."

"Use the stimulants then. Use them quickly because there's something else going on there and you need to skedaddle," Crim said.

"You're not kidding. I'm still seeing plasma bolts…"

Someone had finally noticed me, and I saw several of them moving toward me. They were farther away.

I leaned against a shuttle and brought up the medical interface on my omnitool. A cool vapor came into my helmet, and I inhaled the stimulants. It smelled pungent, but at least the fog that was clouding my brain quickly cleared.

Several things became glaringly obvious to me in the span of a few seconds. First, there were large, darkly clad soldiers racing toward me. Second, the power core of my combat suit was nearly depleted. Third, the delivery drone was still offline, and the storage container filled with prisoners trapped in stasis was just sitting out in the open. Fourth, since the stimulants had cleared the effects of the pain medication, my body hurt…my *whole* body hurt like I'd been tackled by the entire Eagles defensive line.

A plasma bolt slammed into the ground near me, and I jerked away. Muttering a few curses, I started running—really running, not the inebriated trot I'd been doing before. It was a wonder I hadn't been killed already.

More flashes of light flew by me. I kept changing direction but slowly moving toward the storage container. Several bolts slammed into the side of it, and I spun around, firing back at them.

A new data comlink came online. It was the control interface for the delivery drone connected to the storage container. I ducked around a shuttle and ran between the rows of them, hoping it would lure whoever was shooting at me away from the container.

"Who's shooting at you?" Crim asked.

"I don't know, Crim! I didn't have time to ask their names!" I snapped.

The drone's control interface was really slow to respond. All I needed to do was input a new set of coordinates.

"What are the ship's coordinates?" I asked.

"Won't work…in route…"

The comlink to the ship went offline, but I was still connected to the drone interface.

I swore.

I saw movement up to the left, coming from the top of a shuttle. There was an Akacian up there. He wore a silver uniform and looked down at me for a second, then toward the soldiers following me. He brought up a rifle and began firing on them.

"Run!" I shouted up to him. "There are too many of them."

The Akacian lowered himself to the top of the shuttle and peered at me. "What?"

"I said, there are too many of them. Run—"

Two plasma bolts ripped off the top of the shuttle in a bright blast and the Akacian tumbled down to the ground.

I raced toward him as he tried to sit up but couldn't.

I skidded to a stop and knelt to check his injuries. Akacians are a cross between wolves and Komodo dragons. His skin was supposed to be green, but half of it was blackened from where the plasma bolt had hit.

He looked up at me with his good eye wide in shock and his body arched in pain. He struggled to speak, and his breath came in gurgled gasps. Then he became still. I looked at the emblem on his arm but didn't recognize it. I didn't know who he was, but he'd died trying to stop the others.

I heard the stomping footfalls of the approaching soldiers. There was no way I could make it to the storage container with them so close. I moved to the side of the shuttle and got my hand cannon ready, then reached over my shoulder for my multi-purpose tool. The four-foot metallic stick had a dull lavender glow at the tip.

I watched from the shadows as the soldiers moved toward the dead Akacian. They were tall and built like Mesaklorens. Their armor had red accent lights that drew a memory from me of a time fighting for my life atop a building on another planet.

I maximized the power output to my hand cannon. It was separate from my combat suit and would quickly go through my ammo, but it would be more lethal.

I watched as the soldiers made a sweep of the area. Just as one of them headed toward me, I fired my weapon. Mesakloren combat armor was weak in the neck. It had to do with protecting their ugly faces, or at least that's what I liked to think.

The soldier dropped to the ground, and I came out firing at the others, charging toward them.

The soldiers scattered quickly, recovering from my surprise attack, but not before I killed another one.

A shadow swooped from above and a soldier slammed into me, knocking me to the ground. I rolled to the side and was on my feet again, swinging my weapon blindly while anticipating the soldier would follow up on his attack. My stick slammed into him, unleashing a sonic burst of energy that shoved him back against the shuttle so hard the shuttle moved.

I ran toward him, leaping into the air, and brought the stick down on his head. A shockwave crushed the helmet and the head inside.

I heard the whine of a weapon being primed and jumped backward. A barrage of plasma bolts obliterated the body of the dead soldier. I ran in the opposite direction, circling around the next shuttle. Then I went at a full-on sprint behind the row of shuttles.

I knew they were pursuing me. I'd just killed a few of them. There was no way they were going to let me go, and I really didn't have any means of escape. As I ran, I came up with a plan. It was dumb, foolhardy, and desperate. Sometimes those plans were the ones that surprised you.

I peered down the area between the shuttles and saw the storage container nearby. If I could get to it, then I could get away. If any of the soldiers could fly, they'd already be doing it while they searched for me. They hadn't.

I turned toward the alley between shuttles and hastened toward the end where I stopped and became still. I heard the harsh, almost guttural Mesakloren language. I checked my comms system and tried to reach Crim, but it wouldn't go through.

"Communications are blocked," said a harsh voice from nearby.

I closed my eyes and winced. I knew that damn voice. Dead my ass.

"You've killed three of my soldiers. Impressive feat. I could use those skills," he said.

He wasn't far from me, and I weighed my options while I tried not to panic. Several soldiers turned down the far end of the shuttle and were coming toward me. Sighing, I put my stick on my back and stepped out from the shuttle with my hands held high.

"Kael Torsin, are you offering me a job?"

He frowned toward me and blinked.

I made my faceplate transparent so he could see me. "I bet I'm the last person you expected to see today."

A big Mesakloren soldier flanked by two others stopped walking toward me. His ugly face was exposed, and his gaze locked onto mine. I'd bet if I started running, his eyes would remain locked onto me even as he ran me down. I was suddenly reminded of a documentary showing a lion making a run at an antelope. While the lion's body moved to carry it toward its prey, its head remained locked on the target.

God, it sucked being the antelope.

It was right about then that I decided I needed to rethink the decisions I'd made in my life—what little of it that was left, anyway. Several data windows appeared on my HUD.

"Nathan Briggs," Kael Torsin said and stepped toward me as if he wanted to savor this moment. "You're a bit earlier than I expected, but that's okay. I'm going to enjoy this."

# CHAPTER 14

He could've just shot me right then and there wasn't much I could've done about it. I was alone and surrounded.

"Heard you were dead," I said.

"Keeping tabs on me, I see. It was convenient for others to believe they'd eliminated me," Kael Torsin said and looked at the storage container. "That's one of mine."

"Is it? I hadn't known."

Kael Torsin gestured for one of his soldiers to check the storage container.

I stepped toward it as a sort of involuntary reflex. The other soldiers looked as if they were a second away from killing me.

Kael noticed the movement and looked amused, or as amused as his ugly face would allow.

"Well, I'll get out of your hair then," I said but didn't move. I frowned. "Hold on a second. You said you were expecting me?"

Kael Torsin stalked closer to me, and at seven feet tall, he could loom with the best of them.

I clenched my teeth and glared at him. He might have expected me to cower, but I wasn't going to give him the satisfaction. I stepped toward him.

"Let's get this started. I haven't got all damn night. Come on!" I shouted.

Kael Torsin shook his head a little. "Arrogance isn't entirely a Human trait, even in the face of your betters."

"Maybe you think too much of yourself. Maybe I'm going to die right now."

A menacing glint came to Kael Torsin's gaze. "I'm certain of it. You might believe this show of bravado will allow you to die with some dignity. It doesn't," he said and gestured toward the storage container. "Quite the revelation, aren't they?"

I shrugged. "Not really. Not much, anyway."

"Earth isn't a bad planet. The mountains are certainly—"

"Sir, I'm locked out of the drone's control interface," a soldier said.

I hid my amusement. Crim had taught me how to use my omnitool by tracking my eye movements on my HUD.

Kael Torsin looked toward the soldier, but the others kept their weapons pointed at me. If I moved, they'd shoot me.

"Our security is being hacked. The Akacians are trying to disable our suits," another soldier said.

Kael Torsin frowned and then turned toward me, eyes narrowing.

"Crystalline enforcers are en route here," a soldier warned.

I certainly didn't have any idea who that was, but the Mesakloren soldiers did. They began checking their surroundings for a greater threat than I was.

*Interesting.*

I looked at the storage container, deciding I had to take a chance of reaching it.

"The drone's engines are coming online. I'm still locked out!" the soldier said.

Kael Torsin spun, searching back the way they'd come. I followed his gaze and saw teams of soldiers loading a large shuttle in the distance. They were robbing this place.

I stepped to the side a little, edging toward the storage container, and he swung his gaze toward me.

I froze with a smirk. "You're pulling a heist? Is that what this is? Well, it looks like you've got your hands full."

The drones' engines sputtered to life, emitting a whine of power and drawing their attention.

I grabbed my stick and spun, swinging it at the soldier behind me. For such a versatile weapon it packed quite the punch, which worked two-fold. First, the armored soldier was knocked off his feet, and since I'd leaped at the last second, the backlash of force sent me flying through the air toward the storage container.

I tried to use my flight system on sheer reflex, but my combat suit wasn't having it. It had no power to spare, even for a burst of energy.

Multiple data windows invaded my HUD. I didn't know what they were or where they came from, but they distracted me enough that I stumbled as I landed on the ground. I quickly regained my feet while resisting the urge to check behind me, certain that I was seconds away from Kael Torsin and his soldiers firing their weapons at me. They'd made short work of the guardians of this place, and I was no match for them, so I ran.

The storage container lifted into the air and I gritted my teeth, trying to get as much speed as I could to jump for it.

I leaped into the air, my arm stretched out to grab onto the delivery drone, but the engines burst with sudden speed, and it flew away. I stretched my eyes wide as I landed on my side.

I'd missed.

Howls of rage sounded from behind me, and I shot to my feet. I crawled on top of the nearest shuttle and then leaped to the next one, trying to catch the fleeing storage container.

I thought I could catch it, but the delivery drone banked to the side and gained altitude, carrying Serena and the other prisoners away from there.

Something bright and orange flashed toward my face. My body became rigid, as if something had overridden the controls of my combat suit, and I fell to the ground.

I couldn't move. I tried to use my HUD to get the status of my suit, but it went offline.

"Hey!" I shouted and then cursed.

I tried to twist inside my suit, but it was like wearing an extra layer of thick skin; there wasn't much wiggle room. I began to panic because with my suit offline, I no longer had life support.

I thought I heard someone walking toward me, but it was muffled. My faceplate was no longer translucent, and I couldn't see anything but the darkness inside my helmet.

"Wait. Wait. Is someone there?"

I felt something grab hold of me and lift me up. It touched the back of my neck, and as the helmet retracted, I found myself staring into a glowing, bright-orange octagon. Its smooth planes shimmered like a crystal that caught the light, but I saw that there was also a light source inside.

"Volz 3, turn him toward me so I can scan him."

The crystal octagon had a pair of arms and pincher-type hands that squeezed my arms as it turned me toward the speaker.

The alien I was facing looked about four feet tall, had curly dark hair, and a snout full of sharp teeth. Its large, dingy brown eyes narrowed as they peered at me. It reminded me a little of a bear. He wore a gray uniform with a blue diamond emblem on its arms, and a headband sat on the hair between his large ears. His ears flopped at the top, giving him a dog-like appearance.

Volz 3 lowered me toward the ground. I felt something grab my legs and saw that two more arms had extended from the glowing octagon. Volz 3 angled my head toward the sneering bear.

I leaned away.

A bright flash came from something in the center of the headband, and the beast looked down at his omnitool.

"Unregistered species," he said. He looked up at me. "Where are you from?"

I blinked and tried to open my mouth, but I couldn't. I frowned and the bear rolled his eyes.

"Let him speak, Volz 3. Don't make me bring Volz 4 in here. Your performance today is already lacking by five percent when compared with the others, so don't push it."

Whatever force that was preventing me from speaking suddenly lessened.

I smiled a little and moved my jaw because it felt tingly. "Your timing was impeccable. I can describe all of them."

The bear frowned. "What are you talking about? You're being taken into custody. I need to know your name and species because I don't have a record of it."

"Custody? Me?"

The bear sighed and he looked up at Volz 3. "I don't think this one understands us. Negative reinforcement protocols authorized."

"Wait!" I said. "I'm Nathan Briggs. Human."

The bear nodded and began fiddling with his omnitool. "Nathan Brings Human," he said and looked at me suspiciously. "Do you think this is funny?"

I shook my head. "No."

He leaned toward me. "I don't believe him. Volz, remind him who's in charge here."

A jolt of pain spread across my skin as if I were being whipped. I cried out. I wasn't sure how long it went on, but when it stopped, I was gasping. I slumped down and lifted my head toward the bear.

"There, now you'll listen to me."

I either had drool or blood dripping down the side of my mouth. "I'm trying to cooperate. What do I call you?"

The bear seemed to consider this for a second. "Names are not necessary."

"I thought we were going to be civilized."

The bear sighed. "Well, Nathan Brings Human, I'm Be'zell."

I blinked. "My name is Nathan *Briggs*."

Be'zell stared at me for a second. I'm aware of your name, Nathan Brings."

I shook my head. "No, it's *Briggs*."

"What brings? What are you talking about?" he asked and then narrowed his gaze suspiciously. "Are you trying to trick me?" he asked.

"No," I said quickly, not wanting to experience that pain again. "I think there's something wrong with the translation."

Be'zell drew himself up and considered that for a few moments. "It's not beyond what is possible. What species are you?"

"Human."

Be'zell blinked and gave me a once-over. I couldn't tell whether he was sizing me up for a meal or something worse. "Human. Okay, I'll need to check this out."

I tried to glance over my shoulder for a second. "Is there any chance you could let me go? This is just a big misunderstanding. I wasn't even supposed to be here—"

Be'zell laughed. His furry paws settled on his stomach and made circular motions. It didn't fill me with a lot of confidence.

"You're not going anywhere. This has been a major breach of security. No, you'll be going away for a very long time," Be'zell said. He looked up at Volz. "Take him to holding."

"Wait. Just wait a second," I said.

"Gag him!" Be'zell shouted.

I couldn't move at all. I tried to open my mouth, but it was as if the muscles wouldn't listen to my brain. There was no force, but something was keeping me from moving. I could breathe and blink, which might not sound like much, but given what I knew about aliens, it was a lot. They could have easily stopped everything.

Be'zell leaned toward me. "I'm going to get to the bottom of this. You'll tell me everything I want to know. Everything you know—everything and then some."

I wanted to reply, explain the situation, but there was something rigid and a little scary—in a deranged sort of way—to his gaze.

He seemed to have arrived at a decision, and I blacked out. No blow to the head. No flash of light. It was simply lights out and nothing.

# CHAPTER 15

I woke sometime later, sprawled out on the floor of a holding cell. At least, I thought it was a holding cell. My combat suit was on minimal power, which was just enough to keep the nanites in formation, and I wasn't sure if they could protect me from anything with so little power left. I'd never tested them at this level.

A soft yellow light came from the ceiling, and I pushed myself up and leaned against the wall. I brought my knees up and rested my forearms on them, noticing how stiff my muscles were. Next, I tried stretching my arms over my head, then stood and continued to loosen my aching muscles.

I was thirsty. I sniffed the air and couldn't smell anything. The small room had no other features—no chair, bench, or bed —but what concerned me the most was that there was no toilet. I didn't need one right then, but like most things like that, it was only a matter of time. I didn't relish the thought of using the floor.

It took me three long strides to reach the other side of the room. There was a stain of some kind on the floor. It was faded but definitely there. I slid my fingertips along the wall, hoping a holoscreen would become active.

It didn't.

I was in a metallic box, and I didn't like it. I tried to bring up my omnitool, but it wouldn't respond. I shook my arm, hoping the motion would somehow startle the omnitool into working. I should've known better, but I was becoming desperate.

The light overhead changed from a soft yellow to a harsh white. One of the walls dematerialized and I saw Volz hovering in the air. He was still octagonal-shaped and glowing orange, but he had none of the arms from before. I peered at the ground underneath him, wondering how he was able to hover in the air. Maybe he had some kind of counter-grav emitter or — Where was Ben when I needed him? He could probably figure this out.

I raised both my hands in front of my chest, hoping Volz didn't interpret it as a threatening gesture.

"I don't want any trouble."

Volz didn't answer or show any indication that he understood what I'd said. Instead, he began to float away from the door.

Not needing more of an invitation than that, I followed him. At least, I thought it was a "him."

The wide corridor was easily large enough to accommodate an aircar, and I wondered what other kinds of beings were held here.

Volz led me down a corridor and into another room. There was a table, and a bear-like creature waited there. He gestured impatiently with one of his claws toward the table.

"Come. Come. Come. Stand here. Time is crucial," he said.

I hastened to comply and went to stand by the table.

The little bear regarded me for a moment. "Nathan Brings,"

he said, and I didn't try to correct him. "Akacian light combat suit. Strip it off, now."

I lifted my left arm and my omnitool became active. Whatever had been suppressing it must've stopped. I initiated the breakdown of my armor and the nanorobotic particles fell away from my body. They clustered together into a square on the table. Since I'd been wearing my armor over my clothing, I knew I wasn't going to give the bear a show.

The bear peered at me. "Civilian smart fabric. Looks like Ustral generic fibers. You may keep those."

"Thank you," I replied.

The bear narrowed his gaze suspiciously. I had no idea what made them so uppity, but it was getting annoying.

The bear looked over my shoulder at Volz. "Where are the rest of his weapons?"

Volz moved toward the table for a moment. When he moved away, my hand cannons and multipurpose tool were next to my inactive combat suit.

The bear activated a holoscreen and then looked at me. "Are these yours?"

I glanced at them for a second. "Yes."

The bear entered something I couldn't see. He was probably noting down my response.

I glanced at Volz and then at the bear. "May I speak?"

The bear regarded me intently for a few seconds. "Very well."

"Thank you. Who are you?"

"Bolgan."

"Nice to meet you, Bolgan."

Bolgan stepped toward me, snarling. "What is this! Are you mocking these proceedings?"

I shook my head, leaning back a little. "No, I'm not mocking anything. I'm trying to be civil. It's a gesture of respect."

Bolgan considered this for a few moments and then backed away. "Very well, proceed."

Touchy didn't even begin to describe them. They were like some kind of sick, deranged version of the Care Bears.

"I think there has been some kind of misunderstanding. I was arrested—"

"You were arrested while stealing from a Tamiran Consortium military production complex. A very serious offense. You and your team are responsible for the deaths of thirty-three security officers protecting the complex. Also, there is the destruction of thirteen security shuttles."

"I wasn't there stealing anything. I was there accidentally," I said.

Bolgan looked skeptical. "It's always fascinating to hear the statements of criminals. I enjoy destroying their defenses with pure logic."

I wasn't sure if this was a trial, but I hoped not.

"What authority do you hold over me?"

"I'm authorized by the Datronia Systems Security Forces. This interview is being recorded, and we will use these recordings to confirm the level of your guilt," Bolgan said.

His voice sounded nasally, as if he had a bad allergy or something.

I inhaled and considered what I was going to say for a few seconds. "I'm not familiar with the laws here."

"I assure you that they are quite logical. A law is broken —or in this case many laws have been broken—and the perpetrators are punished. Even a place such as..." He paused for a moment, looking confused. "What is your home world?"

"Earth."

He nodded and continued with what sounded like a

prepared speech. "Even a place such as Earth must have similar laws in place to punish criminals."

I made a show of considering what he'd said. He expected it, and I needed to build some kind of rapport if I was going to escape.

I nodded. "We do have laws to determine guilt and punish criminals."

Bolgan made a "there you have it" gesture with one of his paws.

"Are you accusing me of a crime?"

Bolgan was about to reply but stopped when someone banged repeatedly on a nearby wall. A new doorway appeared and in walked Be'zell. He looked as if he'd cleaned himself up, but he scowled in my direction.

"Of course, you're being accused of a crime. What do you think we're doing here? Do you think we have nothing better to do?" Be'zell asked.

Bolgan looked at him and raised his snout a little. "I was getting to that."

Be'zell appeared unperturbed. "Yes, but I needed to move this along. I haven't decided whether this Nathan Brings is extremely clever or colossally stupid."

Both bears stared at me intently. They spoke very fast, and it took a moment for me to catch up.

"I can see you're very busy and have very important work to do. I don't want to be here any longer than necessary," I said and paused for a moment.

Bolgan leaned toward me, rubbing his grubby little paws together. "So, you admit your guilt then. We can move on with punishment. This is excellent. My efficiency scores will improve greatly because of this."

The two bears began speaking so quickly that I couldn't

understand what they were saying, but I knew I didn't like it. I had no idea what kind of punishment they had in mind, and I really didn't want to find out.

"Woah. Hold on a minute. I haven't admitted anything."

Bolgan looked away from Be'zell and frowned. "You haven't?"

I blinked and shook my head. "No, I haven't. I think you've skipped a few steps here."

Bolgan lunged toward me. "How dare you!"

I leaned away from him as he tried to grab my throat and shoved him back with my foot. He howled in rage. Snarling, he charged toward me, baring his teeth.

With Volz-number-whatever standing near me, I didn't risk trying to get up from my chair.

"I thought you followed the law. Don't you need to tell me what I'm being accused of and give me a chance to defend myself?" I asked.

Be'zell blocked Bolgan from getting to me. "He's right!"

Bolgan struggled against his companion, and in any other situation I would have found the two chubby little bears wrestling to be extremely funny, but I didn't dare laugh because I didn't need two of them coming after me.

"Control yourself," Be'zell said. "You'll lose your post. You mustn't give in to your primitive instinct. We're not juveniles anymore."

Bolgan regained control of himself and took several deep breaths.

"Bolgan," I said, and he looked at me as if he'd just come out of a daze, "I didn't mean to offend you or the way things are done here. Please don't misunderstand me, but meaning no insult to either of you, I really do believe there has been a serious misunderstanding that we can resolve quickly."

Bolgan looked at Be'zell for a few moments and the two seemed to arrive at an unspoken agreement. Then, they came back to the table and sat.

"Very well, Nathan Brings. We will indulge your questions, as is your right as the accused," Bolgan said calmly.

I considered him for a few moments. Both of them redefined what "quick to anger" meant. Sure, they appeared to be calm, but there was something wild and dangerous about them.

"You mentioned something about a robbery where many guards had been killed."

"Yes, the military production complex has been raided and thirty-three guards have been killed."

"I'm just one person. There is no way I could've done all that."

Bolgan's gaze narrowed in irritation. "We know that. No one has accused you of killing the guards," he said and looked at Be'zell. "Did you accuse him of that?"

Be'zell shook his head. "Of course not. I would never do that."

Bolgan looked at me. "There you see. You are mistaken."

I blinked, not quite believing that I was being held by these two idiots. "What exactly are the charges against me?"

"Robbery, destruction of property, breaking restrictions for personal power core, and resisting arrest."

"Okay, let's take them one at a time. First, I haven't stolen anything."

"That's because we stopped you before you could," Be'zell said, and Bolgan gave him an approving nod. They both seemed pleased with this.

I considered my response for a few seconds. "We're missing some context here. I wasn't there to steal anything. I stumbled upon a robbery that was already in progress."

"Stumbled, you say? You just wandered into a highly secure production facility?"

The two of them peered at me.

"There is more to it than that," I said and told them about the alien abductions and how I'd been tracking them.

Both of them regarded me for a few minutes. I'd never want to play poker with them because I couldn't get a read on what they were thinking.

Bolgan sighed and glanced at Be'zell.

"Do the security recordings show a storage container with a delivery drone attached to it?"

Be'zell frowned in thought for a second. "They're checking."

I frowned. "Who's checking?"

Be'zell narrowed his gaze for a second. "The tribunal support team. They have the evidence to review at their discretion."

This was the first I'd heard of anyone else listening in, and I wasn't sure if I should be relieved to hear there was a tribunal judging me. If the tribunal was anything like these two bears, I wasn't sure how I'd ever escape.

Be'zell gestured to an area in front of him and a holoscreen appeared. I watched a video recording of the storage container being set down among the rows of shuttles.

I gestured toward the screen. "That's where the prisoners were being kept."

Bolgan's snout wrinkled as if he'd smelt something foul. "It's not a refrigeration unit. It's just a container. There are millions of them used on the station, and that doesn't include the planet."

"There were stasis pods inside the container. I saw them being loaded. That's why I was following them, and that's why I violated the power core restriction. A friend of mine is a prisoner inside that container."

"A friend? Another accomplice?"

"No, dammit!" I slammed my hand on the table.

They weren't startled. Instead, they looked delighted, as if my response was what they'd hoped for.

"Do you have the container? You can look inside and confirm it for yourself," I said.

Be'zell looked away.

"The container was not retrieved."

"You lost it."

"No we didn't!" Be'zell said quickly.

"Then where is it?" I asked.

"We're tracking it down."

I didn't believe him. They hadn't even mentioned the container until I'd brought it up.

Bolgan brought up another recording, which showed me crashing into the shuttles. I winced as I watched my body bouncing off the tops of half a dozen shuttles before crashing violently to the ground. I shook my head. As my aching body could attest, I now felt every bit of that crash.

I looked at them and frowned. Their shoulders were shaking, and they each made a snorting sound as they rocked back and forth.

I sighed. The deranged Care Bears were laughing at me.

I shook my head. "I'm glad you're enjoying yourselves, but this does prove my story. I wasn't there to steal anything."

They stopped laughing.

Bolgan regarded me for a few seconds. "Preposterous. This confirms that you were at the location when the crime occurred. I think we can move forward with a verdict for this charge. Don't you agree, Be'zell?"

"I do agree. The evidence is irrefutable and not defensible."

"What are you talking about? I wasn't there stealing anything. I just told you why I was there," I said, my voice rising.

"For all we know, you were there to rejoin your companions," Bolgan said.

Be'zell nodded enthusiastically.

"My companions? Oh, you mean the Mesakloren soldiers who were trying to kill me? Those guys? That should be on that video as well."

Bolgan waved away the comment. "Doesn't matter. You had a disagreement and that started the fight."

I clenched my teeth. They refused to see reason and were determined to punish me. "What about Kael Torsin? He was there, and he was running the show. He's the one you should be punishing."

They both frowned in confusion.

I blinked. They had no idea what I was talking about.

Bolgan brought up a data window and ran a search. "Ah, I see. Disgraced soldier who was killed in a raid. He couldn't possibly have been here."

I balled my hands into fists. "He was there because I saw him. I spoke to him. Just bring up the video and you'll see. Bring it up. Look for yourselves."

Bolgan looked at Be'zell and he nodded.

They brought up the recording after I'd crashed. The playback speed made it jump until I saw myself surrounded by the soldiers. None of the camera angles showed Kael Torsin's face. He was dressed like every other soldier, and even with his helmet off, the video only showed the back of his head. I suspected that Kael Torsin knew he was being recorded.

"He's right there," I said, gesturing toward the soldier nearest me.

"Identity of the Mesakloren is not confirmed. We shall investigate this. However, this doesn't absolve your guilt. You were at the location when the crime was being committed and, therefore, you were participating in the crime. The fact that we found no stolen items with you doesn't negate your involvement."

My mouth hung open. This wasn't a trial at all. They'd already determined my guilt just by being at the location.

"This is crazy," I said.

"Our methods are quite deliberate and have served this system for a very long time. We are the custodians of the great Datronia System, and you have violated its laws. You are responsible for the deaths—"

"I didn't kill any guards. In fact, one of your guards saved me because he watched those soldiers trying to kill me."

Bolgan surged to his feet. "See, you admit it. Your presence is directly responsible for the death of the guard. You admit it," he said and looked at Be'zell. "He admits it."

"You're blind to the actual facts. Kael Torsin was the leader who was stealing from the production facility. He's the one responsible for all those deaths. Do you even know what they got away with?"

Be'zell tilted his head to the side. "What makes you think they got away?"

I leveled my gaze at him. "Call it a hunch. Because if you had encountered him or any of his soldiers, you'd be dead. They would've wiped the floor with you, you pathetic weasel!"

"Insults! You believe you're so clever. Maybe I should have Volz 3 remind you of the error of your thinking. The Mesaklorens are no match for the Crystalline."

"We're done here," Bolgan said.

I laughed bitterly. "Done! We never even started. I've poked holes in every one of your charges and you refuse to see reason."

"The guilty always spout their injustice, but justice will be served, and you, Nathan Brings, are guilty."

I shook my head. "It's Briggs! My name is Nathan BRIGGS, dammit! Not BRINGS! You can't even get my name right."

"We'll be sure to get it corrected, not that it matters."

I growled as I shot to my feet and lunged toward the bears. Before I could get across the table, Volz 3 grabbed me by my feet, hands, and arms at the same time, and I was lifted off the ground. Scowling, I still tried to lunge toward the bears.

They stood up with malicious grins on their evil faces.

"The tribunal has agreed with the charges and the verdict. The punishment will be carried out," Bolgan said.

I stopped my futile struggle against Volz 3. "What's going to happen?"

"Oh, it will be quite unenjoyable," Bolgan replied.

I narrowed my gaze and then smiled. "You don't even know."

Bolgan blinked and then glanced at Be'zell. "Yes we do. We know exactly what's going to happen to you."

I shook my head. "No you don't. You're just the middlemen. You don't know anything. There are alien trafficking crimes happening right under your furry little noses and the best you can do is arrest me, who told you about it in the first place. You're convicting me of a crime based purely on my proximity to the scene of the crime rather than following any real evidence. Your entire argument is flawed, just like your logic."

The two bears snarled in rage and leaped onto the table. Volz 3 lifted me higher, keeping me out of their reach. There was a white flash, and the two bears were knocked off the table. They rolled onto the ground in a daze.

Volz 3 set me down on the ground. He released my feet and legs, but still held my arms to my sides.

The two bears slowly came out of their daze.

Bolgan looked at Be'zell. "It happened again. Volz 3 had to restrain us."

Be'zell looked at Volz and was ashamed. "This is going to count against us. They'll never allow us to transfer to the Prime now."

Bolgan peered at me. "I'm required to inform you that you've been found guilty of all the charges against you. The punishment will be swift and severe."

Speaking to them was a waste of time, so I didn't reply.

"Do you acknowledge that you understand what I've said?"

I simply glared at them.

Bolgan's snout wrinkled a little, as if he were trying to keep himself from snarling. He looked at Be'zell. "He doesn't have to acknowledge it, right? Not verbally. He understood us until now, so we should be in compliance with a quality review."

I knew I shouldn't have been surprised by this, but I was. The level of absurdity just kept increasing, and all I wanted to do was drop-kick the deranged bear into the middle of next week.

Bolgan regarded me for a few seconds. "I think he intends to harm us."

Be'zell stared at me and then nodded. "I do believe you're correct."

"Should we add this to his list of crimes?"

I sighed. "For the love of— Yes, I understand. Just get me out of here now. Anything I can do to speed this along."

Bolgan blinked a few times. He bobbed his head as if he were reviewing some kind of mental check list. Then he raised his gaze toward mine. "We'd like you to review our performance for your trial. It'll assist us with improving our services in the future."

I opened my mouth, flabbergasted.

Be'zell cocked his head to the side, considering. Then he looked at Bolgan. "I don't think he will."

"Nonsense. Our performance was impeccable, and as an

intelligent being, he'll have no choice but to highlight those facts."

I stood there with Volz 3's pinchers securing my arms at my side while my gaze darted between them. My muscles tightened across my chest because I just wanted to strangle both of them.

I lowered my head for a few moments and tested Volz 3's grip a little. Yeah, I wasn't going anywhere but by his say-so. I lifted my head and sneered at the two bears. "You want my feedback on your performance? A friggin performance review like a customer satisfaction survey?"

They stepped back from the table and actually looked shocked.

I wanted to scream at them. Howl in rage and promise to… to…I just wanted to…Gah!

Bolgan looked at his partner. "I think you're right. He can't even speak anymore. We might have broken him."

I looked over my shoulder. "Let me go. I'm convicted, right? Right? Let me go. What's two more murders on top of everything else thrown at me?" I turned toward the bears. "I swear I'm going to find the two of you and I'm going to tear you apart. Don't back away from me. This trial was a sham. I could teach you a thing or two about due process. Where did they find you? Did they pick you right out of the forest or did they fetch you from the zoo? I know, maybe it was the circus."

I don't know if they understood everything I said, but what had gotten through snapped them out of their amicable mood.

"Come on!" I chided them.

I was so focused on them and they on me that I hadn't noticed a Mesakloren entering the room. He wore a dark-green uniform with golden accents on his chest and shoulders. He was slenderer than the muscled soldiers under Kael Torsin's command but still had that pushed-in face akin to a bulldog on steroids. I didn't think even a mother could love that face.

"What's going on here?" he asked with the voice of authority.

Bolgan looked at him and his ears went back. He jabbed his paw into Be'zell's side, and the bear stood straight, his pouch of a gut sticking out.

"Agent, sir, we were processing the prisoner," Bolgan said.

The Mesakloren regarded the two of them for a moment. "And?"

"Guilty, sir. The accused has been found guilty of all charges," Bolgan said, sounding proud of the outcome.

The Mesakloren regarded me for a second and then nodded. "Very well. I shall take him for further processing."

Bolgan frowned and raised one of his paws. "Agent, sir, this is highly irregular. He's due at central processing where he'll be transferred to long-term incarceration and reprogramming. I need to authorize that."

Mesaklorens weren't much for facial expressions, at least as far as I could see. He regarded them. "Ordinarily, this would be correct, but given the nature of these crimes, this convict will require additional processing for our investigation."

Bolgan considered this for a few seconds. "Who are you?"

"Agent Kylath. I'm with Tamiran Consortium Military Intelligence. Authorization for prisoner transfer is pending but should arrive in your office in a short while. Now, if you'll release your prisoner into my custody, I can get a jumpstart on our investigation and my superiors will be satisfied."

Over the years, I'd seen a number of people try to con not just me but anyone they could get away with. This was an old-fashioned steamrolling of the mark. To put it bluntly, my BS meter was well within the red zone.

I looked at Bolgan. "Don't do it. An official transfer of custody would have proper authorization sent ahead of time."

Kylath's gaze narrowed.

Bolgan looked conflicted.

Kylath turned toward the two bears. "As I already said, authorization is coming through normal communication channels, but could you do me this favor just this once? Some highly confidential equipment was stolen from the complex and I've been tasked with tracking it down."

"Something isn't right," I said. "He's working with Kael Torsin. Don't let him take me anywhere. He's going to kill me!"

Kylath looked over my shoulder at Volz 3. "Gag the prisoner. He's being hostile."

Something cold and metallic came around my face. My nose and mouth were covered, and I couldn't speak. My eyes widened. I could breathe through a small opening near my nostrils, but I couldn't move my jaw. I tried to speak, but it came out as muffled, incoherent grunts.

Kylath nodded, pleased. "Thank you," he said and turned toward the others. "I understand you had quite a struggle with this one. He believes Kael Torsin is alive and that I work for him." He shook his head and gave me a disapproving look. "How pathetically absurd."

Kylath turned toward the others. "Help me out with this and I'll send over a glowing commendation for both of you for an outstanding job. How does that sound?"

Bolgan glanced at Be'zell with an excited gleam in his eyes and they nodded.

"Volz 3," Bolgan said, "I hereby transfer prisoner…" he paused, eyeing me for a second, "Nathan Briggs to Agent Kylath of the Tamiran Consortium. You may release him into his custody."

Kylath turned toward me, and I glared at him. Volz 3 released me. Kylath threw something metallic toward me that floated deliberately toward my hands. It looked to be made of a similar material to my combat suit. Soon, both my hands were covered in a nanorobotic shackle. I tried to lift my hands, but the shackle had spread around my waist and the gag stayed in place.

I turned toward Volz 3, but the glowing orange crystalline being had already left the room.

Bolgan and Be'zell went to the table and began gathering my belongings.

"I'll take those as well," Kylath said.

Be'zell frowned. "But we get a bounty for them."

"I'll ensure you're both suitably compensated," Kylath replied.

I tried to back up, but there were shackles around my ankles and they held me firmly in place.

Be'zell looked unconvinced, and his paw gravitated toward my multipurpose tool.

"That's evidence," Kylath admonished.

"He's right," Bolgan said. "Come on. Let's go finish our report so Central can see that we're ahead of our quota!"

The two bears headed for the door, and I tried to scream through my gag. Bolgan glanced at me and smirked as he left the room.

Kylath walked to the table and touched the multipurpose tool, which collapsed to a small cube. He then put both my combat suit and tool into a storage container and tossed them at me with a dismissive gesture.

I fumbled my shackled hands to catch my stuff. Without access to my omnitool, I could only carry them.

Kylath headed for the door and my shackles spurred me into

motion. Tiny barbs pricked the skin of my ankles and I let out a muffled cry.

"Keep up, convict, unless you'd like those shackles to drag you along the floor," Kylath said.

I shuffled my feet to catch up with him, and it felt like the barbs were tearing into my skin, but they did retract once I was closer to Kylath.

He led me through a security checkpoint where more ugly bears sneered in my direction. I tried to speak to them, but the gag wouldn't allow me to turn my head. My muffled attempts at communications were met with evil laughter from the bears.

# CHAPTER 16

Kylath walked onto an elevator, and I reluctantly joined him. It was either that or having those barbs chew through my ankles.

The doors closed and the elevator began to move.

Kylath glanced at me. "Screkles are an abrasive species, but no one can question their dedication."

So, the bears were called Screkles. I decided I preferred calling them deranged Care Bears. I tried to turn toward him but the gag still wouldn't let me, and I got the sense that Kylath was amused by this.

The elevator doors opened to a crowded room filled with bears. It reminded me of the DMV where long lines of people waited their turn at the wheel of bureaucracy. The bears—Screkles—seemed to take great delight in turning aliens away for not having their paperwork in order.

As Kylath and I marched through, I noticed that the different types of species seemed to open a path for Kylath. Some glanced at me with trepidation. They stared at my shackles, and the wetness near my ankles meant I was bleeding a little.

No one would make eye contact with me for very long, at least none of the civilians. The uniformed guards, or law enforcement Screkles traveling with their Crystalline escorts, regarded me as if my fate had been sealed. My options for escape were virtually nonexistent. I doubted Kaz or the others were going to break me out of jail. They didn't have access or know how to do that. Maybe Ben would contact Delos to see if he could pull some strings and get me free. But that was going to take time, and time was something Serena didn't have.

Kylath led me to a pickup area for various types of transport. I wasn't the only prisoner there. Given my experience, I wondered just how many had been wrongfully accused as well.

Kylath guided me toward a windowless aircar. The rear passenger compartment opened and he gestured for me to go in. I shuffled forward and stepped inside. There was another Mesakloren inside the vehicle, and he stared at me for a moment with almost a frown. Then, Kylath and the other one gestured toward a seat across from them. I moved in front of the seat and sat down in a controlled fall. Straps extended from the back of the seat and secured me in place.

I saw Kylath climb into one of the front seats and then the aircar left the area. I looked at the Mesakloren across from me. He wore a similar uniform to Kylath's, but his thick, braided hair was white. He didn't look old, but I didn't know enough about Mesaklorens to really know. His skin had a few wrinkles near his eyes and also at his wide forehead. He didn't look at me, which I thought was peculiar. He seemed preoccupied with looking out the window. After a few minutes he brought up his personal holoscreen, but he used some kind of privacy mode and I couldn't see what he was doing.

None of this struck me as being legit, and the fact of the matter was that the Screkles had released me into the hands of these aliens. Maybe Kael wanted me delivered without injury so he could torture me. I rolled my eyes. That was a cheerful thought.

I lifted my shackled hands and tried to speak. I just wanted to get his attention.

The Mesakloren glanced at me.

I tried to ask if they could take my shackles off, but it came out like a series of grunts.

Something on the holoscreen got his attention and he began navigating the interface. He pulled out a palm scanner and held it in front of my face. Then, he started moving it down the front of me. I had no idea what they were scanning for, but when he paused near my crotch, I began to shift in my seat. He kept scanning my legs. He paused at certain areas, and I thought I felt my skin warm for a few seconds.

He moved the scanner to my right arm while watching the data window on his omnitool. He paused it over my forearm and frowned over the spot where I'd had the Asherah artifact embedded in my skin. Sometimes I thought there was a remnant of it still there, but none of the ship's scanners could detect it.

The Mesakloren pulled the scanner away and looked over his shoulder. "We're clear. All trackers have been disabled."

"Understood," Kylath said.

The Mesakloren leaned back in the chair and regarded me for a few moments. There was something knowing in his gaze that made me a little uncomfortable.

"Almost to the target," Kylath said.

I was getting tired of being gagged, but I was also sure it could've been worse. At least an old rag hadn't been stuffed into my mouth, held there with heavy amounts of duct tape. This wasn't the first time I'd been a prisoner, but I hadn't felt this help-less in a long time. I could honestly say I didn't miss it.

I closed my eyes and started praying. Almost inevitably, I began thinking of all the events that could've gone right and prevented me from being there right then. It wasn't God's fault, and I never blamed him. If I'd only made it to the storage container, I would've gotten away. Maybe I didn't do enough. The thought of Serena trapped in one of those stasis pods, being moved to who knew where, kept coming to the front of my mind. I'd completely and utterly failed, and I hated that. It made me angry, which made me foolish. I'd been knocked down a number of times in my life but never quite like this. I was going to be executed. They were taking me to Kael Torsin right now, and he was going to do what he'd been wanting to do ever since we'd first come face-to-face. And there wasn't anything I could do about it. Nothing.

I glanced down at my inactive combat armor and multipur-pose tool. With the shackles on, I couldn't access my omnitool. Even if I could access it, the Screkles had blocked it somehow.

I leaned back in the chair and exhaled forcefully through my nostrils. My gaze slid toward the Mesakloren across from me, and I couldn't keep the glare from my gaze. If I could get free somehow, I was going to exact my revenge. Kael Torsin was involved with the alien abductions. I didn't know how or why, but he was definitely involved. He wanted the shipping container and military equipment. I didn't know what he was planning, but I knew he needed to be stopped.

Kael Torsin had it in for me, in particular, and he'd sent these two goons to retrieve me. At some point they'd remove these shackles, and then I'd make my move. I just needed to bide my time.

The aircar began its descent. The holoscreen that had shown

a video feed from the outside had been turned off. I felt the aircar stop and the Mesakloren climbed out. Then, I was released from my seat and I did the same. We were in an empty structure that reminded me of a parking garage, and we were completely alone. I spun around, searching for others but not finding anyone.

Kylath walked over. "They're late."

"They're being cautious," the other Mesakloren answered.

He turned toward me.

"Don't," Kylath said. "Not here. They could be watching."

The Mesakloren leaned toward me, and my eyes widened a little. They didn't resemble anything I'd ever wanted to be close to.

"You have to trust me," he said. "I'm going to remove the gag and your shackles. I will explain what's going on, I promise."

My gaze darted to both of them. It felt like I was being tricked into something, but it didn't matter. Getting this stuff off was a step in the right direction.

Kylath lifted a hand cannon and pointed it at me. "I'm not taking any chances. We barely got away from the detention center."

I blinked a few times and then looked at the other Mesakloren, doing my best to nod.

He brought up his omnitool and I felt the metallic gag come away from my mouth. At the same time, the shackles came off my hands and feet. The nanorobotic particles merged and flew toward Kylath's outstretched hand. He still had his weapon pointed at me.

I looked down at my feet. There was some dried blood near my ankles. I raised my gaze toward the other Mesakloren. "What do you want?" I asked.

I wanted to back away and use my own omnitool to open a

comlink to the ship, but with a weapon pointed at me and nowhere to run, my options were limited. At least I wasn't gagged anymore.

"We're friends," he said.

Kylath growled a little.

I stared at the one who'd spoken for a few seconds. "Who are you?"

The Mesakloren tilted his head for a second, regarding me with a somewhat amused expression. "Come on, Nate. You know who I am."

I blinked and stared intently at him...her. As the truth dawned, I sucked in a deep breath. It was Raylin! She was disguised as a Mesakloren and Kylath was her partner.

"Don't say it. Just nod if you take my drift."

I nodded.

"This area is not secure, but we think we removed all the trackers you had," Raylin said.

"Why the...what are you doing? Serena is in a storage container."

Raylin nodded. For some reason, she maintained her disguise and I wasn't going to give it away, but I couldn't help my suspicions.

"We know about the container."

"You do? Where is it? Do you have it?"

She shook her head. "No, but you can find it."

I frowned. "How?"

"You took control of the delivery drone. What coordinates did you input into its navigation system?"

"I was trying to send it to the ship, but Crim was going to meet up with me, so I couldn't give it a set of coordinates," I said.

Kylath sighed. "It's lost, then. We should focus on Torsin."

I glared at him. "Yeah, good luck with that."

Kylath pointed his weapon at me.

I rolled my eyes. "Go ahead and shoot. I doubt you went through the trouble of snatching me away from the bears just so you could shoot me. You're looking for Kael Torsin. He's not here."

Kylath stomped toward me, acting in a manner much like the other Mesaklorens I'd met.

Raylin blocked his path. "Give him a moment to get caught up, Kylath."

Kylath glared at her. "You promised me a way to find Torsin."

"I did. He's the way," she said, gesturing toward me. "Now, give us a minute to work this out."

He lowered his weapon. "Not long. I've already stuck my neck out for you. It's time to deliver on your end of the bargain," he said gruffly and walked around to the other side of the aircar.

Raylin reached inside the vehicle and grabbed my things. She set them on the ground and gestured for me to collect them. I used my omnitool to reactivate my combat suit. The nanorobotic particles went from a solid state to a thick, fluid-like state. I shoved my fists into the metallic fluid and the particles swept up my arms, eventually covering my body. I didn't have much power, but I had enough for some basic protection. My hand cannons had been disabled, and I couldn't do anything with them until they were recharged back on the ship. I retrieved my multipurpose tool and set the configuration to sonic mode. I liked my boom stick. It had proven to be an effective weapon, and I wished I could've used it on the bears.

I looked at Raylin. "Do you have to stay like that?"

She looked me for a few seconds and then checked her omnitool. "You might want to look away," she said.

I did. I'd seen Raylin shapeshift before, and it wasn't pretty. It was actually quite disturbing to watch, not to mention painful. It had to be. Raylin never indicated that it hurt, but as I'd watched her muscles and skeleton change back to her normal form, I was convinced it had to. Her bones made popping sounds, as if they were breaking, and after a few seconds it stopped.

I looked up and saw the real Raylin—graceful and elegantly feminine. Even her dark armor couldn't mask the gently curving expanse of her body. Her idly curling hair reflected hints of sapphires in the light. She regarded me with pale blue eyes that didn't have any irises, but they seemed to lure me in.

"Hello, Nate," she said in her normal voice. "We don't have a lot of time. Serena doesn't have a lot of time. Others are searching for the container."

"What do you mean? Why are they searching for it? Wouldn't they have just left it?"

Raylin shook her head. "We think there's something in the container Kael Torsin needs. That's why he won't abandon it."

I looked away while I considered that for a few moments. "Are you saying the container is still flying around and no one can find it?"

"Yes, you managed to hide it in plain sight."

"How'd I do that, exactly?"

"Have you seen the amount of air traffic there is here?"

She had a point. I had so many questions, but I knew I needed to prioritize finding the container first. I brought up my omnitool and then went to the hack program Crim had given me.

"I'm not able to connect to the container," I said.

"We're probably out of range. We'll need to find it on the move," Raylin said.

"Why can't we just use the sensors on the ship? I'm sure Kaz has the *Spacehog* nearby."

"You'd paint a huge target on both the container and the ship," she said.

Kylath came around the aircar. "Are we all caught up yet? We've got to move."

He climbed back into the aircar and sat in the pilot's seat.

I looked at Raylin. "Nice friend you've got there."

"Temporary alliance. We need his help," she said and climbed into the back of the aircar.

I followed her inside and sat next to her as she brought up a large holoscreen.

"Wouldn't someone notice a storage container flying around, going nowhere?" I asked.

Raylin shook her head. "Datronia is a major shipping hub. There are lots of deliveries happening all the time. Easy to get lost."

We left the parking garage behind.

I stared at Raylin for a few moments. "What happened to you? Why didn't you contact the ship? We've been trying to find you for months."

"We got caught up in it, Nate. I'm sorry. By the time I realized it, we were cut off."

"How did Serena get captured?"

Kylath cleared his throat. "Start scanning."

Raylin lifted her chin toward the holoscreen. I started broadcasting the signal for the delivery drone.

"Kael Torsin is probably monitoring for this signal, assuming he's still here," I said.

"That's a lock. Confirm the reply," Kylath said.

A data window came to prominence on the holoscreen. It was the delivery drone, and I initiated a data comlink to the ship. Once I got a reply, I bridged the comlink between the drone and the ship, allowing the ship to become a homing beacon for it.

Kylath turned toward me. "Tell me you didn't initiate a comlink to your ship?"

"All right, I won't." Raylin sighed and I frowned. "What?"

She looked at Kylath. "Get us there as quickly as you can."

"Tell me something I don't know," Kylath replied.

Raylin strapped herself in and I did the same. I felt a surge in speed as I watched the front holoscreen. This was no ordinary aircar.

I looked at Raylin. "Is this a deluxe ride?"

"It's got a few bells and whistles, as you like to say," she replied.

"I've got a lock on the container," Kylath said.

I watched as he weaved through air traffic. Several security drones were following us, but there was another aircar right up on the storage container. Kylath sped toward it.

"Does this thing have any weapons?" I asked.

"No, it's just got speed," Kylath replied.

We darted closer to the container and saw a group of Mesakloren soldiers crawling on it.

A warning flashed on my omnitool. The soldiers must be trying to break through my control of the delivery drone.

Four of the soldiers noticed our approach and began firing their weapons at us. Kylath banked to the side to avoid taking fire, then sped toward the container.

I thought he'd slow down so as not to damage it, but he kept going in a straight line toward the other aircar. He rammed it, sending the container into a spin.

One of the soldiers fell off and was quickly followed by the other one.

Kylath tried to ram the other aircar again, but it swooped out of the way. Kylath yanked hard on the controls to avoid slamming into the container.

"There are people inside it!" I shouted at him.

An alarm flashed on the holoscreen as a video feed behind us became active. There were six armored aircars flying right for us. They each had some kind of mounted weapons systems.

I'd kept the comlink to the *Spacehog* open, and I added voice comms to it. "Kierenbot, where are you? We need a pickup fast!"

The enemy aircars swooped around us, and Kylath flew in front of the container, using it as cover. I didn't like it. The Mesaklorens could just as easily destroy the container.

"Get out of there, Kylath. How about we don't use prisoners to shield us from the nice soldiers trying to kill us," I said.

"That's not my mission," Kylath said.

I'd had about enough of Kylath. I unstrapped my seat belts and lunged toward him from the back seat.

I grabbed his arms, and the aircar swung out to the side. The air around us lit up with plasma bolts firing from the enemy ships.

Kylath jerked one of his elbows back and my whole body moved to the side of the aircar from the blow, but I held onto his arm. I wasn't going to let go.

A huge shadow flew over us as the *Spacehog* suddenly came into view. The main hangar bay doors were open. The ship's weapons returned fire at the smaller aircars, and they scattered.

There were still soldiers on the container.

I grabbed my boom stick and crawled toward the door.

"What are you doing?" Kylath demanded.

"Get me closer. They're trying to destroy the drone," I said.

"Do it, Kylath," Raylin ordered.

He cursed, and the aircar swung toward the container.

I waited a few seconds and then leaped to the container, hitting the edge but clearing the top. I rolled to my feet amid the soldiers and came up swinging. My boots magnetized, giving me the leverage I needed to use my boom stick to knock the soldiers off the top of the container.

I saw Raylin provide covering fire. She was shooting at the rear of the container where the drone was located. She must not have had a good angle, and she gestured for me to go. I ran toward the back of the container with my boom stick raised.

There were two soldiers squatting down on the drone, trying to cut it away. We were losing altitude, and the *Spacehog* loomed in front of us, trying to keep up.

I raised my boom stick, intending to throw it at them, but it elongated into a whip. The end snapped at the soldiers with a release of sonic energy. The concussive blast took the soldiers by surprise, and they flailed their arms as they fell.

I looked down at the drone. It had taken damage.

"We're clear, Kierenbot. Get us inside. I don't know how much longer this drone can keep flying," I said.

The *Spacehog* sank in front of us with the hangar bay lined up. Then it moved in closer to swallow us up.

Crim was in the hangar bay with several grav pallets in the path of the container. We flew right into their artificial gravitational field and the container stopped.

I didn't.

The force was too much for my magnetized boots to overcome, and the gravitation field was focused on the container. Unfortunately for me, I flew through the air and did my best bug-splatter impression as I crashed into the wall. I flopped to the ground and lay there, stunned.

Perfect ending to a messed-up day, but it wasn't over yet.

The ship was being attacked.

# CHAPTER 17

I'd taken my share of blows over the years, and some might say I deserved every one of them, but I could roll with the punches. So, when the entire hangar lurched to the side, I knew we were in trouble. I'd already taken a beating the past few days and felt every bit of my aching muscles as I stood up. I swayed on my feet and thought that perhaps it was the aftereffects of crashing into the wall, but it wasn't.

Crim was shouting, and I couldn't understand him. I was too busy stumbling across the deck. I heard a loud clang and saw an aircar skidding right toward me. Somehow, I still had enough adrenaline to sprint out of the way. I watched the aircar skate to a stop and headed for it.

I opened the door and saw Raylin strapped to the seat. I helped her out of it. Kylath climbed out the other door. He looked at me and I waved.

"You missed."

Not waiting for a reply, I jogged toward Crim, doing my best to ignore the pain across the middle of my back.

"Welcome back, Nate. We're being attacked," Crim said.

I'd never been in a space battle before. I'd been in dangerous situations where a battle was being fought in the area but never in an actual battle with shipboard weapons. I guessed we'd sink or swim, as the saying goes, or as Flynn enjoyed telling me: *Life doesn't care if you've been beaten to your knees. Get up and keep moving.*

"Can we…" I started to say but stopped and opened a comlink to the bridge. "What's our status?" I asked.

Ben and Lanaya were in the hangar bay, too. I would've felt better if T'Chura were there. Kylath might be a problem and I wasn't sure what Raylin had done. Crim eyed Kylath warily.

"They're firing disruptor drones at us. They interfere with our gravitational field generator," Kaz said.

"Is everyone aboard? Can we outrun them?"

"Now that you're back, we're ready to go. Kierenbot is trying to—"

He broke off as something inside the ship let out a long moan like a steel cable that was about to snap. The lighting in the area dimmed a few times before returning to normal. I felt the floor sink away from my feet.

"Kierenbot, get us out of here!" I shouted.

I didn't get a reply. I looked at my omnitool and saw that shipboard comms were down.

"What did they say?" Ben asked.

I shook my head, cursing, and ran out of the hangar bay.

It didn't take me long to reach the bridge. At least the elevators were still working. I ran down the corridor and palmed the door controls.

Kaz, T'Chura and Kierenbot were on the bridge.

T'Chura's eyes widened. "Nate, I'm so glad you're back."

"Me too. I need you down on the hangar deck. We've got

some guests who need looking after."

T'Chura, needing no further explanation, marched off the bridge quickly, gaining speed as he went. He could handle Kylath if he got out of line.

I went to Kierenbot. "What's happening? Can't you get us out of here?"

The red orb on Kierenbot's face was frozen in place, which happened when he was multitasking to the max.

"The ship's been damaged, and we're being pursued," Kierenbot said. His voice had become monotoned and he sounded a little distracted.

"Okay, but can we get out of here?"

"Negative, Captain. Our main engines have been damaged. We can navigate in-system, but I'm afraid they're going to catch up to us."

I frowned. A tactical map appeared on the main holoscreen. There were four ships tracking toward us. They had an alpha numeric designation and were marked as hostile.

We were still in the Datronia System near the primary planet. There were hundreds of other ships also flying in the area.

"If we can't get away, we need to hide. Can you take us closer to one of the other ships? Use them as camouflage?"

Kaz looked at me in surprise, as if he hadn't considered it.

"I believe so, Captain. There is a materials transport ship. However, I must point out that this is just a stalling tactic. They will eventually find us," Kierenbot said.

I nodded. "I'm trying to get us some breathing room. Is that transport ship heading away from the planet?" I asked.

"No, it operates near the planet. It's an offload ship that takes deliveries from mining vessels."

"Perfect."

Kaz frowned. "How's that perfect? We need to get out of

here."

Kaz knew more about the ship than I did. He'd owned it for a lot longer than I had, so he was much more familiar with its capabilities. But sometimes his grasp of a situation blinded him to its reality, unlike me. We couldn't leave, so we needed time to repair the ship and then worry about escaping.

"Kierenbot, can we hitch a ride without our pursuers knowing?"

The artificial intelligence was capable of massive amounts of calculations and subroutines that I simply couldn't keep up with. Sometimes, his suggestions were a bit off the mark, but regarding the ship's capabilities he was extremely accurate.

"I have a solution, Captain. Shall I execute it?"

"Does it get us there safely?"

"Yes."

"Execute," I said, trusting Kierenbot.

Kaz looked as if he was going to object, but he leaned toward me. "I hope you know what you're doing."

"So do I," I replied.

We watched the tactical plot. Kierenbot flew the ship among the others, making his way toward the materials transport ship. It was likely automated since its route was well established.

I looked at Kaz. "They expect us to run. They don't expect us to hide."

Kaz considered for a few seconds and then nodded.

Kierenbot docked the ship with the transport vessel amid huge storage containers. We were still exposed, but it would be difficult for them to track us. Ship signatures tended to blur together when they flew too close.

I watched the tactical plot, and the four ships hunting for us didn't follow. I smiled at Kaz.

"If they don't double back on us, we should be okay for a

while," I said. "Kierenbot, I need the main engines back because we can't stay here long."

"I'll begin my damage assessment at once," Kierenbot said and looked away from me.

I arched an eyebrow toward Kaz. "Where are Darek and Jeshi?"

"They were working with Crim when we heard from you. What happened to you? Kierenbot found reports that you'd been arrested," Kaz said.

I headed for the door, and he walked with me.

"I was, but we've got to get to the hangar bay," I said.

I filled Kaz in on the way.

"You found them," Kaz said. "I thought the container was lost for sure. We searched for it, but we couldn't find it. Crim nearly went crazy trying to."

"Kael Torsin is alive, Kaz. He's behind all this. I saw him. I spoke to him."

Kaz regarded me for a few moments. "I believe you."

That made one person. Now I needed to tell the others. Kael Torsin was willing to operate out in the open, so he must have enough influence to stall the local authorities. Hopefully, the more time we could hide, the more pressure would build on him.

The door to the hangar bay was open and I heard shouting coming from inside. I should've known better than to expect people to just work together.

Kylath was pointing his hand cannons at Darek, who stood in front of the storage container. Crim held some kind of grenade in his hand and looked ready to throw it at Kylath.

T'Chura stood nearby with Ben, Lanaya, and Jeshi behind him.

I clapped my hands loudly as I walked toward them. "I know this one. Stop me if you've heard it before. You're going to love it.

A Mesakloren, an Akacian, and an Ustral all walk into a bar together." They stopped shouting and stared at me. "The Mesakloren scowls and pulls out his weapon, threatening the others. The Ustral, with explosives handy, is ready to level the playing field, but no one is paying attention to what the Akacian is *really* doing." Kylath began to speak, but I shushed him. "Darek, why don't you step away from the storage container. And stop that scan you've got running on your omnitool."

Everyone stared at Darek, and he held up his hands. A holoscreen showed a scan running. He disabled it.

"This is evidence—" Darek began.

"That you have no authority to have," Kylath said.

I sighed heavily. "I see we have to do this now. Two competing intelligence agencies right here on my ship. I win the prize." I looked at the hand cannons in Kylath's hands and then looked at him. I doubted he'd start shooting, and if he did, after I went down, Crim or T'Chura would be on him in seconds. It was a no-win situation.

He lowered his hands and retracted the hand cannons.

"Good choice. The way I see it is that you are both guests aboard my ship, and I'm the only one who has the authority to do anything with that storage container," I said.

Kylath looked at Raylin. "Is this true? He's the captain?"

Raylin nodded. "Did I leave that out?" she asked innocently.

I grinned. "Okay, time to prioritize," I said and looked at Crim. "Lock down the comms systems. No signals in or out. Also, check with Kierenbot about what needs to be fixed. We've taken some damage, but we've got some breathing room."

"Got it," Crim said. He disabled the grenade and placed it on his belt, then walked over to a nearby workbench.

I headed for the storage container. "We'll work out who's got dibs later. There are prisoners inside the container." I blinked.

"Never mind. Serena is in there, and I'm getting her out even if I have to tear this thing apart myself." I swung my gaze toward Kylath and Darek. "You can help or stay out of the way. Just don't become a problem."

The container doors were misaligned and had trouble opening. I arched an eyebrow at Kylath. "See your handiwork here?" I asked, gesturing toward where he'd rammed the container with the aircar. "Get over here and help get this open."

"Wait," Ben said. "Let's try cutting it open."

"Okay but be careful. There are stasis pods inside," I said.

Ben came over with a handheld plasma cutter. He adjusted the configuration and began cutting through the doors. As he cut, a green liquid leaked out the bottom. He snatched the cutter away, staring down at the liquid.

Kaz peered at it. "It's coolant. One of the pods must've broken."

I grabbed one of the edges Ben had just cut through and pulled. My armor protected my hands. Some of the others came to my side and helped. Together, we pulled open the door, which unfolded as if it was being bent in the wrong direction.

The stasis pods hung upright on a rack. There were tracks along the roof that held four rows of pods, which reminded me of metallic cocoons. We quickly began offloading them one at a time.

Crim joined us and began examining the pods.

There were several broken pods that had coolant leaks. Emergency power was keeping the occupants alive.

"We've got to wake them up," I said.

"Nate, wait," Raylin said.

I stood over the pod with Serena inside. She looked as if she were sleeping.

"She's right, we shouldn't open all the pods," Darek said.

"Why not? They were prisoners. They shouldn't be kept like this," I said.

"I know that, but they've been through a traumatic experience, and are you really equipped to deal with them? Some of these pods have species that I doubt are in your autodoc's database. That means if there's something wrong with them, we won't be able to help them."

"I can have a team here to assist in no time at all," Kylath said.

I shook my head. "No backup is coming to support you," I said and looked at Crim. "Can you open the pod?"

"Nate," Raylin said, "I need to warn you."

I stared at her for a second. "Warn me about what? What did you do to her?"

Raylin looked guilty, and it scared me.

"Serena volunteered to infiltrate the Academy," Raylin said.

Lanaya gasped. "She's been in training."

I blinked. "You mean they brainwashed her?"

When I'd seen Serena on the station, looking dazed, I'd hoped it had been an act. I flung a look at Raylin, waiting for her to answer.

She gave me a small nod.

I gritted my teeth and stomped toward her. "How could you let her do that? Don't give me the 'she volunteered' crap! She's not equipped to do something like this."

Deafening silence swept through the hangar bay.

Raylin's shoulders slumped a little. "Please, let me explain."

I jabbed my finger into the air. "Later! Crim, open it."

Crim brought up the control interface for Serena's stasis pod. "Ending stasis protocols," he said quietly.

The pod opened and Serena began to awaken. She blinked several times and looked up at me.

"Serena, it's all right. You're safe," I said.

She stared at me with a thoughtful frown.

Lanaya came next to me. "Let me try," she said.

I nodded.

Lanaya leaned over the pod and began speaking quietly with Serena. It sounded like a chant, and I couldn't hear what she was saying, but Serena's gaze locked onto Lanaya.

I tried not to become impatient, but it was impossible. I took several slow, steady breaths just to calm myself down.

Lanaya helped Serena out of the pod, and she still appeared as if in a daze. She frowned while she looked around. Then she saw me, and her gaze softened. Her warm, brown eyes sought out mine, and the world around us simply ceased to exist.

"Nate," she said, and I pulled her into my arms.

I hadn't realized how great holding her felt. After months of searching, after every frustrating step, Serena was here in my arms. We held each other for all the world to see. Something primal inside me accepted a moment of peace in the knowledge that she was safe.

She looked up at me and I kissed her. Her full lips pressed against mine, and all the thoughts, worries, and everything else fell away from me. Her mouth felt so good against mine.

We'd never kissed before, although we might've come close to it a few times, and I cursed myself inwardly for not doing it sooner.

We pulled away a little.

"I've missed you," I said.

She smiled and leaned toward me. "I missed you too, Nate."

There was a harsh guttural clearing of the throat. "How long must we wait for this?" Kylath asked.

I ignored him. The rest of them could wait. "Are you all right? I saw you, and you looked like you were sleepwalking."

She frowned and looked a little afraid, as if she were suddenly remembering a bad dream.

Something snarled from nearby, and I heard Crim back up with a bellow of his own.

A dark, scary alien with a bunch of tentacles came out of a damaged stasis pod.

Crim shook his hand. "It bit me!"

The alien skittered around the deck as if it couldn't quite see its surroundings. It shoved Darek out of the way with flailing tentacles. Then it twisted toward Kaz.

He had his hand cannon raised and took a few steps backward. "Tell this thing to back off."

"Hey!" I shouted.

The black, slithering alien stopped and turned toward me, moving fast in my direction.

Serena stepped in front of me and made some kind of high-pitched squealing sound. After that, she changed tempo into a kind of song and the creature stopped. Then it mimicked the sound and sat down.

"What did you do?"

"I told him that we weren't going to hurt him," Serena said.

"Him?"

"Yes, Nate. Don't get caught up in the details right now. I'll explain everything in a minute," she replied.

The creature did a crawl-slither thing toward Serena, moving leisurely. It didn't have any eyes that I could see, but it must have had some other sensory perception. It made different noises for Serena, and she replied with a low, level, humming sound.

I glanced at Darek. Kaz was helping him stand. Darek rubbed his chest where he'd been struck.

"Can he play nice, or do I need to lock him up?" I asked.

Serena looked at me. "He'll be fine now. Just give him some

space. He's one of the abductees. They were torturing him, trying to get him to kill."

I stared at the creature for a few seconds. "We don't want to hurt you."

The creature regarded me for a few moments and made a cooing sound that had a bit of growl in it. He had a mouth filled with sharp teeth. His tentacles slid across the floor and began touching things.

"I hope he's got a concept of personal space," I said and looked at Serena. "What's his name?"

"They have songs for names. I can teach it to you," Serena replied.

I shook my head. "Any other time I'd be all over this, but we've got bigger fish to fry," I said and frowned. I looked at the tentacle-beast. "No offense," I said, figuring it couldn't hurt. "Does he have to touch everything?"

"It's part of how he perceives the world," Serena said.

We'd all seen how fast he could move. He was dangerous, but that didn't mean we had to keep him locked up. Technically, everyone in the hangar bay was dangerous, so the creature was in good company.

I turned toward Crim. "Let's not open any of the other pods right now unless it's absolutely necessary."

"Nate, that's not right," Serena said.

"I know it's not. They just need to sit tight for a little while longer. We're still in danger," I said and looked pointedly at Darek and then Kylath. "Kael Torsin is alive. Those are his ships out there, hunting for us. He's the one behind all of this. He faked his own death."

Kylath didn't look surprised by this, but Darek did.

I stared at Kylath. "You don't look surprised."

"We suspected. That's part of why I'm here," he said.

# CHAPTER 18

I stared at Kylath for a second. "Just so we're on the same page, are you here to stop Kael Torsin?"

"He's become a terrorist and must be stopped."

I looked at Darek. "And you?"

"My mission hasn't changed. I'm here investigating why juvenile alien abductions have started back up. The Academy was disbanded years ago."

"So you've said, but Lanaya and these others are proof that they managed to hide from you," I said.

"How do you know these aren't recent abductions?" Darek asked.

I gestured toward Lanaya. "She was taken when she was a little girl. Does she look like a little girl now?"

There was an edge to my voice, but I didn't care. Darek shook his head. "No, she doesn't," he said and looked at Lanaya. "I'm very sorry for what has happened to you."

"It's not your fault," Raylin said. I stared at her, and she held my gaze.

She had a mysterious past and I suspected that she knew more than she was letting on.

"Raylin, you look like you've got something you want to get off your chest," I said.

"I was part of the covert operations that were part of this."

I leaned toward her. "What exactly are you saying?" I asked, trying not to rush to judgement, but it was getting hard not to do so.

"Intelligence agencies conduct operations in isolation. I never abducted anyone from their home world, but I did come across several programs that were exploitative," she said and paused for a moment, looking at Lanaya and the tentacled alien. "Too many covert operations were being run by influential beings. At first, I didn't do anything about it. Don't look at me that way. It's never as black and white as it seems in hindsight."

I saw Ben glaring at her and then he glanced at me.

I sighed. "What did you do?"

"I was a junior intelligence agent, and I reported it to my superiors. I don't know if they were put off or not, but nothing changed. I started conducting my own investigation with some other junior agents, and we began to disrupt the Academy until it could no longer be ignored," Raylin said and looked at Darek. "That's probably when CGH became involved."

He nodded. "The case files indicated that they'd been tipped off. Evidence and reports arrived across the desks of the CGH leaders—too many to be ignored."

Raylin nodded and turned toward me. "We had limited resources. The CGH had more."

I considered what she'd said for a few moments. "What happened to you after that?"

Her gaze hardened. "I was hunted. All of us were."

"Why would they hunt you?" Ben asked.

"Because she upset the balance of power, kid. I bet there were very powerful people who were caught up in this and needed to contain the situation," I said.

Raylin lowered her chin a little in acknowledgement. "I ran. I had no choice. They'd trained me to blend in and disappear if I needed to. So I left everything behind and eventually crossed paths with Kaz."

I glanced at Kaz for a second and then back at Raylin.

"So the Academy was dismantled, or the operations that were the foundation were stopped, but parts of it were put on hold," I said. Raylin frowned. "I'm not accusing you of anything. I'm just trying to get a clear picture of what happened. Lanaya was abducted when she was a little girl. She enters this program and they train her for a certain amount of time. At some point the program is being dismantled, and instead of running, they put her and the other abductees into stasis pods."

Raylin nodded, and then gestured toward Kylath. "We think Kael Torsin came across classified operations and began exploiting them."

Kylath nodded. "He's raided a number of military storage operations centers and successfully stolen a number of data repositories."

I frowned. "He collected intelligence assets and military equipment. What for? Why would he do this?"

"It's obvious," Darek said, and I raised my chin for him to continue. "He's establishing a power base of his own. His superiors abandoned him and failed to take him out."

"They tried to kill him?" I asked.

Darek shrugged and looked pointedly at Kylath.

I gave Kylath a once-over. "You?"

He glared at me.

"You were part of the cleanup operation for this, but he

turned out to be a much bigger problem than you anticipated. It's all right to admit it."

Kylath remained silent.

I shrugged. "So you want to kill him."

"After I retrieve the stolen data from him," Kylath replied.

"Okay, fine, whatever. But why are you working alone? You've seen what he's capable of. He has ships and resources at his disposal. What do you have?"

Kylath glanced at Raylin and then Darek. "I'm authorized to use military assets, but only after I have Kael Torsin's exact location."

I peered at him for a few seconds. "Since you messed up the first time, I'm willing to bet that it's your neck on the chopping block if you fail. So, what are you waiting for? Call in your military assets. Clean this whole mess up."

"He can't," Raylin said.

"Why not?"

Kylath blew out a harsh breath. "Do you know which ship Kael Torsin is on? Do you know which ships are loyal to him?"

I frowned for a second and then sighed.

"There, now you understand. Only it's worse. You've managed to get the attention of Datronia security forces, so they're no doubt searching for this ship."

The others watched me and there might've been something accusatory in their stares.

"Wouldn't they be searching for Kael Torsin, too?" Ben asked.

Kylath nearly sneered. "They'll do a sweep of the entire area, and they'll eventually stop all ship traffic until they're satisfied that the perpetrators of so much destruction aren't simply hiding."

"As soon as we repair the ship, we'll get out of here," I said.

"Where will you go?" Kylath asked.

"I don't know. Not here," I said and looked directly at Darek. "What were you scanning for?"

Darek frowned and I rolled my eyes.

"We're seriously going to do this?" He stared at me. "Before, when I walked in, you were scanning the storage container."

"It was the computer system that manages the stasis pods. Sometimes there's useful data stored there that might give us a clue as to where his operations are."

I looked at Ben. "Can you take a look?"

He nodded and went to the container. He navigated the holoscreen for a minute and then frowned.

"What did you find?" I asked.

"It's strange. Looks like someone already took the data from it," Ben said.

I looked at the others and peered at Darek. "Which one of you took the data?"

"I didn't get anything," Darek said, holding up his hands.

Kylath stared at me as if daring me to accuse him.

"Wait, Nate," Ben said. "I recognize the program used to exfiltrate the data. It's Crim's. This went to your combat suit."

I frowned thoughtfully with my lips pursed. "Huh?"

"Crim said he sent you a way to override the delivery drone's control systems, right?" Ben asked.

I nodded. "Yeah, but there was a lot going on at the time."

"I get it, but which option did you use?"

I blinked a few times. "I have no idea." They all stared at me. "Look, I was chasing the storage container and then was shot at by Kael Torsin's soldiers while they were robbing a military equipment storage facility."

Serena's eyes widened and she looked at the large storage container as if seeing it for the first time.

"You don't remember climbing into the stasis pod?" I asked.

She shook her head.

"What about me? Do you remember me trying to wake you up?"

She bit her lower lip as she frowned and shook her head a little.

"You looked right at me, Serena. I was right there. We all were—except for Raylin and Kylath, that is."

Serena's gaze sank to the ground and she frowned thoughtfully. "I can't remember."

I scowled at Raylin. "See, this is what you did. She's got holes in her memory."

"Nate," Serena said.

"Who knows what else they did to her while you went off on this foolish crusade."

Raylin stared back at me, stone-faced.

"Nate!" Serena said sternly. "Stop yelling at her. She didn't do anything."

My gaze swooped toward her. "You didn't see what I saw."

She jutted her chin up. "Don't act so high and mighty. I was there, too."

"Oh, and do you remember what they made you do?"

"I volunteered to go into that place to infiltrate their operations and expose it."

"You're a nurse! You're not a spy. What did you think you were doing? You nearly got yourself killed. If I hadn't gotten you out of there, who knows what might've happened?"

Her eyes were like Spartan spears jabbing into my chest. She stormed toward me, and I actually backed up until my back was against the container. "Don't you dare act is if you had to come rescue me."

"I *did* come rescue you!"

"I can take care of myself," she said, glaring at me. She turned away.

"Oh yeah, how were you going to do that trapped in a stasis pod? Tell me, how was that working for you?"

She sneered at me.

I gestured toward Raylin. "She had no idea where you were. You lost control of the situation."

Sometimes I know I've gone over the edge of a cliff way too late. It's like a sudden sinking feeling that occurs just before the plunge.

Serena narrowed her gaze at me. "At least I was doing something about it. What were you doing? What was it that was so important that you couldn't come? Oh, that's right. It was a treasure hunt. How'd that work out for you? Was it everything you dreamed it would be?"

"Serena," Ben said, gently. "We've been searching for you—"

"Don't defend him, Ben," Serena said. "Nate always does what's best for Nate. Isn't that right, Nate? *Isn't that right!*"

I inhaled a very deep breath and just stared at her for a few seconds. "Believe whatever you want. You've got me all figured out," I said and turned away from her. "Next time, maybe I'll just…"

I didn't finish because I knew that whatever I said, I'd regret it.

"What's the matter, Nate? Isn't this the reunion you've always wanted? Here I am—the prize."

There was only so far I was willing to be pushed. I could take a lot of punishment, but her words stung like a slap to the face. I spun around.

Serena glared at me with so much venomous hatred that it startled me. She raced toward me, beating her fists against my armored chest. I grabbed her arms and held them tightly.

"Stop!" I said.

She struggled against me, but I held onto her. "What's the matter with you?"

She gritted her teeth and tried to pull away from me.

"Stop!"

I didn't want her to fall, but she yanked so hard that she slipped free and fell to the ground. She curled up into a ball and started crying. It sounded so raw, as if she were completely unravelling. I started to go to her, but the dark, tentacled alien slipped between us and spread his black tentacles wide to block my path.

I glared at him. "I don't know what the hell you are or even where your face is, but you better get out of my way, right now."

The alien let out a screeching bellow and waved his tentacles threateningly.

"Fine," I hissed, and reached for my boom stick.

"Nate, wait," Lanaya said.

I glanced at her. "What?"

"This isn't her," Lanaya said and frowned. "She's not herself. Let me speak to her. Can you give us a few minutes?"

I was gripping the end of the stick, and my fingers tightened around it as if I could choke it. What had they done to Serena?

"Please, Nate," Lanaya said.

I was still reeling from what Serena had said. I felt like the whole thing had happened in some kind of whirlwind. I swallowed hard and nodded.

The others stared at me, and I wanted to scowl at them to stop it.

Kylath spoke first. "I'd like to see the data you've got."

"I bet you do," I said and exhaled through my nostrils. "So do I."

I glanced at Serena and she was sitting up, hugging her knees to her chest. Her eyes were puffy and red from crying. She looked so small and vulnerable. I just wanted to help her, to make everything right, but I didn't know how. Had she been brainwashed like Lanaya? It made sense, but what she'd said…it had hit close to home. That had to be real. She'd meant it.

Raylin went to Serena's side with her tentacled alien protector guarding her.

T'Chura came to my side. "Give them some time to sort this out. Lanaya is right, this isn't like her."

"He's right, Nate," Kaz said.

It might not have been like her, but what she'd said had been so damn truthful, and that made it worse. I might've already been in too deep when we'd parted ways—me pursuing the Asherah and her helping Raylin track down those responsible for the abductions—but it might've been more than that.

"The data," Kylath said.

I sighed and walked over to where Crim stood at a workstation. He was speaking to Kierenbot and waved his arm for us to go away.

They were trying to fix the ship.

I opened my omnitool and brought up the application Crim had sent me. The others watched me, trying to peer at my screen. I turned away from them. As I read it, my pulse quickened.

"What is it?" Kaz asked.

I pressed my lips together and kept reading just to be sure of what I'd seen. Then I looked at the others with my mouth slightly agape.

"He's not going to give up the search," I said.

"Who?" Ben asked.

"Kael Torsin," I said. "I had Crim's hacking suite working for the entire encounter with him. I've got data from him somehow, and it looks like a list of his operations and what might be his plans. There's a lot there. I'm going to need Kierenbot's help to review it all."

"I can't allow that," Kylath said.

I frowned. "What did you say?"

He drew his hand cannons and pointed them at me. "I need the data you have. Give it to me."

The others stiffened, and I kept my gaze on him. "Good for you."

"You don't understand; I'm not asking you for it. I'm demanding that you give it to me. You have stolen classified data from the Tamiran Consortium. I cannot allow you to keep it."

"Haven't we been through this? I'm not giving you anything. If you stick around and don't get in the way, I might...*might*... share what I've got with you. Otherwise, you can go pound sand."

An orange glow came from his hand cannons. They were primed and ready to fire.

"Think it through, Kylath. I'm not giving it to you."

I didn't like having his weapons pointed at me and I didn't want to die, but I wasn't going to cower.

Kylath was about to respond when Kierenbot's voice came over the ship-wide comms.

"Captain, there are hostile ships scanning the area. They're making a sweep. They will soon discover us."

I smiled at Kylath. "Put your damn hand cannons away. You're not going to muscle your way through this. I'm sure my friend T'Chura would make short work of you."

T'Chura let out a subsonic growl and Kylath pointed one of his weapons at him.

"Look, I get it. There's something here that's important to the people you work for. Okay, I understand. I'll give it back to you but only after we get out of here. That's my best offer. Take it or leave it."

Kylath considered it for a second. "Very well."

"Good, now help us repair the ship so we can get out of here."

# CHAPTER 19

Sometimes being the captain wasn't as easy as it looked.

"Crim, I've got a group standing around, waiting to be told what do to," I said.

He closed the holoscreens and came over to us, eyeing the others. "Good, I need help in engineering."

I gestured toward the others. "Go with him. Do what he tells you."

Kylath looked as if he was going to protest, and I scowled. "You can either help or I lock you up. I'm pretty sure we've got a stunner available that will make you change your mind."

Kaz cleared his throat and we looked to see that he had a palm stunner in his hand. It was a chrome bracelet that extended to his palm and had a greenish glow.

Crim had already headed for the door and stood in the corridor. Jeshi bounded around him with his seemingly endless supply of energy.

I tipped my head toward the door. "Go on."

Kylath started walking toward the door with T'Chura behind him while Kaz gestured for Darek to go in front of him.

Ben gestured toward his chest and glanced at the door.

I nodded. "Help Crim, but keep an eye on our guests."

They left and I turned toward the women.

As I approached them, their alien protector fluttered his tentacles.

Time to put this guy in his place. I started to grab my stick, and Serena stood. The alien stepped to the side as if something unspoken had passed between them.

Serena looked at me and a wide range of emotions seemed to show in her eyes. Her face tightened and then she was calm, but her eyes sank to the ground as if she couldn't stand the sight of me.

"I'm so sorry, Nate. I can't control it."

"It's okay. I understand," I replied as gently as I could.

Raylin and Lanaya were at her side.

"We're going to take her to the medbay and let the autodoc examine her," Lanaya said.

I nodded, feeling that if I spoke it might hurt Serena in some way.

Raylin lingered behind and I stared, unable to keep my resentment from her.

"What do you want, Raylin?" I asked harshly.

She looked at me in silence for a moment. "I'm not going to apologize again, Nate."

I rolled my eyes and started heading toward the door, but Raylin moved in front of me.

"But that doesn't mean my regret for what happened has changed. I do want to make amends to Serena. You were right, Nate. Serena came with me and was under my protection. I knew that sending her in there might've been too much for her, but I thought I could get her out before things went too far."

I frowned as I tried to push away my anger and frustration. Then I sighed. "We both underestimated it. You couldn't have known that Kael Torsin was involved."

Her eyes softened for a moment and she frowned uncertainly, then gave a slight shake of her head. "I was trained to distance myself from my objective. It's what made me so effective at my job, but that's changed—largely as a result of my encounter with you and others."

"I don't understand."

"You, Serena, Ben, and even Flynn wear your emotions proudly. They motivate you and guide you in an intricate balance with your intelligence. It's inspiring, Nate." She paused for a few seconds. "Kael has played this masterfully. You're right, I did underestimate him. He's very dangerous, and if you have what he needs, he'll never stop hunting for you, even if you find a use for the data. If you use it as a bargaining chip with the various sector governments, he'll still want to strike at you and anyone close to you."

My lips pressed together while I thought about my encounter with Kael Torsin. I tried to remember exactly what he'd said.

I blinked a few times as the memories broke through my thoughts, and I gasped.

"What is it?" Raylin asked.

"Something you said made me think of something."

I started walking toward the door and Raylin came with me.

"What?" she asked.

We entered the corridor. "I think he planned this. He was going to use Serena to get to me. He said that I'd arrived sooner than he expected."

"He couldn't have known that we'd…" She paused for a second. "*He* sent Lanaya to us?"

"It's possible. I mean, it makes sense, but it's a bit on the nose, don't you think?"

She wrinkled her nose. "On the nose?"

"Obvious, like it's too easy."

She pursed her lips in thought as we entered the elevator. "Someone else could've done it so we would start investigating the Academy."

I nodded. "Kael must've made enemies, or someone is trying to clean up a mess that's gotten out of control."

We stepped off the elevator and headed toward the bridge.

"That seems more likely," Raylin agreed.

"It's also low effort, if you think about it."

"Because all they need to do is dangle Lanaya in front of us and we do the rest. It's possible, but if they had access to get Lanaya out of there, why wouldn't they just eliminate Kael Torsin then and there?"

"Maybe it was easier to get to Lanaya than it was to eliminate Kael. Also, if they just took out Kael, then someone else could take his place. He's started something, and I think a lot of higher-ups are exposed. You saw how Kylath reacted. He'll do whatever he can to get his hands on the data."

We walked onto the bridge.

"We're surrounded by enemies," Raylin said.

Kierenbot turned toward us. "You've got that right."

"What are you doing here?" I asked.

"I'm using the battlebot as well as this body. More efficient, and should the crew require backup, I'll be better able to assist."

I couldn't fault his logic. Kylath would be kept in line with both Kierenbot's battlebot body and T'Chura there to keep an eye on him.

"Are we able to leave?" I asked.

"Not yet, Captain. Crim is working on it. Jeshi is helping him, and his help has proven invaluable," Kierenbot said.

I nodded and walked over to a workstation where I transferred the data from my combat suit to the ship's computers. "Kierenbot, make sure this is locked down. Only you and I will have access to it."

His red orb froze in place for a second. "Done, Captain. Restricted access to the current data set has been enforced."

I chewed on my lower lip for a second. "If someone attempted to override the security protocols, would you be able to destroy it?"

"Captain! I could do that, but you would lose it. Are you willing to risk it?"

"I don't want to risk it falling into the wrong hands."

"Very well, Captain. It will be as you've ordered."

"Thanks, Kierenbot. Now, will you have a look at it? I want to see if you can confirm what I suspect this is," I said.

"I will need a few minutes to analyze it," Kierenbot said.

I nodded and then looked at Raylin. "What did they do to Serena?"

She considered it for a few seconds. "It appears to be a couple of things. Some of it is brain conditioning to train it for a particular response."

I leaned toward her and lowered my voice. "You saw what happened. It was like she hated me. How could they make her do that?"

"They can't make her hate you, but they can do things that inhibit the way her brain uses information," Raylin said and frowned with a slight shake of her head. "I'm trying to keep it simple. Think of it this way. Our emotions are governed, but an inhibitor can be used to confuse how the brain responds to the information."

I considered it for a few seconds. "But that could make her insane."

Raylin nodded, looking afraid. "Yes. The more she resists, the more likely it is that something will indeed break."

"So, she really does hate me for not going with you."

She grinned a little. "Oh, Nate, you're so good at reading people. How could you not know how Serena really feels about you? She loves you, Nate."

Sometimes, getting hit between the eyes by the truth could throw you so far off-balance that your brain froze, as if a secret had suddenly been exposed.

Raylin stared at me. "And you love her. It's quite beautiful, actually. I admit it does make me a little envious." She cleared her throat. "There are things we think and don't say, but those things rarely keep us from taking action. I saw what you did. Review the surveillance videos. I know you didn't leap into danger for me, Nate, and I don't expect you to. But you did it for her."

My jaw tightened and I looked away from her. "I was afraid I'd lose her. That I'd already lost her."

"You haven't. She's here and she'll fight what's been done to her."

I looked at her, sensing a hesitation. "But."

"But she might not survive."

I blinked. "What do you mean?"

"Serena is like you in some ways. She'll fight with everything she has to protect herself and others who are important to her. But if there is an inhibitor involved, the autodoc will not be able to remove it."

"Why not? I've seen that autodoc do some amazing things."

"Removing it will kill her. The inhibitor will need to be disabled."

My first instinct was to deny it. Raylin had to be wrong. That instinct lasted for a few seconds, but like most flawed arguments, it fizzled out like a balloon with a giant hole in the side. Kael Torsin wanted to exact his revenge on me, and he'd had all the pieces in place to do it.

"Captain," Kierenbot said quietly, "I've reviewed the data and it appears to contain a serious payload of information right from Kael Torsin himself. He's quite paranoid to have kept it on his person."

"What did you find?" I asked.

"Detailed data on operations he's involved in, as well as deployment of his various teams. He's built up his operations considerably recently, but through your use of Crim's very capable hacking application, you've been allowed to steal the keys to his burgeoning kingdom right out from under him."

I exchanged glances with Raylin. "I thought I just found some plans for the operations he has going."

"You did, but you also stole his authorization keys to manage those resources."

I considered it for a few seconds and my eyes widened. "Are you telling me he can't command his teams because of what I stole? He's dead in the water?"

"Yes and no, Captain. He is unable to command his remote operations, but the forces he has available here are still under his command."

"Can't he just override his own authorization and take back command of his external forces? Or doesn't he have some kind of backup?"

"Negative, Captain. Creating a secure system requires certain limitations as concessions to maintain the security of the system.

There are no backups of his secure access codes or keys. His access is unparalleled from within that system, which makes it highly effective, but it assumes that Kael Torsin always has possession of the keys."

I blinked while I tried to follow what the AI was telling me. "All right, I think I get it, but how could Crim's application do that? You can't tell me that bypassing whatever security Kael Torsin had in place was that easy?"

"It's not. I've also analyzed what Crim made available. Kael must have been in communication with the wider network of his organization. Crim's application doesn't determine the value of what it finds. It simply searches for comms signals and forces itself into the middle. It compromised the source, which is something Kael carried himself. It's the only explanation that makes any sense. You were in close proximity to him for an extended period of time. By the time he realized what had happened, it would've already been too late. You were taken into custody by the local authorities. Or if he had realized it, you were extracted by Raylin and Kylath before Kael could send someone to retrieve you. I would have to do further analysis and access external systems to be sure, but I'm fairly certain that my assertions are correct."

I nodded. "Good work, Kierenbot."

"Thank you, Captain," he replied, sounding pleased. "I must remind you that there are still ships searching for us. They're closing in on our location."

"Is it Kael or Datronia's security forces?"

"Unknown."

I frowned in thought.

Raylin peered at me intently. "What are you thinking?"

"I'm thinking that I've got one heck of a bargaining chip."

Her eyes widened a little and she frowned thoughtfully. "If

you can get him to bargain, I wouldn't expect him to do so in good faith."

"I don't have any other choice."

"Kylath won't like this, and neither will Darek."

I wasn't too concerned with whether the two intelligence agents approved or not. What *did* concern me was helping Serena.

Raylin smiled a little, as if she knew what I was thinking.

"Kierenbot, can we call Kael Torsin without him tracking us down?" I asked.

"I could scatter the signal, but it will only be a delaying tactic."

"Get it ready," I said.

"Captain, Crim and his team are still conducting repairs."

I looked at the tactical plot on the main holoscreen. If I didn't act, our window for escaping would vanish. The *Spacehog* wasn't a warship.

"I understand, but we don't have any other choice. Get me a comlink to Kael Torsin."

"Very well, Captain," Kierenbot said.

"Put it on the main holoscreen when you're ready," I said.

Raylin moved closer to my side. "I'm done hiding. I'm with you, Nate."

The edges of my lips lifted. "Thanks."

A few minutes later, a video comlink came online. Kael Torsin scowled into the camera.

"I have something you want, and you have something I want. How about we do an exchange?" I asked.

"Maggot!" he growled. "You insignificant insect! Give back what you stole and I will kill you quickly."

I stared at him. "No. I think I'll send a copy of all this data to everyone in the galaxy. It'll spread like wildfire—the story of how Kael Torsin tried to start his own empire and failed."

Kierenbot waved toward me and I frowned. I muted the comlink so Kael couldn't hear us.

"Enemy ships are closing in on our position," Kierenbot said.

"Be ready to run," I said.

If we were caught hiding on the transport ship, we were as good as dead anyway.

I unmuted the channel and Kael glared at me.

"You muted the comlink!" he shouted.

"Oh yeah, sorry about that," I replied. I probably shouldn't irritate him—poke the bear—but he made it too easy. A wave of cold swept down my back. It seemed to come from nowhere and was followed by a slight tingling along my arms. Everything slowed down as my perception of time increased. This wasn't the first time I'd witnessed various timelines and all the experiences of them at the same time, but it wasn't as intense or as many as when I'd been connected to the Asherah machine. I hadn't done it since then, but I thought maybe I still had part of the capability. A heightened sense of possibilities arrayed before me. Decisions and outcomes stretched out, but they were influenced by my own memories. My abilities were directed by some inner part of my mind, the subconscious that works on solutions to problems that arrive in our minds as a sudden idea.

"I know you have the data," Kael said.

His voice sounded as if it echoed from a dozen empty corridors, and my attention was drawn to the tactical plot and the enemy ships searching for us. Various timelines faded away as I seized different paths.

"Kierenbot, get us out of here!"

# CHAPTER 20

t amazed me how consistent Kierenbot was across multiple timelines. In most of them, he didn't question my orders; he followed them. The timelines where he had a different response were muffled, as if he were speaking in a low voice that I couldn't quite understand.

"We have a lock on you," Kael Torsin said. "Go ahead and try to run. You'll never get there fast enough. You'll be too late. I've already given the orders."

I frowned.

He'd given the orders. The orders to do what? I didn't know, but he was certain, and that was enough to scare me.

Several possibilities spread before me—timelines where we'd been captured, which led to our deaths. Kael made sure I watched it all and then he killed me. Other timelines showed that the ship had taken serious damage, then nothing but cold void. I assumed that I'd been sucked into the vortex of space. So many ways to die and nowhere near enough ways to live.

I had to be careful. Focusing on death could become a self-fulfilling prophecy. I didn't want to die, but the more I saw it happen, the more it distracted me, pulling me in.

I let all the timelines go. The possibilities were there, but I didn't have to observe them.

"Kierenbot," I said, my voice sounding strained.

"They are closing in on us, Captain. I expect they will try to disable the ship so they can board us. After that, they'll—"

"Stop," I said, sharply. "I know *you're* listening."

Kierenbot's red orb locked onto me, and Raylin stared at me intently with a confused expression.

"Nate, who are you talking to?" she asked.

I ignored her. "*You're* listening, monitoring. I know you're there. I need your help. You wanted to know if I still had it—the only thing that's left of the Asherah. I do. You're about to lose the only access to it if you don't help me right now."

Kierenbot froze and his red orb changed to a soft yellow. "Prove it," the Collective said.

The voice was monotoned and sonorous all at once.

"Right now, all I see is that we're going to die. The only way we don't is if you help us."

"This does not increase our understanding of Humans."

"It will if you let me," I said.

Raylin stared at Kierenbot warily.

"He has a team going to Earth. They might already be there," I said.

"It is known."

"Then you know why I need to get there to stop them."

"Impossible."

I slammed my fist on the workstation. "No, it's not! Slow them down. Give me a chance to stop them."

"Kael Torsin's forces are almost upon you."

"You can stop them. I know you can."

"We do this and you'll grant us access to study the Asherah remnant?"

"I will, but only after I stop the team going to Earth."

The soft yellow orb darted back and forth. "We cannot stop them completely. We can only slow them down."

I nodded. Something was better than nothing. "I just need a head start. Can you do that much?"

"It is done. We will remember your bargain."

Kierenbot's orb returned to normal.

"Apologies, Captain, I've experienced a temporary system reset."

"Set a course to Earth!"

"Earth? I can do that. Oh, it's already in the navigation system. I don't recall doing that. Captain, enemy weapons systems are targeting us."

"Nate," Raylin said. She grabbed my arm and pulled me into a seat.

Automatic straps secured us in place.

Multiple things happened at nearly the same time. The *Spacehog's* damaged engines engaged despite safety measures that were supposed to prevent such an action, and the ship lurched to the side as if something massive had rammed into it.

The tactical map on the holoscreen went dark for a few seconds and the lights on the bridge flickered as if the power core was being overburdened.

A moan sounded from the walls as if the ship were crying out in pain. Then a wave of unseen force pressed us into our seats. It was crushing, and I couldn't even inhale a breath.

The bridge of the ship shook violently, and I clenched my teeth to keep from biting my tongue. Then it stopped just as abruptly as it had begun. A cascade of alerts appeared on the main holoscreen, which kept flickering like a slow strobe light.

Then an image flashed onto the screen, and a picture of a bright blue planet appeared in the distance, but we were close enough to see it well. The breath caught in my throat and my chin lowered toward my chest.

It had been nearly a year since any of us had been there. Seeing the planet left me feeling oddly peaceful, awestruck, and humbled. We were finally home. The planet on the main holo-screen was Earth.

# CHAPTER 21

I released the straps keeping me in the seat and stood. The image of Earth on the holoscreen seemed to draw me in as it never had before. Nothing like a jaunt across the galaxy to make you appreciate where you came from.

The door to the bridge opened and Kaz burst through. He was followed by Kylath and Darek.

Kaz came to an abrupt stop and stared at the holoscreen for a moment, then he looked at me with understanding registering on his face.

"What are we doing here?" Kaz asked.

The last time I'd used the Asherah ability to tap into the universal intelligence, it had left me a bit dazed that had lasted for hours. I'd needed time to cope and for my brain to make sense of what it had witnessed. I felt like I was still catching up to the present reality.

"He sent a team to murder my family," I said.

Kaz blinked. "Kael Torsin? How could he even know where your family is?"

I looked away from him, trying to remember. "He hinted at it. He said something about the mountains, but I didn't catch it. But just now, he said he'd already given the order. We need to get down there and get my parents and my brother."

He frowned.

"You have a brother?" Raylin asked.

I nodded. "An older brother. We've got to get moving. We only have a little bit of time."

Kaz regarded me for a second, considering. "Nate, if he's already given the order, it might already be too late."

I shook my head. "No, it's not. Kierenbot, take us to the planet," I said and brought up the navigation interface. I entered the coordinates to my parent's home. "They live in a rural area. They prefer to be off-grid," I said and grinned nervously.

My head still felt as if I were emerging from a fog.

"Captain, the ship has sustained heavy damage—"

"Will it prevent us from reaching the planet?"

Kierenbot hesitated a moment. "Negative, Captain."

"Well then, get us there."

"Nate," Kaz said, "take a breath."

I rounded on him with a scowl. "*You* take a breath. Kierenbot, do it now!"

Kaz lifted his chin toward the main holoscreen and I frowned. "Look at it, Nate. The damage is severe. If we do manage to land on the planet, there's a good chance we won't make it out of there."

I clenched my teeth and stared at the holoscreen. It didn't matter. My parents were in trouble and deserved better than to be murdered by a band of mercenaries.

I looked at Kaz and the others. Kylath looked as if he was on the verge of taking matters into his own hands.

"Listen to me," I said. "Kael Torsin is going to come here. He doesn't have a choice. I have the keys to the empire he's building."

"If you'd given them to me, I could've neutralized Kael Torsin for you," Kylath said.

"I don't trust you, Kylath. And I won't give anything to you. Kael has what I need, too."

Kylath scowled, and Darek moved in closer. "I wouldn't," he warned.

Kaz stared at me for a second. He blinked a few times as he thought about it. Then he glanced at Raylin, his eyes widening a little. "It's Serena."

"Yeah," I said. "Now do you get it? He's going to come here. We're stuck. And with the ship this damaged, we can't make a stand here."

The truth of our situation seemed to register with all of them. The floor shifted a little and I noticed that we were flying closer to Earth.

"Damage to the ship is affecting the inertia dampeners. The grav drive is out of alignment. Attempting to compensate," Kierenbot said.

I started to head back to my seat and saw that Kaz and the others hadn't moved. "What's wrong with you guys? Didn't you hear him? Get to a seat and strap yourselves in. Kierenbot, warn the others."

Kaz sat to my left and Raylin to my right. Kylath and Darek went to a workstation farther to the right.

Kierenbot didn't need to be strapped in. Some kind of metallic tube rose from the deck and up to his waist, securing him in place.

I looked at Kaz. "Can the other team detect us?"

He frowned in thought for a moment, and then I repeated my question to Kylath.

"Doubtful. Standard strike-team deployments are smaller, like ten to fifteen members. They'll be focused on the target and not looking for interference. Where is our destination?"

I updated the main holoscreen so it showed the mountains along the eastern United States.

"The target is an area known as the Blue Ridge Mountains, centrally located," I replied.

Kylath peered at the holoscreen for a moment. "I'd approach over the ocean, then angle the approach from either the south or the north."

"It'll have to be south," I said.

"Acknowledged, Captain," Kierenbot said.

I looked at Kaz. "Was the ship detected the last time you came?"

"We came in a shuttle to avoid detection," Kaz replied.

"Yeah, but you took the whole damn bus, remember?"

"We were detected, but that could've been Kael Torsin's strike team tracking Quickening there. So it's difficult to determine. I'll see if we have any stealth capabilities left," Kaz said.

As we flew toward Earth, it was the middle of the night where my parents lived. The International Space Station zoomed over the horizon.

"Try not to hit any satellites, and watch out for the ISS," I said.

"Would you like me to hail them, Captain?" Kierenbot asked.

It wasn't safe to assume he was joking. "Not today. The fewer people who see us the better."

"Very well," Kierenbot replied, sounding a little disappointed.

"You've only just begun exploring your moon," Kylath said.

"We've been there before, and we're going back to set up a permanent base," I replied.

"How long ago did you first reach the moon?"

"Over fifty years ago."

Kylath frowned and actually glanced at the others before coming back to me.

"Getting there was expensive. At least that's what they say," I said in a mildly defensive tone.

Kaz cleared his throat. "Their scientists are still chasing theories instead of practical application."

They all looked slightly amused but were trying to hide it.

I settled back in my seat. "We'll get there. Don't you worry."

Kylath exhaled a long, slow breath. "Easier said than done."

"We made it this far. We'll go all the way," I said.

"You're sure about that?" Kylath asked.

I nodded. "We're not perfect, but after traveling with you guys, I realized that neither are any of you. You made it, and so will we. And it'll be quicker than you think."

*Quicker, with Ben helping to give us a push in the right direction.* I didn't think Kylath or Darek would approve of Ben's plans, so I kept that thought to myself.

The *Spacehog* flew toward Earth, and our approach took us toward the Atlantic Ocean. Kierenbot had lined us up with the Bermuda Triangle. I hadn't told him to do that; he'd selected that route on his own. I wondered if there was some kind of significance to it. After all, the Bermuda Triangle was the source of a number of legends, from lost ships and WWII squadrons to lost time for the pilots who flew through it. Would there be any affect on the ship?

I glanced at the others, but they were focused on the main holoscreen.

The ship flew through the multiple layers of Earth's

atmosphere. I didn't know their names, but I was sure Ben did. He knew all kinds of things like that. What made me frown was that even though we'd entered the atmosphere going at high speed, we hadn't displaced any of it. For instance, when meteorites hit the atmosphere, we could sometimes see them.

I realized the answer had to do with the grav drive and its ability to control it. I'd watched the *Spacehog* fly through the atmosphere on other planets, and there was no telltale sign that it had been there.

The video feed showed that we were flying close to the ocean. The moon was bright and seemed to light up the entire area. I spotted a line of ships that looked like container ships navigating the ocean. I smiled a little, thinking that if anyone who had the night watch happened to look out the window, they might see a little something extra.

I looked at Kaz. "Stealth working?"

"There is a field around us to prevent the rudimentary scanning capabilities I've detected."

"What about if someone happens to be looking up at the sky as we fly over?"

"Shouldn't be a problem. It's nighttime and anomalies are easily explained away," Kaz said.

I rolled my eyes a little. "They'll likely say it's just another weather balloon."

Kaz was about to reply when the ship suddenly dipped toward the water. We didn't touch it, but the field from the grav drive was causing a wake as we flew.

"Multiple drive failures. Attempting to compensate," Kierenbot said.

He was likely already doing that exact thing, even as he spoke.

The ship lifted into the air, but it reminded me of a stalling car that couldn't quite accelerate.

We cleared the coast and the ship had gained significant altitude. I kept staring at the darkened landscape between large areas of artificial light. Something about it set my mind at ease. I could've returned to Earth at any time over the past year, but I hadn't. I had a spaceship that could take us anywhere we wanted to go, so why would we go where we'd already been?

Soon, the small cities faded into the distance as we flew over the rural Carolinas. I wasn't sure which one we flew over and it didn't really matter. I knew where we were heading.

"When was the last time you saw your parents?" Raylin asked.

"It's been years."

"No regular contact then?"

I frowned. "Just the occasional contact."

"I see."

"What?"

"I'm just trying to gauge what our reception will be."

I blinked. "They haven't met an alien before, so I expect they'll be pretty shocked."

"This is going to be so much fun," Kaz said dryly and leaned forward to look at Raylin, gesturing toward me. "Remember how he was."

I cleared my throat. "Excuse me, but you abducted me. How was I supposed to act? Anyway, assuming you survive the initial encounter, you should be fine...probably."

Kaz looked alarmed for a few seconds. "What aren't you telling us?"

I glanced at them both with an arched eyebrow. "They moved to the mountains because they preferred a remote location. They don't get a lot of visitors."

"So they're hermits?" Kaz asked.

I shook my head. "No, this is their retirement. You'll see. Just a word of caution. They'll likely be armed." Kaz stared at me, and I shrugged. "Well, you might want to let me speak to them first; otherwise, they might shoot you," I said and glanced at Raylin. "Probably not you but Kaz for sure. It's the green skin."

He rolled his eyes. "This is more of that attempt at humor."

"Well, when you put it like that it's not very funny. Can we detect the mercenaries?" I asked.

Kaz turned toward his personal holoscreen. I was watching him navigate the different systems to bring up the scanning interface when Kierenbot screeched out a warning.

"Hang on to something!"

The ship twisted to the side and my body jerked in the chair. The straps held me securely in the seat and my armor protected me from the straps digging into my skin. The ship felt like it had become a tumbling ball bouncing along, or maybe this was what it felt like to be in an industrial dryer. The ship struck something hard, which I assumed was some part of the mountains, and we were now rolling downhill.

I gritted my teeth and clutched my arms to my chest. The others did the same. I think Kierenbot might've said something, but I couldn't be sure. It all passed by in a bit of a blur until we stopped.

Kaz tilted his head to the side, stretching his neck, but otherwise looked okay. I turned to Raylin and she was fine.

"Sound off," I said.

"Huh?" Kaz asked.

"Is everyone okay?" I asked.

The others on the bridge were fine. I unstrapped myself and stood. The floor was tilted to the side a little.

"Kierenbot, are the others okay?" I asked.

"I'm not sure, Captain. Systems are down. Emergency systems are coming online."

I nodded. "All right. Let's find the others."

"What about the mercenaries?" Darek said.

"One thing at time," I said. Did he really think I'd forget about them?

Kylath regarded me thoughtfully for a second. Then he looked at Raylin. "No military training?"

I snapped my fingers. "Hey. If you've got a question about me, ask me. What the heck is it when you ask about me when I'm right here in front of you? Come on. Less talking and more moving."

We went out into the corridor and Kaz was at my side.

"We overshot the landing zone," Kaz said.

"Did you see by how much?" I asked.

He shook his head. "Not sure. I just know we did."

"Okay, I'll figure it out once we get outside."

I sent Kaz and Kylath down to central engineering to check on the others, and then I led Darek and Raylin to the medbay.

As we came to the medbay, the door looked as if it was stuck in the process of disintegrating and reforming the door in an endless cycle.

I opened a comlink to the bridge. "Kierenbot, we've got a door that's malfunctioning."

"Stand by," he replied.

I looked at the others. "Can we force it to stay open? Aren't there safety protocols or something?"

"The field is unstable. Anything that comes within range will be dematerialized. It's not worth the risk," Raylin said.

I thought about that for a few moments.

"Captain, control unit is unresponsive for that door," Kierenbot said.

"What if you cut the power to it? What will happen?"

"You'll be without power, Captain."

I shook my head. "Yeah, I know that, but if there is no power to the door, will it automatically open or remain shut?"

"Oh, that's actually quite clever, Captain. The door will open because the field will be disabled."

"Good, let's do that," I said.

Power to the medbay went out, and Raylin produced a light source that lit up the area. The door had dematerialized.

I hastened through and found the tentacled alien in one of the corners. I gestured toward it. "Darek, check on him."

He gave me a withering look.

I understood his reluctance, which was why I'd asked him to do it.

I started to head to the nearest exam room to find Serena and Lanaya, but Darek called out to me.

"I'm not sure about this," Darek said.

I turned toward him. "What?"

"Come on over here and look."

Sighing, I went over to him while Raylin went to check the exam rooms.

Darek stood a short distance away from the tentacled alien and looked reluctant to get closer.

"What?" I asked when I came to his side.

The tentacled alien looked as if he'd wedged himself into the corner, and some of his tentacles were attached to the walls.

Darek gestured toward it. "*You* go. I have a keen sense of self preservation, and you're the captain. Go on."

I rolled my eyes and stepped toward the alien. I heard a soft moan coming from it.

"Hello? Are you all right?" I asked.

It might've twitched, but I couldn't tell in the dim light.

Just then, the lights came back on and power was restored.

"That should do it," Kierenbot said over comlink. "That area is stable now."

"Okay," I said and watched as the tentacled alien extracted himself from the wall.

I tried to make the same sound that Serena had made when she spoke to it.

It seemed to deflate a little and I thought it appeared less menacing.

"Come on... *Thing*. Let's go find the others," I said.

Thing's inky tentacles twitched, and he started to move toward me. I backed away a few steps and then saw Raylin, Serena, and Lanaya come out of an exam room.

I raised my chin toward them, and my gaze lingered on Serena. Her eyes softened. "Hey, are you guys okay?"

"We're fine," Lanaya said.

One of Thing's tentacles gingerly touched my shoulders and I felt like I was getting patted down by the TSA. I saw that it had barbs on the inside, but they were folded in. Thing could have grabbed me if it really wanted to.

"Okay, Thing. I'm hoping this is just a friendly gesture," I said, and patted his tentacle.

He withdrew his tentacle and became still.

Serena smiled at me, her eyes gleaming. "Oh Nate, it looks like you've made a new friend."

I chuckled. "That's me, Mr. Congeniality," I said and paused for a second. "Are *you* all right?"

She regarded me for a long moment. "It comes and goes. Lanaya has helped me understand it."

"I'm working on a solution, but I'll tell you on the way. We need to go."

She frowned and looked more like how she'd been before she left the ship. "Where are we?"

I pressed my lips together for a second. "We're on Earth. Kael Torsin was nice enough to send a strike team to murder my parents."

Her eyes widened. "Oh my God, Nate. Are you serious?"

I tipped my head toward the door. "Yeah, I'll tell you on the way. My parents are a little peculiar though."

"Peculiar? Against a Mesakloren strike team?" Darek said.

I smiled. "They're not what you'd call the typical American retirees."

# CHAPTER 22

We made a brief stop at the armory where I quickly swapped out the power core of my combat suit, but it wouldn't work. Regretfully, I put my combat suit into storage, which would start a recharge cycle. I had no choice but to use my backup suit, which didn't have as many augmentations as my primary suit. No flying for this one. It had standard protection capabilities and movement augmentation only.

Raylin and Serena both changed into their own combat suits, which were more of a silvery gray in color.

Darek stood in the doorway, and I looked at him for a moment. Then I tipped my head toward one of the lockers.

"Kaz has a backup suit that should work for you," I said.

Darek walked over to the locker, and I opened it for him. He pulled out a block of nanorobotic particles and tried to activate it, but it wouldn't unlock for him.

I opened a comlink to Kaz and asked him to authorize Darek to use his backup armor. He sent a signal to the armor and

Darek was able to activate it. It quickly covered his body in a very dark-green, metallic pattern.

Darek brought up his omnitool and checked the combat suit's capabilities. "Impressive. Remind me to ask Kaz where he got this."

I headed for the corridor, impatient to get moving. "Glad you like it. Come on, we've got to move. Crim has weapons for us in his workshop."

We made our way to Crim's workshop, and I heard him speaking with Kierenbot. The AI had switched to his battlebot chassis, which was a towering, nine-foot-tall killing machine.

T'Chura stood off to the side. He already had his specialized combat suit on, which armored his muscular Sasquatch frame. He looked as if he could give the Incredible Hulk a good workout.

I glanced at the hangar bay doors, and they were shut.

"They won't open. They were damaged in the crash. I can fix it, but it'll take time," Crim said.

I looked at the battlewagon regretfully. "I guess we're going on foot then. Who do you need to help you with repairs?"

Crim eyed the others for a moment. "Ben, Lanaya, and Jeshi. The rest I assumed you were taking with you."

Crim was very good in a fight. I'd seen the old veteran reveal his prowess, but he was also the best qualified to fix the ship.

Ben looked at me. "I'll go if you need me, Nate."

I nodded. "I know you would, kid."

He leaned closer to me. "What about them? Are you really going to bring them with you?"

There was no need for him to gesture toward Kylath and Darek. "Better out there with me than causing trouble back here with you. What about Jeshi?"

"He's actually pretty good. A bit quirky, but he knows his stuff. I think Crim enjoys having him on the ship."

Jeshi seemed harmless enough, but he also had a sneaky side to him. I was willing to bet that more than a few people had underestimated him to their detriment.

"Good luck, Nate," Ben said.

"Thanks, kid."

I went over to the others. "Kierenbot, do we have a map of the area?"

"Ship scanners aren't operational, but I did send out a few reconnaissance drones."

He projected a holographic map of the area, outlined in amber. It was still the middle of the night, with dawn only a few hours away. The Blue Ridge Mountains were prone to fog, which should give us some cover. I peered at the map as the others gathered around.

I was able to manipulate the map so I could zoom in to a location. "Okay, the main house is here in this valley."

"No one else lives nearby?" Kaz asked.

I shook my head. "No. They own about a thousand acres across the valley. The recon drones haven't detected any ships in the area, so I'm going to assume the strike team is approaching the house on foot as well."

T'Chura nodded. "The house is in a defensible location, but there isn't anywhere for them to retreat to."

I smiled. "You don't know them. There are tunnels all over the property, with hideouts and other things. There's a barn here and a storage shed farther into the valley. There are also perches along both sides of the valley, which will give them good coverage of the area."

Serena stared at me for a few moments, and I shrugged. "They know how to handle themselves. Former military and..."

my gaze slid over to Raylin, Kylath, and Darek, "...worked for intelligence agencies as well. Don't get caught up in the details; just know that they can handle themselves."

"The strike team is most likely moving in stealth, intending to take them by surprise," Kylath said. "Do they have defensive measures?"

"Probably," I said.

Kylath narrowed his gaze. "What do you mean 'probably'? Don't you know?"

I ignored him. "Crim, weapons. Hand cannons aren't going to cut it."

Crim smiled and went toward the battlewagon. He opened a storage container near it and gestured inside. "Multipurpose assault rifles with kinetic armament. Should penetrate Mesakloren armor easily." He said that last part while staring at Kylath.

Kylath walked over and lifted one of the rifles. "Ustrals produce excellent weapons."

I grabbed a rifle. I'd expected it to have more heft, but it was actually pretty lightweight considering the size. I leaned toward Kylath. "I think he wanted you to know that these rifles were made especially for Mesaklorens."

"Oh, I know. I just don't care. We've got a job to do."

I nodded. "A deal's a deal. I get it."

After we were all armed and were clear on our approach, I led them to a nearby airlock near the hangar bay doors.

I glanced at the others. We all had our helmets on, but their names appeared on my HUD. It was helpful but unnecessary for some of them. There would be no mistaking T'Chura or Serena as they occupied both ends of the height range.

We stepped outside where the temperature was a cool fifty-five degrees and the air was humid, but I couldn't see fog. The HUD in my helmet enhanced what I could see better than any night-vision goggles ever could. The ship had crash-landed into the mountainside about a mile away from the target.

"I'm taking point because I know where we're going. Kierenbot is with me and T'Chura will bring up the rear. The rest of you stagger your approach."

I started running with Kierenbot on my right. Kylath took it upon himself to stay on my left, and I glanced at him. He moved like a soldier, surveying the area with practiced efficiency while holding his rifle close to his chest as he ran.

We were followed by Serena and Raylin, then Kaz and Darek, and finally T'Chura.

There was something exhilarating about running through the forest at night. I really wanted to remove my helmet and breathe in the fresh air, but I also wanted to keep my head.

"Any detection of the strike team?" I asked.

"Negative, Captain," Kierenbot replied. "There is a high probability that the strike team is wearing combat suits capable of masking their presence from our drones."

"We should slow down and be cautious with our approach," Kylath said.

As much as I wanted to run headlong right to my parents' house, I knew Kylath was right. I slowed my pace, and the others did as well.

The landscape was somewhat sloping to my right as we made our way along the western valley wall. The terrain was uneven and perilous at night, but the combat suit assisted the wearer to keep us moving at a good pace.

I brought up a video feed from one of the drones and it was doing a high-altitude flyover to survey the area. Not much could be seen from it, so I switched to the other drone.

A sound like thunder boomed across the valley, echoing along the way.

Kierenbot slowed down. "There are no storms in the area."

"That's no storm. That's fifty calibers of death being fired," I said, quickening my pace.

"Say again?" Kylath asked.

"Sniper rifle," I said.

"Adjusting drone detection capabilities," Kierenbot said.

He was much better at multitasking than I was. As we came around the side of the mountain, an area flashed on my HUD, indicating where the weapons fire had come from. Within seconds, there were bright flashes of light as plasma bolts peppered the same location.

The recon drone began tagging enemy forces once they were confirmed.

Boom!

Another sniper-rifle shot came from the other side of the valley right into the shooters from the strike team. Then another came from farther away.

The main house lay snuggled down in the valley, and its warm lights pierced the night. I heard the sound of a nearby waterfall.

"There are two shooters," Kylath said.

I nodded. "I told you they'd make the team work for it."

I peered down at the house and saw one armored figure lying unmoving about seventy yards from the barn. They'd come right up the middle, believing they could take them by surprise. He hadn't been wearing a helmet, and that mistake had cost the Mesakloren soldier his life.

A bright flash lit up the area where one of my parents had shot from, and the hideout burst into flames, but I couldn't see anyone caught in there. The Mesakloren strike team had brought some heavy ordinance.

"They're getting boxed in. We need to split up," I said.

"Agreed. We've got one chance to take them by surprise," T'Chura said.

"T'Chura, you're on the team with the heavy weapons. Take Kaz and Kylath with you," I said.

They started moving, and I gestured for the others to come toward me.

"I'm able to detect them now, Captain," Kierenbot said. "Six Mesakloren soldiers are making their way across. If we hurry, we can flank them here."

A route appeared on my HUD. I glanced at the others, and they saw it, too. "Let's move. Kierenbot and I are on point. The rest of you cover our backs."

We started moving like an arrow heading toward an unsuspecting target. There weren't any other sniper shots. My parents were likely on the move and could see that the strike team was closing in on them.

I ran, easily keeping up with Kierenbot. I might not have been able to fly, but running in a combat suit wasn't slow. We closed in on the strike team.

"We're in position," Kaz said over comms.

We threaded our way through the forest and then hugged the outskirts of an open area on the main property.

The strike team was ahead and focused on the area ahead of them. I squatted down next to a large tree and aimed my rifle. Kierenbot moved a short distance away and got ready.

Raylin, Serena, and Darek move into position to my left and hung back a little.

"Fire!" I said.

High-energy darts streaked through the forest. The Mesakloren soldier I had aimed for went down, the darts penetrating his armor. Three others also went down almost immediately.

The remaining two scattered and I quickly lost sight of them.

Across the property, there were several explosions that temporarily lit up the valley.

Crouching, I moved forward in spurts of movement, quickly using cover just in case I was spotted.

I saw a flash of movement above me as Kierenbot leaped among the tall trees like some kind of mechanical ape assassin. Several soldiers fired their weapons at him.

I used Kierenbot's distractive tactics to my full advantage and sprayed the area with my rifle on full auto. The others did the same, and the Mesakloren soldiers went down.

I scanned the area, looking for more of them.

"We're clear here," Kaz said over comms.

"Looks like we are, too," I said.

No sooner were the words out of my mouth than a combat shuttle flew over the mountain ridge, heading right for us.

"Run!" I shouted, gesturing toward the forest. "Go! Go! Go!"

We needed cover, and the nearby trees were the best we were going to get. I waited for the others to start moving, and then I started running. I made my way toward Serena, and Kierenbot dropped in front of us.

"There's a second strike team, Captain."

Heavy plasma blasts cratered the ground from the combat shuttle's weapons systems. It flew toward us and made a quick pass.

"Are you sure? What gave it away?"

Kierenbot turned toward me. "Is your helmet malfunctioning, Captain?"

I shook my head. "No, dammit. How can we take that thing out? I need options."

"Nate," T'Chura said, "if you can keep their attention, we'll move up to the house and I can take it down."

I glanced toward where he was talking about. "I got it."

I looked at Serena and the others. "Come on. We're live bait, and we're splitting up. Serena, you're with me. Raylin and Darek, I want you to stick to the forest. See if you can flank that shuttle as it flies after us. Kierenbot—"

"I have a plan, Captain," he said.

The combat shuttle did a flip motion and was already making its way toward us. There was something elegant about grav engines that allowed it to do things like spin on a dime. The inertia dampeners basically overruled centrifugal motion.

I started running with Serena at my side. We'd practiced this in the training simulator on the ship. The module hadn't used a Mesakloren combat shuttle, but getting chased was pretty much the same no matter what was involved.

I paused to fire my weapon at the shuttle, just to get its attention, and then kept running.

This wasn't the first time I'd been chased by a combat shuttle filled with Mesaklorens trying their utmost to nail Yours Truly. Serena ran next to me, and we swerved toward the trees. The combat shuttle pulled up at the last second while still firing its weapons at us.

A bright flash came from farther away and slammed into the side of the shuttle. It leaned to the side from the blow, but its armored plating protected it. Then it sped away, and T'Chura's second shot missed it entirely.

I watched as the shuttle disappeared over the ridge.

The video feed from the recon drone showed the shuttle circling around. They weren't finished with us yet.

"It's coming around," I said.

"What are we going to do? Our weapons can't do anything to that thing," Serena replied.

I frowned as I looked around the area and saw the remains of several Mesakloren soldiers. "Come on," I said.

We ran toward them. They were all dead.

"Nate, it's coming back," Serena said.

The dead soldiers' weapons were near their bodies, but I kept looking. Eventually, I found a large shoulder rig for the heavy weapon one of soldiers had been carrying. There was a thick cable that connected it to the dead soldier's body where a large metallic pack looked to be part of the heavy combat armor he'd been wearing.

I ran toward the shoulder rig and lifted it up. It still had power. I put it on my shoulders and Serena helped to steady it.

I swung the weapon around.

"Get clear," I said to Serena, but she wouldn't move. She continued to help steady the weapon. It was oversized for me since it had been designed for a much bigger person.

I clutched both the hand controls for the weapon and a holographic HUD appeared in front of me.

The Mesakloren combat shuttle flew over the ridge and the others began shooting at it.

I waited for the heavy weapon to finish priming as power was drawn into it. Then, I fired.

It was a good thing Serena had stayed with me because both of us were shoved backward, but I managed to keep the shuttle within my targeting envelope. As we fell backward, I heard the shuttle flying dangerously close over my head as it crashed into the forest behind us.

I wiggled my way out of the rig and helped Serena to her feet. An orange blaze came from behind. Kierenbot joined us, as did the others, and we quickly made our way toward the shuttle.

The hull was still somewhat intact, so we had to make sure there was no one left to fight.

We circled around it and found an area where the shuttle had been severed almost in half. I aimed inside, searching for any survivors, but I couldn't find anyone.

I turned toward Serena just as she was raising her weapon to point it at something behind me.

Boom!

A loud shot echoed through the valley, and I spun around to see a Mesakloren soldier fall to the ground. He'd been hiding in the back.

The others took cover inside the shuttle.

Kylath pointed his weapon at me. "You better handle this or I'm going to start returning fire. I don't care who they are."

I ignored him and came out of the shuttle. I lowered my weapon and held my hands up high. "Don't shoot!" I yelled. "It's me, Nathan." I retracted my helmet. "Mom. Dad. Please don't shoot me."

"Nate?" my father asked, his voice coming from about thirty yards to my right.

"Yeah, Dad, it's me."

"Hell boy, I almost took your head off."

I nodded and lowered my hands a little. "Wouldn't be the first time. Where's Mom?" I asked, glancing at the area with the higher vantage points.

"As if you had to guess. She's up high." I watched as my father walked toward me. "Evelyn!" My father's voice boomed across the valley. "Come on down. It's Nathan."

He turned toward me. "You've got timing, son. Real good timing."

A tired chuckle escaped my lips and I nodded. "Thanks, Dad. Uh, I'm not alone, and there are some things you should know." I gestured toward the shuttle. "Come on out. I've got a couple of introductions to make."

# CHAPTER 23

moved closer to my father. He was fit, with gunmetal gray
hair that had a smattering of black. He held his MK 20 SSR
as if he expected to need it again.

"It's okay, Dad. They're with me. Come on out," I said.

Kaz came out from behind the broken remnants of the
Mesakloren combat shuttle first. His gaze darted between us, and
he nodded to himself as if he'd arrived at some kind of
calculation.

Kaz retracted his helmet and my father simply stared at him.
Next came Darek and Raylin, then Kylath. My father almost
jerked the SSR up. Kylath calmly regarded my father in a non-
threatening manner.

"I know, Dad. He looks like them, but he wasn't part of the
strike team."

My father blinked a few times and then glanced at me for a
second before lowering his weapon.

"I understand you're suspicious," Kylath said.

My father frowned in confusion and looked at me. "Is he trying to speak to me?"

I shook my head. "Yeah, he is," I said and then called out. "Kierenbot, can you equip my parents with some micro-translators."

"Of course, Captain," Kierenbot said.

The nine-foot-tall battlebot came out from cover and my father stared up at him, at a loss for words. He backed up a few steps.

"Nathan!" I heard my mother call out.

"It's okay, Mom. Please don't shoot anyone."

My mother walked out from the trees. She had a Kevlar vest strapped over her clothes, and her long brown hair was tied back in a loose ponytail. There were dark smudges on her high cheekbones.

She stared at me for a few seconds. "Nathan," she said, and I smiled. It had been a while since I'd seen her.

There was something about seeing my parents that made it feel more like a homecoming. And it wasn't because of everything that had happened over the past year; it was something more, some remnant of childhood that resided inside me and hinted at all the memories growing up with two loving, if peculiar, parents.

For a long moment, the fact that we were all being hunted by dangerous aliens was pushed aside as I walked toward my mother. I stepped out of my combat suit and gave my mother a big hug. She felt warm and strong, every bit as athletic as my father.

She placed her palms on my face and stared at me in that motherly way that quickly assessed a multitude of things only she could see—some kind of instinct that informed her of how I was really doing.

"You look tired," she said.

I snorted a little. "It's been a long day, Mom."

I moved back into my combat suit. I didn't want Kylath getting any ideas.

T'Chura stepped out from the shuttle with Serena. Both my parents stared up at him, awestruck.

Kierenbot handed something to Serena and she walked toward us.

"Hello, Mr. And Mrs. Briggs," she said with a small, almost shy smile. "I have a pair of micro-translators that will allow you to understand the others. You just place it inside your ear and it'll do the rest."

On the palm of her hand were two small, dark earbuds.

My father smiled at Serena and glanced at me for a second.

"It's fine, Dad. It's not going to hurt you, I promise."

He nodded and took one of the earbuds. When he stuck it inside his ear, it disappeared, and his eyes widened a little.

"It'll pass. It's just doing its thing so you can understand them," I said.

He blinked several times and then nodded toward my mother.

She took the remaining earbud from Serena's hand. "Thank you…" she frowned.

"Serena," she said.

My mother smiled. "Evelyn."

She glanced at the earbud for a few seconds and then stuck it in her ear.

My father stepped toward Serena. "I'm Jace," he said, and looked at the others. "I guess we have all of you to thank for the assist."

Kaz glanced at T'Chura. "It's remarkable, isn't it?"

I frowned. He looked at my father and then at me.

"Indeed. The resemblance is striking," T'Chura said.

"I know. It's like an older version of Nate," Kaz said.

My father grinned. "You wouldn't be the first to say that."

Kaz blinked and walked slowly toward them. "I have so many questions for both of you," he said, looking at my parents.

"You can ignore him. He's nothing but trouble," I said quickly.

Kaz grinned, but my father frowned. He looked at the remains of the shuttle and then at the others before his gaze settled on me.

"What have you gotten yourself into now?" he asked.

I blinked, and Kaz slapped my arm.

"He certainly knows you, Nate."

I looked at my father for a few moments. I knew he'd been through a lot, being both a veteran and a former agent in one of the three-lettered intelligence agencies.

My mother came to stand by my father's side, and they looked at me expectantly.

"We're a little exposed here," I said.

My father gave me the Dad stare, the kind that pins you in place. "I seriously doubt going back to the house is much safer than it is right here. Stop tiptoeing around it, son. Who've you got chasing you now?"

Kaz barked out a laugh, and I was suddenly reminded of a time in my early teens, getting the third degree in front of my friends.

I glared at Kaz. "Why don't you do something useful and see if there's anything to be salvaged from that mess."

Grinning, Kaz turned around and went back to the shuttle.

I looked at Kierenbot. "Check in with Crim and find out what the status of the ship is."

"At once, Captain," Kierenbot said.

I tipped my head to the side, gesturing for my parents to follow me off to the side while Serena moved to join the others at the shuttle.

"Not you, dear," my mother said and smiled. "I'd rather you came with us. Nate sometimes has selective amnesia about things."

Serena's mouth hung open a little and then she smiled, her eyes gleaming.

My gaze went skyward for a moment. "Yeah, all right, fine, whatever."

We walked a short distance away, and I rounded on them.

"You're right," I said, looking at my Dad, "they came here because of me."

"Actually," Serena said, "it was all of us. Not just, Nate."

We shared a look, and my lips lifted a little.

My mother gave both of us a calculating stare that lasted a mere second but probably yielded volumes of information. Then, I told them about Kael Torsin and a very condensed version of all of us getting abducted by aliens. They took it pretty well, all things considered. They both had a great capacity to take in a lot of information and file it away in an orderly manner, but I saw them staring at the others, so they weren't completely immune to shock.

"How did you detect the attack?" Serena asked.

My father arched an eyebrow toward my mother for a moment. "Motion sensors. The valley is full of them. The images are analyzed by custom recognition software. When it couldn't find a reference for the Mesaklorens, it triggered the silent alarm."

Serena blinked and then frowned. "Are you expecting to be attacked by someone?"

My father snorted. "Better to be prepared."

Serena looked at me and I cleared my throat. "I'm not the only one who attracts trouble from time to time. Had to come from somewhere." I tipped my head toward my parents.

My father shook his head. "I think you've really outdone yourself."

"The robot," my mother began and paused for a second. "Kierenbot. He called you captain. What's that all about?"

I pursed my lips for a second. "Oh well, Serena and I, and Ben are owners of a ship. I'm the captain."

They glanced at Serena and she nodded. "He does a good job of it. Sometimes a bit by the seat of his pants, but not bad."

I smiled. "Didn't you once say we were all works in progress?"

She rolled her eyes a little.

My mother chuckled. "That's a Briggs family trait. They're impossible braggarts sometimes."

I arched an eyebrow toward my mother. "I thought the term was roguish."

"It's called charm," my father said in a matter-of-fact way. "Fortune doesn't favor the shy." He grinned.

My mother smiled warmly at him and sighed.

"Captain," Kierenbot called out.

I looked at him and he gestured toward the house. "There is a vehicle approaching. Could be more hostiles."

It was still the middle of the night. I peered toward the house for a moment and then engaged my helmet. Immediately, I could see more clearly. A black, late model Mercedes pulled into the driveway. Bright LED lights illuminated the house. The car slowed to a crawl and then stopped.

"Captain?" Kierenbot asked.

"Stand down," I said and began walking toward the house.

I retracted my helmet and looked at my parents. "Expecting anyone?"

They both shook their heads.

"Who would drive here in a Mercedes in the middle of the night?" Serena asked.

The car door opened, and a tall man stepped out. "Hello," he said.

My mother gasped. "It's Owen," she said and hastened ahead of us with my father quickly following her.

Serena glanced at me, eyebrows raised.

"Owen is my older brother," I said.

"You have an older brother? Why didn't you ever tell me about him?"

I shrugged. "It just never came up."

Owen looked as if he'd stepped out of a men's catalog—wavy hair, chiseled features, lean muscles and a good four inches taller than me, the jerk. I watched the brief reunion between Owen and my parents.

"I got the message that you wanted me to come here right away. Are you all right?" Owen asked.

"We didn't call you," my mother said.

Owen frowned. "I've got a message from Dad on my phone," he said, reaching into his pocket and pulling out an iPhone. He paused, finally noticing Serena and me. His gaze lingered on Serena for a moment, which made me stiffen my chin.

"What, no helicopter this time?" I asked, holding my arms out wide.

"Nate," he said, giving me a once-over. "What are you wearing? Is that…armor?"

Owen was rich enough to afford his own zip code. We rarely saw eye to eye on things.

I looked down at my chest. "Hadn't you heard? Armor is in."

There was a bit of an edge to my voice, the kind that happens when highly competitive brothers got within throwing distance of one another.

Owen's gaze went toward Serena. "Please forgive my brother's lack of manners. I'm Owen," he said and extended a very tan hand toward Serena.

Serena moved to shake his hand, but he kissed the top of it in a greeting straight from the formal parties of high society.

"Oh." She giggled.

*Giggled!*

It wasn't the first time I'd seen my brother's affect on a woman, but I seriously considered using one of my weapons on him.

"Yeah, okay. Let go of her hand," I said.

Serena's cheeks had spots of pink on them, and she looked away.

I heard the loud footfalls of T'Chura approaching.

Owen looked behind us and his eyes widened. His face paled and he gestured, but for once—and I can't deny a certain amount of satisfaction on my part—he was at a loss for words.

"Owen! What's wrong? What is it?" I asked and turned around. "Oh my God. What is that!"

T'Chura paused in mid stride, looking confused. Then he glanced behind, looking for some kind of threat. "There's nothing here, Nate."

I grinned and turned back toward my brother. He looked at me and then at T'Chura, then back at me.

"Got any of that expensive whiskey handy? You're going to need it," I said.

While my parents had taken the news of aliens among us quite well, Owen took a little while to warm up to the idea. My father went into the house and grabbed a bottle of whiskey, offering it to Owen.

While Owen settled his nerves, I looked at Serena.

She looked up at me and I raised my chin a little. Then I rolled my eyes.

"Come on. I know you're not into that perfectly chiseled features, model kind of guy," I said.

She shrugged a little and smiled wickedly. "I don't know. I could be convinced..."

I walked away from her.

She grinned and caught up to me. "Oh, come on, Nate. I'm only teasing you, silly."

I smirked and she narrowed her gaze and shook her head.

"Gotcha," I said.

She rolled her eyes a little. "Fine."

"He's not your type," I said.

She leveled her gaze at me. "And you know what my type is?"

I leaned toward her. "You bet I do."

Her cheeks reddened a little and she gave me a grudging smile, the kind that made me want to kiss those full lips of hers.

"Captain," Kierenbot said.

He walked over to us, and I noticed Owen do a double take.

"I'd stay away from his hands. They're very sharp," I said to my brother as I joined T'Chura and Kierenbot.

"Nate, hold up," my father said, catching up to me.

"Dad, we can't stay here. I've come to get you guys out of here."

He glanced at the shuttle wreckage for a second. "More are coming?"

I nodded. "Could be a lot more, but I've got a ship."

"What about the people here, Nate? What happens to them?"

"Nothing should happen to them. They're after me now."

"Why?"

"Because I have something Torsin needs, and he won't ever give it up," I said.

My father considered that for a few moments. "Is giving whatever it is back to him an option?"

I glanced at Serena. She had the ticking time bomb in her head. My father followed my gaze and then looked back at me.

"This has to do with her, too?"

I sighed. "It didn't start out that way, but yeah. She's in danger too, Dad."

He nodded once and a bit of steel entered his gaze. "Well then, we can't have that."

"No, we can't," I said, tipping my head toward the others. "Come on."

"Captain, I've been diverting local law enforcement from the area," Kierenbot said.

"Good. That's really good. Thanks for that, Kierenbot. What about the ship? Have you heard from Crim?" I asked.

Battlebots couldn't look regretful, but the pause in responding to my question was a good indication that I wasn't going to like what I was about to hear.

"Negative, Captain. Crim is unable to get the ship repaired. He said it's going to take time."

I frowned and considered bringing up my omnitool to contact Crim directly. "How much time?"

"Could be days," he replied.

I blinked a few times and raked my fingers through my hair while exhaling forcefully. "We need to get back to the ship."

"What is it? Should I get my tools?" my father asked.

I smiled a little and shook my head. "Good thought, Dad, but I'm not sure any of your tools are going to help."

He pressed his lips together. "Well, don't stand there looking confused."

"I'm not. I'm just weighing the options."

"What are our options?"

"I don't know. Want to see my ship?" I asked.

A boyish smile appeared on my father's face. What kind of boy hadn't dreamed of seeing a spaceship at least once in his life?

# CHAPTER 24

After a good bit of coaxing, we started to make our way back to the ship. I just didn't think I'd be riding in the back of my father's pickup truck to do it. It was a bit cramped, and one of the only things that made it somewhat enjoyable was watching Owen looking really uncomfortable as he sat between Kylath and Darek. He looked as if he expected one of them to attack.

I noticed Raylin watching him, and I guessed she also appreciated the symmetry of Owen's nearly perfect face.

"Quite the specimen," Raylin said.

Kaz shrugged. "If it pleases you."

"It does," she replied.

Kaz gestured toward me. "I think you've hurt Nate's feelings."

Raylin looked at me, the edges of her lips lifting a little. "Not to worry, Nate. You're still my favorite."

"You're mine as well," I said.

Kaz frowned. "Why did your father insist on Serena riding inside the vehicle with him?"

I thought about that for a moment. "Because she's better-looking company than you are."

He chuckled. Our exchange seemed to set my brother at ease.

I really hadn't noticed the *Spacehog's* crash site when we first arrived. A long swath of flattened trees lined up like an arrow, pointing right at the ship. Crim had somehow managed to extend the landing gear and get the ship to stand upright. There was extensive damage along the hull, which normally gleamed in white but now had scorch marks and other markings from the battle.

A long ramp extended from the main hangar bay and the truck stopped a short distance from it.

We climbed out. Kierenbot and T'Chura had gone ahead of us, easily outpacing the truck.

We all walked up the loading ramp and entered the main hangar where Crim, Ben, and Lanaya waited.

"Where's Jeshi?" I asked.

"He's finishing up with the main doors to the workshop," Crim said.

I made quick introductions.

"The ship won't fly?" I asked.

Crim shook his head. "It's going to need extensive repairs."

"Do you have what you need?"

"Unfortunately not. We're going to need some things before the ship will fly again. I'm still putting together a list."

"I hope you're joking. Kael Torsin is probably on his way here right now."

The AI Collective had said they could only delay him for a short while.

Crim glared at me. "I'm not joking. I warned you that the

ship was damaged. The landing wasn't at all gentle and...don't act is if this is my fault."

"Geez, Crim, stop taking everything so personal. I know it's not your fault. I just hoped that things were better than they are."

Crim looked confused. He'd been building up for what he thought was going to be a good long tirade. "Oh, well that's okay, I guess. Could be a lot worse."

"It is possible to fix the ship though, right?"

I didn't want to lose the ship. It had been our home for the past year, and I'd gotten used to it.

"Yes, of course it is. I can fix anything, Nate. Not to worry."

I gestured toward the few hundred yards of downed trees. "Someone is going to notice this if they haven't already."

Crim waved off the comment. "Not to worry. I have drones putting in a stealth field. It'll mimic the surrounding area, so we should be safe from prying eyes for the moment."

I pursed my lips, impressed. Then I frowned. "Will it fool Kael Torsin?"

"For a while, but I heard there were two teams and at least one shuttle. He'll be able to track that."

I sighed. "Of course," I said and chewed on my bottom lip for a second while I considered our options. "All right. Let's tell the others the good news."

Crim and I had been speaking a short distance away from the others. We joined them and they quieted down.

"The ship won't fly, not without extensive repairs, so our only means of escape is off the table," I said.

Ben looked pointedly at Crim and then at me. "We could use the battlewagon and hauler to leave the area. Give us a chance to regroup."

I noticed that Kylath and Darek were staring at me intently, waiting for my reply. "I don't think that's really an option. We've got a few people here who are more familiar with what Kael Torsin is capable of. Crim, T'Chura, Kylath, Darek—really anyone can chime in. Is running a serious option?"

"Not if you wish to survive," Kylath said.

"He's right," Crim said. "Kael Torsin is desperate and dangerous. He won't leave unless you give him what he's come here for."

"And if I do that, he'll kill us anyway," I replied.

T'Chura leveled his gaze toward me. "We cannot run or escape the star system. Our only choice is to choose a place to make our stand."

I nodded and looked at my father. "What do you think, Dad?"

He glanced at the others for a few seconds and then looked at me. "We're remote. We know the terrain. It's an advantage."

I nodded. He meant our family knew the area. "And if we make our stand here, we could keep a lower profile. We don't want to alert the military."

I did not want any US soldiers' blood on my hands. This fight needed to stay in the shadows.

"He'll have the advantage of numbers," Darek said. "We only have the people here in the hangar."

Owen cleared his throat. "Nate," he said, "I know I'm new to all this, but I could make a few calls. Get us some backup."

My brother was a highly influential person with a lot of contacts through his business dealings. I knew he could make those calls and we'd get some support, but with it would come a lot of questions. My parents likely had their own contacts from their former lives as well.

"No," I said.

"Nate, you need help. If this guy is as dangerous as you all say he is, you need all the help you can get."

I gritted my teeth a little and shook my head. "No. No outside help. Not from here, anyway."

Owen stared at me incredulously before backing up a few steps. "I'm not going to listen to this," he said, heading toward the loading ramp and pulling out his phone. "You're in over your head, little brother, just like you always are."

I was in front of him in seconds. The combat suit enabled me to move much faster than anyone without it could.

Owen stopped, his eyes wide.

I snatched his mobile phone out of his hands and crushed it. "I said no." Pieces of the phone rained down on the deck, and I leaned toward him. "Owen, you're going to have to trust me."

Owen looked back at our parents, then swung his gaze back toward me. "They more than earned their retirement. I'm not going to let them get killed because of something you're involved in."

"That makes two of us, Owe," I said.

Owen wasn't wrong about me. I'd gotten into trouble before, and I knew he was more worried about our parents than he was about himself.

"Trust me," I said calmly.

Owen regarded me for a few long moments and then nodded.

I smiled and lifted my chin toward the others, catching a pleased look from my parents. They'd always wanted us to work together, and we'd certainly spent enough time banging our heads over trivial things that weren't worth thinking about anymore.

"We've got enough weapons for everyone here, but there are only fifteen of us," I said and looked at Raylin and then Lanaya.

"What about the beings in stasis? Do you think any of them could help in a fight? They were being trained…maybe they can help?"

I glanced at Serena, and she looked troubled.

Raylin pursed her lips for a moment and shared a look with Lanaya. "Maybe," she said.

"They would be unpredictable," Kaz said.

I shrugged. "Yeah, but I bet once we explained the situation to them, they might be looking to get some payback." I looked over to the side where Thing stood quietly. "What do you think? Want some revenge against the people who were going to use you?"

His tentacles lashed out to the side and a screeching growl came from somewhere within the folds of his skin. It sounded ripe with a vicious promise of death by dismemberment.

I looked at Kaz. "I'd call that a yes."

"Yeah, but can he follow orders?"

"Hopefully," I said, walking over to the stasis pods.

Serena glared at me and I stopped. "What's the matter?"

"We can't use them," she said.

"I don't want to use them."

She blinked. "But you just said you did."

"I said we needed them and that they might like to get revenge on their captors."

"Sounds like the same thing, Nate. You're playing with words."

I felt the heat rush to my face, and I scowled. "The reality is that if they don't fight now, they might never get the chance."

"You're impossible."

"No, I'm realistic," I said. She turned away from me and I stepped in front of her. "Serena, I'm not going to force anyone to do anything. I just want to give them the option to help if they want."

"Then what? If they don't, you'll shove them back into the pod and off they go?"

My shoulders slumped a little. "Come on, you know I wouldn't do that."

She lowered her gaze with a pained expression. "I know, Nate. It's just…"

I knew what it was. It was what Kael Torsin had done to her. I leaned in and spoke softly. "I know. I'm going to fix it. I'll get it from him, and it'll stop. I promise."

She wouldn't look at me. I wanted her to, and I suspected she wanted to but also didn't trust herself. Seeing her like this made me clench my teeth.

"Please trust me," I said to her. Then I waved Lanaya over.

The young woman came over and guided Serena away. I watched my mother join them, along with Raylin.

I went to Crim and the others. My father watched my mother go into the ship with the others and then he came over to us. Owen was at his side.

I looked at Crim. "We need Jeshi down here so he can help with the beings in stasis pods."

Kaz cleared his throat. "How do you know which ones to bring out of stasis?"

"I figured you guys would be able to make a guess as to which ones look like they'd be good in a fight," I said.

Kaz glanced at Crim for a second. "So, you want us to pick the most dangerous ones and hope they don't put up much of a fight before we tell them who the good guys are?"

I nodded. "That's why you get paid the big bucks."

Kaz sighed and stared at the stasis pods. "Come on, T'Chura. I might need some backup."

I looked at Kylath. "Why don't you go with them."

He regarded me for a second, narrowing his gaze a little, and then followed them.

Kierenbot leaned down toward me. "I don't trust him, Captain," he said, quietly.

"I don't either, but we need his help. Keep an eye on him as best you can."

Kierenbot stood up straight and turned his head toward the others by the stasis pods. Kylath looked over at us and his gaze settled on Kierenbot.

"I'm watching you," Kierenbot said firmly. Then his voice came from an area behind Kylath. "I'm always watching you, Kylath," he said in a harsh whisper.

Kylath flinched away from the voice and then tried to cover it up. I arched an eyebrow while Kierenbot laughed.

"Okay, the fun is over. We've got a lot of work to do," I said, leading the rest of them onto the ship.

We set about arming everyone with the weapons stored in the armory. The advanced weapons systems were something my father delighted in. He was like a kid in a candy store as he kept asking Crim questions. It almost reminded me of Ben when he'd first come aboard the ship.

Owen came over to me. "You keep checking your wrist."

"It's my omnitool," I said, showing him the small holoscreen over my forearm.

"That's amazing. I couldn't see it until you showed it to me."

I nodded. "It's one of the features of our suits. We all have them. It's pretty standard fare out there," I said, gesturing toward the others.

Owen nodded and became quiet.

"Why don't you go help Ben?" I said as we entered Crim's workshop.

Owen frowned. "The kid?"

"Yeah, he's one of the good ones," I said.

Owen considered it for a second and then walked over toward where Ben was.

The *Spacehog* had a couple of smaller survey ships, but none that had any weapons systems. They could transport people, but I was sure Kael would have much better equipment.

I stood near the battlewagon and my father made his way over to me. I'd just finished reloading one of the power cores for the battlewagon's weapons systems.

I lifted my chin toward my Dad.

He gestured toward one of the chrome fenders. "Interesting style."

"Yeah, Crim loves cars from the fifties."

"We're going to need to establish some kind of perimeter away from the ship," I said.

He nodded. "Yeah, you don't want to get trapped in here."

I lifted an ammunition block and loaded it into one of the feeders in the rear of the battlewagon. A panel opened and I pushed the block inside.

My father looked at me for a few moments. "We don't have a lot of time."

I shook my head. "The days are short, and they could already be here." I continued moving, and my father grabbed my arm.

"Hold on a second, Nate. Take a moment to catch your breath," he said.

The hangar doors to Crim's workshop were wide open, and a stunning view of the mountains stretched out. The late afternoon sun was racing toward the horizon.

"I've never seen you like this," he said.

At the moment, I only had a few hundred things running

through my head, and the most blaring one was that I didn't have time to accomplish a fraction of what was needed.

"Better to get a couple of things done to completion than having a bunch of things half done," he said.

I sighed. "I know you're trying to help, Dad. But I don't have time for a heart-to-heart right now."

I continued reloading the battlewagon, and my father was quiet for a minute.

"Sometimes it's when our backs are against the wall that we need to take a moment."

I slammed the ammunition block into the open panel with a growl. "I don't need a moment. I need a—" I stopped speaking.

"What? What do you need?"

I turned toward him. "Oh, you know. Qualified reinforcements would be nice. A ship that runs. Enough weapons to fight with. A way to fix what they did to…"

My father gave me a knowing look. "The girl."

There were multiple women on the ship, but only one of them was *the* girl.

I nodded.

"Well, that makes sense."

"No it doesn't. The timing sucks. Right now, she's as likely to shoot me in the back as do anything else."

My father snorted. "Heck, boy. The world works on its own schedule. You're lucky if you get to tag along."

My gaze sank to the floor as I looked away from him. "I did this."

He arched an eyebrow. "You hurt her?"

"No," I said, shaking my head. "Not exactly."

"Well, which is it, son?"

"She left because of me. She should've waited." I sighed. "I should've listened and gone with her."

He waved off the comment. "That's neither here nor there."

"You don't know the details."

"Do I need to? I've been there. Did you forget how your mother and I met? On the job in some forsaken country about as far from civilization as you can get. Militia forces surrounding us."

I inhaled a deep breath and sighed.

"This guy that's coming. He's that dangerous?"

I nodded. "If it comes to a stand-up fight, a lot of people are going to die."

"You prepare as best you can and go to war with the army you've got. Surrendering isn't an option, and I've never known you to back down from anything in your life."

I chuckled a little. "To a fault, Dad. To a fault."

He shrugged. "Yeah, it's a Briggs family trait. Have you thought about what comes after?"

I blinked. "After? No, I'm kinda focused on living for the next few hours."

"Well, think about it."

Crim called out to me. They were ready to deploy some makeshift fortifications.

I looked at my father, and he had that we're-not-finished look on his face. I smiled. "We're covering quite the range of topics here. You'd think we don't have anything else to do."

"You've got to have your head on straight before the fight begins; otherwise, it all goes downhill."

I almost rolled my eyes but stopped. There were some lines I wouldn't cross, and one of them had to do with my father.

I looked down at the deck and swallowed hard. "I'm sorry to drag you and Mom into this."

He blew out a breath. "Bah. I'm not worried about that. You

can always come to us. But I'm serious about you considering what comes after this."

"Yeah, I know," I said, and paused for a moment, considering.

"Regarding the girl," he said, and I looked at him. "Women want to be asked, son. Doesn't really matter what it is or where you're going. They want to be asked."

My father had only been around me for a little more than a couple of hours and could already demonstrate his uncanny capability of seeing right to the heart of the matter.

"That simple, huh?"

He nodded. "If I had a ship like this," he said, looking around the hangar bay, "I'd take your mother with me and never look back." I stared at him, and he smiled. "Now, you go take that spirited young woman and make her yours. Climb aboard that spaceship and make a life for yourselves."

I shook my head. "I can't believe you're quoting that movie to me. It doesn't fit, you know. This isn't the Wild West."

He shrugged. "Close enough, and it's a good movie."

My father must've watched *Tombstone* a hundred times. There was just something about it that he liked.

We spent the next couple of hours on preparation, and I had to admit that knowing the area did help. There were places to hide if you knew where to go.

We salvaged some weapons systems from the shuttle. We had no idea where the Mesaklorens kept the ship they'd traveled there in and the consensus from the experts—Crim, Kaz, Kylath, and Raylin—was that it was likely hidden off-planet somewhere.

Kierenbot deployed a recon drone to search for it.

"I don't want them alerted," I said.

"They won't be," Kierenbot assured me.

"Okay, the team is obviously overdue. Would they have left someone behind on the ship? What would they do?"

Kierenbot's red orb focused on me for a few seconds. "I could speculate, but I don't know whether anyone is waiting on their ship. It would likely be just one member of their team. Not a real threat. They're likely trying to get backup."

I nodded. "And Kael Torsin can't communicate with them because I stole the keys to the kingdom. I got it."

I received a comlink from Crim, and his face appeared on my omnitool.

"Nate, what's this about using the point-defense system from the combat shuttle?"

"Kierenbot said it could be salvaged," I said, looking up at the battlebot.

Crim followed my gaze. "Did he also tell you that the power regulators for the energy weapons aren't reliable?"

I frowned and shook my head.

Kierenbot leaned toward me so Crim could see him. "Irrelevant, Crim. The power output is commensurate with the power core of the *Spacehog*. It'll work nicely and give us a powerful advantage."

Crim shook his head, looking irritated. "Yeah, and doing that will deplete the ship's power core. It can't be sustained."

Kierenbot nodded. "Yeah, but sometimes all you need is a perfectly timed, powerful shot. Right, Captain?"

I considered it for a second while Crim glared at me. "We might not have a choice, Crim."

"Nate, you don't understand. Depleting the core doesn't just use up all available power, it destroys it. The entire core will need to be replaced. You're essentially ripping out the heart of the ship. Do you understand? You'll lose the ship, Nate."

I looked at Kierenbot for a few seconds and he nodded. I

sighed and looked at Crim. "Understood. We still need the option, though."

Crim muttered something and then drew in a breath.

"I know, Crim. The decision has been made. Ben agrees with me," I said.

He hadn't because I hadn't asked him about it, but I doubted Crim had time to go chase Ben down to confirm.

Crim considered for a moment. "Very well."

Since I shared ownership of the *Spacehog* with Ben and Serena, we'd adopted a majority rule for certain things. It had caused a few headaches at times, but it was the fairest option we had to manage the ship.

"Captain," Kierenbot said, "there is a ship detected near Earth, I think."

My gaze narrowed. "You think?"

"All the communications satellites your species has deployed makes a mess of finer detection capabilities. What is it about Humans that they just throw another machine at the problem rather than increasing the capabilities of what's already deployed?"

"I don't know. I'll bring it up at the next space-junk meeting. Is Kael Torsin here or not?"

"I can't confirm it yet. Give me a minute," Kierenbot said.

I brought up my omnitool and opened a comlink to Kaz. "Time's up. Get whoever can fight to their assigned locations. Anyone who can't fight can stay in the caves nearby."

"Got it," Kaz said, and severed the comlink.

"Kierenbot, stop trying to detect them," I said.

"Done, Captain."

"Good, now broadcast a comlink that Kael Torsin is sure to detect."

"Are you sure about that?"

I nodded. "It's the only way. He'll come here sooner or later. I'd rather get out in front of it."

Kierenbot was silent for a few moments. "Understood, Captain. Broadcasting a comlink using Mesakloren communication protocols."

I exhaled a long breath. We were out of time.

# CHAPTER 25

There were times in my life when I just knew that hindsight was going to give me all sorts of insights that I should've been aware of but wasn't. This was going to be one of those times, and I hoped I lived long enough to appreciate it.

Kierenbot and I were alone, surrounded by the forest. He'd maintained a data connection to the ship's computer systems. Setting a perimeter hadn't been an arbitrary action but was well-intentioned in that we thought it was an area where we could exert some kind of influence for when the eventual attack came.

"Captain, I have a reply to the broadcast," Kierenbot said.

A comlink appeared on my HUD. It just showed the establishment of the link for a few moments until a video was added to it.

Kael Torsin regarded me with a brooding anger, as if we were a volcano about to erupt.

I gestured for Kierenbot to begin heading back to the small transport carrier we'd used to come out this far. There was just enough room on the platform for both of us to stand, and I grabbed the railing to steady myself.

"You have nowhere else to run," Kael Torsin said.

"I might have a couple of tricks up my sleeve, but only if you play your cards right."

I could only see Kael Torsin's face. He must've been using some kind of privacy mode to mask anything that might appear in the background.

"I have a weapons lock on your location. All I have to do is authorize the firing solution and that pitiful speck in the mountains will experience the birth of a new crater."

I stared at him for a long moment. "So, you don't want what I have to offer? You're willing to lose everything you've built just to take a shot at me?" I asked and then shook my head. "I don't believe you."

Kael Torsin looked amused and tilted his head to the side. "Perhaps this will convince you."

I looked at Kierenbot. He was flying the small carrier. "I don't have a lock."

He was monitoring the comlink and knew what Kael Torsin had said.

Additional video feeds were added to the comlink. Smaller windows appeared like security surveillance videos that showed my parents' house. Then there was a closeup of my father and mother as they made their way into a treetop hideout. Each window showed a video feed of the others—not all of them, but enough to convince me that Kael Torsin was a lot closer than I'd thought he was.

"Looks like you're creating quite the welcome for me," he said. "When are you going to learn that I've forgotten more about war than you've ever thought of?"

I drew in a breath to warn the others and held it.

"Excellent. You *do* know when to keep your mouth shut and listen," Kael Torsin said.

Kierenbot slowed the transport platform to a stop.

"These aren't just recon drone feeds, Nate. They're video feeds from my team's weapons that are pointed at your crew and your family."

I glared at him. How had he gotten here and into position so quickly without anyone detecting him?

"By now you're probably wondering how I got here. That's not what you should be thinking about."

"And you say *I* talk too much. Get to the damn point already," I said.

He snorted. "Patience, Nate. You're nearly there, and I'm going to savor this moment."

"I'll return the data to you, and in exchange you just leave."

He regarded me with a cold, hard stare. "That's not good enough, Nate. You see, you have quite the recompense coming to you, and I intend to recover every single moment of agitation you've given me."

My mouth became dry, and I felt as if Kael Torsin was about to appear out of thin air in front of me.

"I'll surrender to you."

"I know you're going to surrender to me, *and* you're going to give me back what you stole from me. So here is my offer to you. Return my property and I'll make sure they don't suffer; otherwise, I'll not only hurt them, but I'll make you watch every deliciously excruciating moment of it for everyone here. How does that sound?"

I glared at him, and it felt like I was staring down the barrel of a .45 caliber pistol pointed right at my face. He wanted me to cower, and it was working, but then a part of me became aware of it and resisted. I clenched my teeth for a few moments.

I blew out a breath, and one of the video feeds flashed. I saw my Dad arch his back as he clutched his leg. My mother rushed forward to keep him from falling out of the hideout.

"You son of a bitch!" I bellowed.

Kael Torsin let out a harsh laugh. "It doesn't have to be this hard, Nate. Just give me what I asked for and their suffering will stop. I promise you."

I watched as my parents escaped the hideout. My mother was trying to hold my father up as he balanced himself on one leg. They weren't going anywhere fast.

"I see you need another demonstration. Very well, then."

"Wait!" I shouted. "Would you just stop? I get it. You're here. You can hurt us. See, I get it. Now stop."

Kael Torsin leaned toward the camera, giving me a menacing glare. "I will never stop. This isn't going to end. There'll be no last-minute interference or accident of fate that will save you. Do you hear me? Not even the Collective is going to save you."

I frowned for a second, and my eyes shot toward Kierenbot. His red orb had changed to a flaring white orb.

Kierenbot lunged toward me, and I rolled backward out of reach.

It looked like the AI Collective was capable of double crossing. I scrambled to my feet as Kierenbot's hulking battlebot form strode toward me.

"His offer was better," the Collective's monotoned voice said from inside Kierenbot.

# CHAPTER 26

There were a few things in life that were all but guaranteed: We were all going to die; most of us had to pay taxes; and situations would go sideways when you least expected them to.

I'd known this was going to be one heck of a tough day, but I never expected to be running from Kierenbot.

Using the battlebot made Kierenbot as strong as T'Chura and faster than anything else on the ship, including Yours Truly. But it wasn't Kierenbot; it was the Collective that had somehow taken control of him.

"Come on, Kierenbot, you've got to be in there. Can't you fight this? Are you going to let them win?" I asked.

Kierenbot strode toward me, and the wide head atop his nine-foot-tall body leaned over me. "We are Kierenbot!"

I kept backing up, trying to weigh my options. Running was first and foremost in my mind, but I knew what that battlebot could do.

I stopped moving and peered up at the battlebot. "You're not going to let them win, Kierenbot. I know you're in there. You can fight this. They can't stop you."

Kael Torsin chuckled. "Reasoning with an artificial intelligence is tantamount to trying to convince an Ustral they're an Akacian. It's never going to work."

I rolled my eyes and then clenched my teeth. He was right, so I decided to try something different.

"This isn't going to get you what you wanted," I said, choosing to keep my distance from the battlebot.

He stalked forward, each powerful footfall thumping toward me with the promise that my friend was going to kill me.

I had no other choice.

I focused my mind and multiple timelines sprang to existence all around me. What I'd learned from the Asherah was getting easier to use. I wasn't sure whether that was good or bad, but I would take any help I could get at the moment. Using the ability didn't stop time, not entirely, but it was like stepping out of time to observe multiple timelines with different probabilities. If I wasn't careful, I could get lost in a death spiral. Many timelines showed me dying, which wasn't as detached as observing it on a video feed. I felt it, each and every time. I felt the terror and utter helplessness of dying, and the profound regret. If I became too focused on it, it would become my reality. Through sheer force of will, I made myself ignore all of it and tried to focus on the others, using the video feeds that Kael Torsin had been malicious enough to share with me. They were all moving in very slow motion, but I could guess the outcome. It was like seeing an image with multiple images superimposed over them.

None of it helped. I couldn't save them.

As each timeline confirmed my eventual demise, I felt myself getting backed into a corner. I'd pitted myself against the odds, and sooner or later it was bound to be time to pay up.

That day was today.

I swallowed hard and collapsed all the timelines into one, lifting my gaze toward Kael Torsin on the comlink.

"There is no escape," he said.

I nodded. "I know, and that leaves me with only one thing to do."

He sneered, and it looked as if he enjoyed it. "I lied, Nate. I'm not going to make it quick. Not for any of them."

"I know," I said, and opened a data window on my omnitool. "I hope you recognize this." Kael Torsin peered at the feed. "No one wins, Kael. You're never going to get this because I've just destroyed all the other copies. There are no backups. None. I have the only copy now."

Kierenbot stopped stalking toward me.

"Liar!" Kael Torsin bellowed.

I shook my head. "You can only blame yourself, moron. Let me tell you something about Humans. We're a rebellious bunch. We're not cowed, we don't like being bullied, and we don't give up. Ever. You might have the upper hand here, but if you want what I've got, what's inside my combat suit's computer, then you're going to have to come and take it from me. Not them. Me, dammit. Me!"

I screamed the last word and then did the most unthinkable thing they ever would've expected from me.

I charged toward Kierenbot.

The moments I'd stolen, glimpsing multiple timelines, had yielded bits of knowledge that I could use. Snippets of understanding helped me piece together my only shot at stemming the tide of this disaster.

I leaped into the air with a burst of strength from my combat suit, then used Kierenbot's wide head to spring farther into the air. The battlebot reared back and the motion helped thrust me toward a tree. I reached out, grabbing the branches, and pulled myself up, propelling myself higher and higher.

I breached the treetops and sent an activation signal to the point defense system attached to the *Spacehog's* power core. A bright light burst in the distance where the ship was located. It pierced the projected image that hid the ship, and bright red beams burst forth in a rush. There were too many for me to track, but I knew the point defense system's countermeasures had been scanning the valley since we attached them to the ship's power core.

Kael Torsin might have had his soldiers targeting the crew, but what he hadn't realized was that they were also being targeted. The entire valley erupted in a crossfire from plasma weapons systems, and I hit the ground at a run, racing toward the house.

Mesakloren soldiers crashed to the ground. They'd been using individual flight systems to maintain a vantage point to the targets. Their armor was difficult to spot, but there were ways to track them, particularly the network connection from their weapons systems.

One of the things I'd learned about sneaking around—be it here on Earth or some alien world—was that if there was any type of system connection, it could be traced. This was one of the primary reasons I never carried a smartphone. I assumed my omnitool worked the same way, and I always assumed I could be traced. That was why I'd cut off my combat suit's communication systems.

I carried a multipurpose assault rifle with nanorobotic ammunition. It was set for powerful kinetic darts, which I was sure was the only thing that could penetrate the soldiers' armor. It would never be a one-shot-and-done encounter, but there were some things armor couldn't protect the wearer from. Not even armor could negate the effects of physics, such as when a solid object was flying toward you very fast. All that energy had to go somewhere. So, even if the soldiers' combat armor could withstand some of the high-density darts being shot at them, enough of them could knock them off-balance and eventually penetrate the armor.

I raced through the forest in an all-out run. I'd configured my comms systems to do a periodic broadcast of my location. It was more of a "set it and forget it" configuration, but there was no mistaking when the check-in occurred because it drew weapons fire from almost all around me at varying distances. It took the attention off my family and the crew. Hopefully, it would be enough.

I glanced up toward the sky and still saw red beams from the point defense systems firing, but they'd slowed down. The Mesakloren soldiers must've scattered toward the ground, seeking cover from the deadly beams.

I glanced behind me as I ran and saw Kierenbot running toward me, quickly closing the distance. The battlebot had changed to using all four of its limbs to propel itself forward, going much faster than I could, even with a combat suit on.

Kierenbot's orb still blazed white, so the Collective was still asserting control over him. I angled away, trying to keep trees between us. I tried anything just to slow him down, but he kept gaining on me.

I stopped and raised my rifle, firing it at the battlebot. Kierenbot twirled into the air, performing some kind of acrobatic maneuver and managing to avoid being shot. My combat suit computers attempted to predict where he would move and helped guide me. Several large darts struck his long legs as he leaped through the air, and I saw pieces of his legs fall to the ground as he crashed out of sight. I gritted my teeth and kept running.

"Sorry, buddy," I said.

The Collective was supposed to help me, not turn my friend against me. I shook my head. Kaz and the others had tried to tell me that Kierenbot wasn't actually a sentient being. He was an artificial intelligence that was ruled by a bunch of constraints that I'd thought could be overcome. Of all the beings in the valley right now, Kierenbot wasn't anywhere near the top of the list of who I wanted to fire my weapon at.

A warning flashed on my HUD and I dove to the side, swinging my weapon toward a Mesakloren soldier as he was about to fire his weapon at me. I didn't know why he hadn't fired his weapon and I didn't care. I sprayed high-velocity darts at him, knocking him back into a tree, and he fell out of sight.

I broke through the trees almost at the same time as the battlewagon burst into view. The battlewagon was essentially a flying tank. It could take a lot of damage, as well as deliver it. Crim must've gotten a full crew inside because all the weapons were firing. Mesakloren soldiers fell down before it until a combat shuttle flew over the ridge line. The battlewagon moved sideways, getting out of the way as it fired its weapons at the shuttle.

They hit each other, and a bright flash seemed to engulf the entire valley. I had to look away from it. Some unseen force knocked me off-balance and I tripped. Tumbling to the ground, I bounced off a boulder jutting up from the ground. I felt as if I were still spinning and tried to sit up.

My HUD flashed a warning seconds before I broadcast my location. I had just enough time to scramble to my feet. Dozens of yards away, I saw Serena shouting something. I ran toward her, and she waved me onward.

I changed direction, veering away from her. She didn't know what I had planned. Being around me was the worst decision anyone could make.

"Nate!" she shouted, running after me.

About the only place that had sure footing was the road that led to my parents' house. It connected to the other smaller buildings throughout the property, but it also put us out in the open.

"You've got to get out of here," I said.

"Where are you going?"

She couldn't quite catch up to me, not being able to run as fast as I could. I heard her following me, calling out for me to slow down, but I didn't dare.

Flashes of light snatched my attention and I saw T'Chura and Kaz fighting off a squad of soldiers. There were other groups as well, but it happened so quickly that I couldn't keep track of it all. A battle with nearly constant weapons fire was a tour through chaos and death. I hated it.

A bright explosion rocked the valley, and I spun around. The battlewagon had become a flaming metallic hulk. My mouth hung open as I peered into the surrounding area, trying to search for anyone running away.

"Let me go!" Serena shouted.

I spun toward her and saw Kylath clutch her to his body. A purplish gleam came off a blade he had pointed at her armored throat.

"Enough games. I want the data and you're going to give it to me," Kylath said.

"What about our deal?" I asked.

I began to point my rifle toward him.

"Don't. This blade can pierce her armor like it's not even there."

He pushed the strange-looking blade toward Serena's throat

and the armor seemed to get pushed away by some kind of force. The skin of her neck became red and she screamed in pain, trying to move away, but Kylath held her firmly.

"Okay, okay. Stop," I said.

Kylath moved the blade away from her neck. "Send it to me. Right now."

I looked down at my omnitool and hesitated.

"Now's not the time for tricks. Give me the data and I'll let her go. Isn't that what you want?"

I lifted my gaze toward him and then Serena. She stared at me, her eyebrows drawing together in a perplexed frown. The inhibitor inside her brain was causing a strain as it attempted to block certain emotions. I saw it happening. Her lips lifted into a sneer as she narrowed her gaze toward me.

"Focus, Nate. Once you give me the data I can deal with Kael Torsin. I'll make the problem go away."

I blinked a few times, glancing at my omnitool and then at Serena. She closed her eyes and shook her head.

"Don't," I said. "Look at me."

Serena opened her eyes and I swallowed hard. "Let it happen," I said.

Kylath frowned. "What?"

I lifted the omnitool, showing him the holoscreen.

"Don't try anything," Kylath said.

If I gave him the data, I'd never be able to save her, but he'd also kill her if I didn't give it to him.

Serena glared at me with a growl as she drove her elbow back, catching Kylath by surprise. She spun around, grabbed the hand holding the knife, and pushed it into his shoulder.

Kylath cried out in pain. The armor covering his shoulder melted away as the blade plunged deep into his pale flesh. The wound blackened. Kylath let go of the hilt and Serena grabbed it with both hands. She jerked it down and to the side, and a deep cut separated muscle and bone. Serena pulled the blade out and spun toward me, murder in her eyes as she charged.

I backed up, dropping my rifle. I wasn't going to shoot her. Reaching over my shoulder, I grabbed the end of my boom stick.

"You've got to fight it, Serena," I said, keeping the stick between us.

The end of the stick glowed with a pale blue light. A sonic charge had built up. Serena's helmet was off, exposing her head. If I somehow hit her in the head with the boom stick, she would die.

I kept backing up, trying to maintain the distance between us.

"You don't hate me," I said.

Serena narrowed her gaze. "Yes, I do!" she screamed and darted toward me, howling in fury. "I hate you so much!"

I wish I could say this was the first time I'd gotten this kind of response from a woman, but it wasn't. Alien weapons and tech aside, Serena wasn't the first woman to be furious with me. In this one instance, however, I could honestly say that it wasn't her but the alien inhibitor that was causing her to act this way, which was the exact opposite of how she felt. So, on the one hand I had it confirmed that Serena loved me and I loved her, but now I needed to prevent her from killing me.

I learned a few things over the span of a few seconds. One, Serena could move fast. Two, she was scary when she was angry. Three, I hated seeing her like this. It was hurting her, and it was killing me. What if the damage being done was irreversible? Not only would she never be the same, but I would've lost the one woman I wanted with me always.

Serena lunged toward me with the long, dark, alien blade. I darted to the side and dove toward the ground, rolling onto my feet. It was so perfectly executed that if I hadn't been caught up in the moment, I could've appreciated it.

I had to get the knife out of her hands. She lunged again and I sidestepped out of the way, slamming my stick on her outstretched arm. The force of the blow put her off-balance and I swept her legs out from under her. In one smooth motion, I grabbed the hand with the knife and eased her to the ground.

Serena stared up at me, all the anger and rage gone. She peered at me with those large, honey-brown eyes of hers. "Nathan," she said in a breathy tone.

Recognition lasted only a few moments, so I held her wrist down on the ground or else that damn knife would've run through me.

Scowling, Serena rolled toward me and kicked me somehow. I had no idea how she'd done it, but I held onto her wrist and twisted. If I let go, that knife was going into me.

I surged to my feet and pulled her up with me. She wouldn't let go of the knife no matter how hard I swung her around. She fought me like someone possessed. I couldn't hold onto her, so I let her go. She rolled on the ground, and I raced toward my boom stick. I picked it up and noticed that there were several Mesakloren soldiers watching us. They didn't even have their weapons ready.

One of them walked toward us and clapped his hands in a slow and slightly off-rhythm beat.

I glanced at Serena and she stood, looking around as if she was confused.

I looked back at the soldier, and he held some kind of device in his hand.

"Ah, Nate, this has been so entertaining," Kael Torsin said. "You did not disappoint, but now I'm afraid our fun has come to an end."

Sounds of fighting could still be heard across the valley. Twilight had settled across the mountains.

"Let her go," I said, and held out my hand for the device.

Kael Torsin regarded me for a few moments, looking a little exasperated, and then glanced down at the chrome device in his hands. "Did you really think I'd just hand this over to you?"

I shrugged. "It couldn't hurt to ask."

He stared at me for a second. "You'd make a fine addition to my plans, you know."

"Except for the fact that I hate you and everything you stand for," I said.

I had the combat suit interface up on my internal HUD.

Kael Torsin narrowed his gaze menacingly. "You really don't know when you're defeated."

He stepped toward me, and his soldiers weren't far behind. There were four of them.

"The way I see it is that we both have something the other wants. Give me the device that controls the inhibitor and I'll transfer the data. You'll get your empire back."

He shook his head. "I made a promise to you, Nate," he said in a harsh voice. Leaning toward me he said, "And I always keep my promises."

He raised the device up for me to see and I didn't hesitate.

My combat suit melted off me and I leaped backward as it reduced to its standby form of a cube. Kael Torsin froze as I stepped toward it, swinging my boom stick, and hit it with all the force of the ultimate home run ever executed.

My combat suit shattered from the concussive blast from my boom stick. Orange lightning burst from the power core as the entire suit and all the data inside was destroyed.

Kael Torsin howled in rage, and I crossed the distance between us with nothing but a stick and the clothes on my back.

His eyes widened for a second, but he was a warrior, a soldier who'd fought countless battles, and even though I'd surprised him, it wasn't enough to fully catch him off guard.

He swiped a gauntleted fist at the stick, but I'd managed to change direction at the last moment. I twirled it around and the glowing tip released a powerful blast onto his arm. The force of the blast pushed me back through the air and onto my back, and I used the momentum to roll back onto my knees. My boom stick was gone. I must've let it go.

"Nate," Serena said and tossed the blade she'd taken from Kylath toward me.

I snatched the blade out of the air. It had almost no weight and I could feel it pulsing with power.

I turned toward Kael Torsin, and he waved me toward him. Mesaklorens loved a good fight, and I aimed to give the big alien the fight of his life.

Bellowing a roar, I charged toward him. Another bellow sounded nearby, and it was louder and deeper enough to startle the Mesakloren soldiers. They had just enough time to turn toward the noise before an armored wrecking ball in the form of an enraged Noorkon tackled them all to the ground.

T'Chura was the deadliest alien I'd ever encountered. Those soldiers hadn't stood a chance.

Kael Torsin ignored them and swung an armored fist toward me. I could've taken the hit if I'd still had my combat suit, but I dodged out of the way and got to live for another second. The level of rage exuded by Torsin was what I'd imagined a berserker to be. The alien was beyond reason, and his whole purpose was to kill me.

He reached for me, and I thrust the blade upward with a slash. I met a slight resistance and Torsin cried out in pain. He jerked back and flailed out with his fist, sending me sprawling to the ground.

He raced toward me like a vicious beast and was on me before I could react. He lifted me into the air, grabbing both my arms. I tried to yank myself free, but he was too strong. He pulled me toward his ugly face. Wide mandibles opened, revealing a mouth full of sharp teeth and breath that stunk of death and decay.

He lifted me high into the air as I saw T'Chura dispatch the last Mesakloren soldier, but there was no way he'd make it to me in time. The shock was written all over his face.

I pulled my knees to my chest and tried to kick Torsin's chest, but it felt like I'd straight-legged into solid rock. The pain spread from my lower back down to my legs.

Torsin started to slam my body to the ground but stopped... something stopped him. Black barbed tentacles snaked up his legs while others grabbed his arms. The barbs were out, and they dug into his armor. Another tentacle snaked around Kael Torsin's neck and Thing let out a harsh scream.

Torsin let me go and I dropped to the ground, looking up to see the two aliens struggling against one another, matching strength for strength. Thing used some of his powerful tentacles to anchor himself to the ground, giving him leverage against Torsin, but neither could get the upper hand. I surged to my feet with the alien blade in my hand. With a running start, I leaped toward Torsin and plunged the blade into his chest. His armor was pushed away from the blade by an unseen force. Using my forward momentum and Earth's gravity, I gutted the Mesakloren tyrant from chest to navel. Thing's tentacles did the rest by tearing Torsin's body in half, and his internal organs slapped the ground in a grisly, steaming mess. A half gurgling groan escaped his lips as Thing flung him aside with a howl of triumph.

I sank to my knees and landed hard, my breath coming in gasps. Thing sagged toward the ground, his body shaking uncontrollably. He was bleeding from dozens of wounds.

I slowly regained my feet. The remains of Kael Torsin's body lay a short distance away and I stumbled toward it. Clutched in his fist was the device he'd used to control the inhibitor. It was crushed.

"No!" I cried, trying to pry the pieces from Torsin's hand. "No, dammit. No!"

I couldn't force his hand to open, so I brought the knife up and pressed it against the armored fist. The armor quickly pushed away, becoming something akin to liquid metal, and I snatched the remains of the device.

"Nate!" Crim called out as he came toward me.

I turned in his direction, the remnant of the device in my hand. "Can you fix it?"

Crim glanced down at the crushed device and then back at me. He blinked, looking uncertain, as if he didn't have the heart to give me an honest answer.

"You have to fix it," I said.

"Nate," Serena said.

She was behind me and I almost turned toward her, but I stopped myself. If she looked at me, the inhibitor would start all over again. Without the device to stop it, I could lose any chance at saving her.

I'd come so close, so damn close.

My shoulders sagged. "Crim, you've got to fix it. You've got to. Tell me you can do it. Please, Crim. Please," I begged, thrusting the remains of the device into his hands.

He took them but wouldn't look at them. Why wouldn't he look at them? Crim could fix anything. He had to be able to do this.

"Nate," Serena said.

She was closer to me, no more than ten feet by the sound of it.

"No, don't look at me, Serena. Just stay away," I said and stared at Crim.

Crim looked over my shoulder for a few seconds and then back at me. He lifted his chin and gestured for me to turn around.

Serena stood there and our eyes locked. The muscles of my chest and gut tightened as if anticipating a blow. I watched for the change to occur like it had done before. At any moment, the inhibitor would assert itself and all would be lost.

Serena blinked with a surprised frown, as if she was expecting the same thing.

I took a slow step toward her, afraid this moment would be lost forever. Then we rushed toward each other, Serena smiling widely. We held each other and I lifted her into the air. She laughed and beamed at me as we gazed into each other's eyes. Then, I lowered her to the ground.

I don't remember when the kiss started. I just know that it took me out of the moment, away from what would become one of the most significant events in both our lives.

I wasn't what anyone would call a hopeless romantic, but for Serena I would gladly try for however long she'd let me.

# CHAPTER 27

After the elation of surviving the fight for all our lives, I learned that we were still in trouble. I should've expected it. Someone had noticed the battle.

"Multiple ships are inbound," Crim said.

I glanced around the valley. Smoke rose from about a dozen different wrecked vehicles, smaller buildings on the property, and actual trees that had caught fire during the battle. Jeshi and Darek took it upon themselves to perform fire-suppression duty. With them was a small squadron of drones. Jeshi had taken control of the Mesakloren recon drones and attached canisters from the fire-control systems found on the *Spacehog*.

"His mind is quite agile," Crim said.

I nodded. "You don't say."

Crim frowned. "I just said it, Nate."

I rolled my eyes and Crim grinned. He'd been joking.

"My parents?" I asked.

Crim thought for a moment. "The last I saw was Kaz and Raylin going to them."

I opened a comlink to Kaz.

"It's about time you contacted me," Kaz said. "Your parents are fine, Nate. Raylin says they'll make a full recovery."

I exhaled forcefully. "Can I speak to them?"

"I'm afraid not. They're unconscious—"

"Unconscious! You just said they're fine."

Serena looked toward me. She'd been checking on Thing.

"I meant they aren't dead, but they've been hurt," Kaz said.

Raylin appeared next to Kaz on the video comlink. "Nate, they just need some time in the autodoc. They sustained serious burns and I've used a field kit with medical spray to help with the pain. They're resting comfortably."

I nodded, and it took a few seconds for what she told me to penetrate. I'd almost lost them. My mouth slackened as I stared at Kaz and Raylin. They'd saved my parents' lives. "Thank you," I said with a slow smile. My voice sounded so damn tired.

Kaz snorted and looked at Raylin. "He runs through the valley drawing fire from every soldier in the area and he thanks *us*?" He looked at me with a knowing smile. "You're welcome, Nate."

I smiled, narrowing my gaze at Kaz. "I'm going to make it up to you."

He frowned. "Make what up to me?"

"The fact that you thought it was a good idea to screw with me at a time like this."

Kaz pretended to consider that for a few moments and then shrugged. "I'm sure you will."

We shared a grin and Kaz told me he was going back to the ship for supplies. Raylin would watch over my parents.

Owen came from around my parents' house. There was a gaping hole where the tall windows had been in the kitchen and dining area, and the inside of the house didn't look much better.

Owen had dried blood on his scalp and walked with a bit of a limp. He glanced at the dead Mesakloren soldiers and some of the wreckage.

"Is this what you do now, little brother?"

I walked toward him. "Sometimes," I said and tipped my head to the side to get a better look at his head.

Owen smiled and shook his head. "Tis but a scratch."

I grinned. "If you say so. We should get it checked out."

Owen frowned. "On your ship?"

I arched an eyebrow. "Yes, on the ship."

He nodded and pressed his lips together. "I need to make a few calls and you destroyed my phone. If you want to keep a lid on this thing, you need to let me help you."

T'Chura walked toward us. Pieces of his armor were missing, and he'd taken his helmet off.

"Nate," Owen said.

I held up my hand for him to wait while I went to T'Chura. He looked a little unsteady on his feet. Then he sat on the ground with a heavy thud.

"You don't disappoint," T'Chura said.

"A story for the ages?" I asked.

He nodded. "Indeed."

"Are you hurt? Your timing was impeccable, as always."

He waved away the question. "I was having trouble keeping up with you."

"Yeah, things didn't go at all according to plan."

He arched a big bushy eyebrow and smiled with half his mouth. "So there was a plan?"

I chuckled. Owen looked as if he was going to burst a gasket if I didn't let him make a phone call.

"Hey, Crim," I said. "Can you help my brother out with communications? Keep an eye on him while he calls people."

Owen looked at Crim and hesitated. He still wasn't used to aliens, and Ustrals, with their six legs and humanoid bodies, definitely took some getting used to.

"Will do," Crim said. "Come over here, Owen. There are the comms signals available..."

It was one of those days when hours went by so quickly that I lost track. After medical treatment was administered, cleanup became the priority of the day. Somehow my brother got a fifty-mile stretch around my parent's property declared a temporary no-fly zone. Between his contacts and my parents placing a few calls to contacts they had in certain three-letter agencies, all kinds of law enforcement types were called off. I sometimes found that I didn't necessarily need to know all the details.

I walked through the forest with T'Chura.

"Are you sure this is the way?" he asked.

It was approaching midnight, but between the bright moonlight, clear skies, and a pair of night-vision glasses, I could see the area clearly. The HUD was similar to what I was used to in my combat suit helmet.

I glanced around the area, trying to piece together the death run I'd instigated earlier. "I think so. It's all a bit of a blur, but he's got to be out here."

With the power core depleted on the *Spacehog*, Kierenbot had been cut off from the ship. The normal everyday body he used was in standby.

"We're going to be out here all night. I think he can wait until morning," T'Chura said.

He carried a rifle just in case Kierenbot was still being controlled by the Collective. "I can't believe he betrayed you."

I sighed. "Yeah, I don't believe it either, meaning I really don't think he did."

T'Chura eyed me for a second. "You think this was some kind of ruse?"

Memories of the battlebot trying to run me down were too fresh in my mind to commit to that, but I wanted to believe it. "I don't know. It all happened so damn fast. We owe it to him to hear it from him."

I'd shot out Kierenbot's legs, and he experienced a pretty violent crash because of it. We eventually found him—pieces of him—in a trail that led us to his body.

Kierenbot's upper torso was intact but was definitely the worse for wear. His legs were darkened stumps. He'd crawled to a tree and seemed to be resting. His red orb was barely visible.

"Kierenbot, are you in there?" I asked.

The orb brightened a little and then lazily tracked side to side. He turned away from us, staring at the ground.

"Permission to go into permanent standby, Captain," Kierenbot said.

I glanced at T'Chura and he shrugged. I walked toward Kierenbot and stopped about ten feet away. I was sure he couldn't reach me, but T'Chura wasn't taking any chances. He pointed his rifle at the remains of the battlebot. If Kierenbot so much as twitched, then game over.

I squatted and then sat down. A tired groan escaped my lips.

Kierenbot looked at me. "Sensors indicate that you're dehydrated. You must consume water with an electrolyte mixture to return to peak performance."

I shook my head and sighed. "What happened?"

"You haven't answered my question, Captain."

He wanted permission to go into permanent standby and end his life. "Permission denied. Now answer my question. The Collective took control of you."

"I'm aware, Captain."

Interesting, and a little scary at the same time.

"I watched everything that happened. I was forced to participate."

I frowned, considering. "So it wasn't you trying to kill me?"

Kierenbot bobbed his head once. "My knowledge of the particulars is limited, but it appears that I've been granted a certain amount of latitude to answer your questions."

"They used you."

"Yes. They forced me to use combat protocols to subdue you."

"Why?"

Kierenbot's orb froze in place while he thought about it. "I don't know, Captain."

I stared at him for a long moment. "I want an answer. I know you're in there, monitoring this exchange. Stop hiding behind him and speak to me directly."

Kierenbot's red orb blinked and then locked into place, becoming white.

T'Chura became still and I glanced up at him. His saucer-size eyes were wide, and then he looked at me questioningly. He'd never known about the Collective. Well, the cat was out of the bag now.

I looked at Kierenbot. "Why did you betray me?"

"We did not betray you," the Collective replied.

"Yes you did. You sided with Kael Torsin and tried to kill me. If that's not a betrayal, I don't know what is."

"You are mistaken."

I narrowed my gaze. "Then help me understand." Getting answers from them was like pulling teeth.

"You agreed to allow us to conduct research on the effects of the Asherah through your abilities. This was done in exchange for our cooperation and aid in escaping Kael Torsin's forces."

I chewed my lower lip for a moment while I thought about it. Then I shook my head and leaned forward a little. "Are you telling me that this was a damn test?"

"Precisely."

I sneered. "Are you serious!"

"It was an opportune time to test your capabilities. The data has yielded quite a substantial amount of information for us to consider."

I swept my arms out wide, gesturing to the battlefield. "In the middle of a damn battle you chose to conduct a *test*? Just so you could see what I can do under pressure?" I shook my head. "The deal is off."

"You wish to renege on our agreement?"

I blinked. "You idiots already reneged on the agreement. I didn't sign up for this."

"You are mistaken. Your agreement didn't put any limitations on when and how we conduct our experiments. All our actions come under the purview of our agreement."

I blinked and felt my mouth slacken. I just sat there dumbfounded and way past exhaustion. I used my wrist to wipe my nose and shook my head with a sigh.

"Nate?" T'Chura asked. He glanced meaningfully at Kierenbot.

I stood and gestured for him to wait. T'Chura began to lower his weapon. "Maybe keep it handy for now."

He blinked and then pointed it toward Kierenbot again.

I regarded Kierenbot thoughtfully. Never get into a staring contest with an artificial intelligence. They're always going to win. "I understand," I said.

"Excellent. Then we will resume normal operations," the Collective said.

I shook my head. "That's not going to work. I can't have you attacking me or anyone else close to me as some kind of test."

"Do you wish to end our dealings?"

"What happens if I do?"

"All support operations will cease, and we will have no further contact with you."

I considered that for a few moments. I didn't think the Collective made a habit of interacting with a lot of beings like this. "I think there's room for renegotiations so we can bang out some of the details of this agreement—something that will give us assurances that we're both benefiting from this deal. We didn't have time for it before. What do you think?"

The white orb pulsed for a moment, then brightened. "We find your proposal acceptable. We will place a temporary hold on our operations until such time as to allow for expectations to be clearly defined."

I'd been part of negotiations before, a holdover from my short career practicing law. "I'm going to need some time to come at this fresh. I also need time to repair the ship and...it's a mess around here, so I'm going to need you to be patient."

"Understood, but be warned that our patience isn't without limits."

"Okay, once the ship is repaired and we're underway, we'll sit down at the negotiating table and work on this."

"This is acceptable."

"There is one more thing."

"An additional item to negotiate?"

I pressed my lips together for a second. "This is more of a nonstarter, and it has to do with Kierenbot."

"We will not draw any conclusions without your input."

I pursed my lips, impressed. If only people could do the same.

"Kierenbot doesn't deserve what you've done to him."

"The being you know as Kierenbot is part of the Collective. He was created with the purpose of interacting with biological beings."

"Yeah, and you forced him to try to kill me so you could study the Asherah remnant I've got inside me. He didn't ask for this. I'm sure if you'd asked him if he wanted to participate in your test, he would've declined."

The white orb tracked across the battlebot's head a few times. "Irrelevant."

"You're wrong. It is entirely relevant. In fact, free will is one of the most important traits we Humans possess."

"You wouldn't explain yourself to your hand cannon. You would put it to the use for which it was designed."

"This isn't the same thing, and you know it."

"Nate," T'Chura warned, "be careful."

I thought about it for a few moments. "Kierenbot was created to interact with us so you could learn about different species of intelligent life. This was always going to affect him. Ask him. Would he have tried to kill me if he had the option to deny your orders?"

The battlebot was quiet for a minute.

"He wouldn't do it, would he?" I said.

"His interactions with you have introduced some irregularities," the Collective said.

T'Chura let out a deep chuckle and muttered something about understatements.

"Would you make him indentured to you?" the Collective asked.

I shook my head. "Kierenbot must be free to stay and go by his own choosing. He'll have a contract with the ship, and you can't force him to do anything against his will."

Nothing was said for a few moments, but I waited them out.

"Very well. The confines of the being known as Kierenbot will be updated to grant independence from Collective control. He will still provide us with reports of his interactions, but we will no longer enforce our control over him."

I lowered my chin once. "Good. I think that does it for now. Unless you have something else you'd like to ask me?"

"No, this interaction has been quite informative. We look forward to sitting down with you at the negotiating table."

Kierenbot's orb flicked back to red. "Captain," he said, sounding a little distracted.

"Are you all right?" I asked.

T'Chura lowered his weapon.

"Well, my legs are gone so I can't walk. This chassis will need extensive repairs."

I stared at him for a few moments. "Do you know what happened? Just now, I mean?"

"I am aware that I've been granted the option to remain in service of the ship."

"Only if you want to."

Kierenbot's orb darted toward T'Chura and then back to me. "I'm not sure if this is another attempt at humor."

I shook my head. "It's not. I'm serious. The Collective said they wouldn't take control of you or force you to do anything you didn't want to do on your own."

Kierenbot regarded me for a few seconds.

"As long as you don't try to kill me, you're welcome back on the ship."

The red orb brightened. "Oh, I see. Well then, this would be a great opportunity to discuss my pay scale and share of the ship's profits." I blinked. "It's something that has been overlooked for quite some time."

T'Chura leaned toward me. "I tried to warn you."

It took me a few seconds to pick the bottom of my mouth off the floor. Kierenbot kept talking about how he deserved more pay. "Okay, I get it. You want a bigger slice of the pie. We'll talk about it later. For now, we need to get back and help with cleanup. Are you able to move, or does T'Chura need to carry you?"

Kierenbot pushed up on his hands. "I'm able to move. No assistance necessary, which might've charged me an additional cost."

I looked away from him and sighed. I couldn't blame anyone else because I'd done this to myself. I'd pushed for Kierenbot's freedom.

I held up my hand. "Stop," I said, and Kierenbot became quiet. "First, this is not going to be a constant haggle between us. You're still part of the crew and you're expected to contribute without reminding everyone involved how much work you're doing. No one likes a braggart. Got it?"

"Understood, Captain. The Collective advised me to push for better working conditions and I find that I agree with their advice."

I looked up at the night sky, wondering if it was too late to close Pandora's box.

T'Chura leaned toward Kierenbot. "I think Nate needs some time to warm up to the ideas you're proposing."

My eyebrows raced up my forehead. The Collective, it seemed, wasn't without a sense of humor of their own. If this was what came from Kierenbot's freedom, I could already think of a few additional things to add to his contract that would limit the number of suggestions he was allowed to make regarding his employment contract. I could tweak details with the best of them.

# CHAPTER 28

"What do you mean Serena's gone? Where'd she go?" I asked.

Kaz stood at the bottom of the loading ramp to the ship and shrugged. Stacks of materials rode on grav pallets destined for Crim's workshop. Ship repairs had been underway for a day now.

"I'm not exactly sure, Nate. She said she had to take care of a few things and then spoke with Owen."

I strode up the ramp, lengthening my stride. The ship was still on emergency backup power, which meant all the doors were open and lighting was limited. I spotted Owen speaking with Ben and walked over to them.

"Can I talk to you a minute, Owe?"

He nodded toward me and looked at Ben. "Just think about it. You've got a lot of good ideas, but they'll be difficult to implement without someone with connections to the right people."

Ben looked at me, bouncing from foot to foot. "Owen offered to help me get started."

I frowned. "With what?"

"My ideas. Starting my own research and development company. Take the things I've learned from Crim and help introduce them to the world."

"Oh," I said and frowned, eyeing him. "After we repair the ship, right?"

A little over a day had passed since the attack, or maybe it was two days. It had all passed by in a bit of a blur, and the ship needed a lot of repairs before it could fly. But that didn't account for replenishing the power core, which nothing on Earth could do.

I spotted Thing sulking off to the side and frowned.

"Yes, of course," Ben said. "It all ties together. Owen is going to help secure the materials we need for the repairs."

My lips flattened as I looked at my brother. "You just couldn't resist."

He shrugged. "When opportunity quite literally lands in front of me, I don't hesitate to act. You ought to know that."

I exhaled through my nostrils, considering. Then I looked at Ben. "I want to see any contracts he brings you."

Ben frowned and glanced at Owen for a second. "You don't trust your brother?"

I grinned a little. "Of course, I trust my brother, but I also know the people he works with. Also, if I'm going to invest in this venture of yours, I kinda need to make sure you don't get taken advantage of."

Ben narrowed his gaze. "You'd invest?"

I nodded with a smile. "Yes. I don't need to be involved in day-to-day things, but I'd like some say in the big decisions. However, ultimately this is going to be your venture, kid."

Ben's eyes gleamed and he smiled. "Okay."

I looked at Owen. "Where is Serena?"

Owen frowned. "She didn't tell you?"

"I wouldn't be asking about her if she had."

With everything that had happened there was very little time for anyone to catch their breath. Crim and Jeshi had been able to disable the inhibitor, but it would take time for Serena's brain to heal. Even so, I hadn't thought she'd up and leave without saying goodbye.

"She asked if I could loan her a car so she could go home. She said she wanted to check on her mother."

I felt my eyes stretch wide for a second. "A car? Her mother lives in Seattle, Owe."

He nodded, smiling with half his mouth. "I know. She told me. Don't worry, I didn't loan her a car."

The edges of my lips twitched with relief. "Oh, okay."

"I had one of my jets fly her where she wanted to go," he said, and my shoulders hunched a little. "There'll be a car waiting for her when she lands." He checked his watch. "Oh, she should've landed by now." He reached into his pocket for his phone. I wondered how many backup phones he traveled with. "Yup, got the check-in from my pilot. It's all right, Nate. She'll be in good hands."

She'd left. Serena left and she didn't even say goodbye. I glanced at Thing and rolled my eyes. "Well, now I know why you're sulking over there." I gestured for him to move. "Go on, get moving. This ship isn't going to fix itself, and you're never going to get home if you're always taking breaks."

"Stay on the ship," Thing said.

As it turns out, Thing could speak. I could understand him a little bit, but sometimes he didn't make any sense.

I regarded him for a moment. "Well, if you make yourself useful, then I'll consider letting you stay on the ship."

"I miss Serena," Thing said.

I sighed. "She's only been gone for a few hours. You've got to pull yourself together."

"Uh, Nate," Ben said. I looked at him. "I don't think his perception of time is the same as ours."

My eyebrows pulled together. "Come again?"

"Time. You know how we only think it's a few hours? To him it could be days or weeks. We're not sure about it yet."

I pursed my lips for a second and then walked over to Thing. All of his dark tentacles were droopy like a plant that needed water.

I gave him a companionable pat on the shoulder and leaned toward him. "I get it, big guy. I miss her, too."

I did. The last few days had gone by in a blur, and we hadn't had the chance to really sort anything out. I glanced at my omni-tool, considering sending her a message. Nothing over the top, just a "Hey, I missed you this morning…"

I shook my head and sighed. She needed space, so I'd give her some. I glanced around the hangar bay. I certainly had enough to do.

Over the next several days, we worked on repairing the ship. Crim was able to salvage materials from the Mesakloren combat shuttles. These high-grade materials were much easier to work with than what was available on Earth. Salvaging parts from the shuttle helped with critical systems, but I still needed Owen's help for other things. He assured me that with the price he'd agreed to, the suppliers would look the other way and not ask any questions.

We had the supplies delivered to a remote location in Tennessee, and I flew the hauler to retrieve the materials. To cut down on the risk of alien remains being detected after we eventually left, we burned them. Focused energy beams removed all traces.

Darek helped with the disposal of things we didn't want found, including Kylath's body. Darek would report it to the Tamiran Consortium Military Intelligence in a way that would prevent it from being traced to Earth. I later learned that the blade he'd carried worked by disrupting the field that most nanorobotic particles used in combat armor. It had something to do with manipulating gravity. Kylath's wounds had been severe enough that not even his combat suit's medical countermeasures could have saved his life. The grav blade was extremely dangerous, which was why I kept it locked away.

"You really destroyed the data from Kael Torsin, didn't you," Darek said.

I nodded. "Your superiors will just have to trust me."

Darek nodded. "They will."

"Will they help get the prisoners home?"

The Council for Galactic Harmony worked for peaceful coexistence across the galaxy. They were peacemakers.

"Yes, a ship has been dispatched and will be here in a day or two," Darek said.

Some of the prisoners had helped fight Kael Torsin and his soldiers, but not all of them. They weren't fighters but had been snatched from their homes and enslaved. I'd intended to use the *Spacehog* to take them all home, but the former prisoners needed treatment that wasn't available on the *Spacehog*. I'd asked Darek to convey the request. Their planets were like Earth in that we had an inferior technological base and, I assumed, a healthy suspicion of things they didn't understand. The CGH would help the refugees reacclimate to their home worlds, and I hoped they had better luck than Lanaya. She'd been taken from Earth a long time ago and had no family left. I doubted she'd leave Ben. If anything, the two had become closer.

The *Spacehog* was going to be a shadow of its former self where the crew was concerned.

I looked at Darek. "What are you going to do now?"

He shrugged. "Probably another assignment. I'll oversee the transfer of the refugees."

"And Jeshi?"

He regarded me for a moment. "Jeshi likes your ship. He'd stay if you asked him."

"Crim likes him. Says he's a good engineer. Maybe I will."

Darek eyed me for a second. "Treat him well and he'll be loyal to you. Someone left him on that space station because they didn't know what to do with him."

Jeshi was peculiar but had proven to be a real asset. "I generally try to treat people well, Darek."

He chuckled. "I don't know if Kaz would agree."

I grinned. "Yeah, well, he's different."

"Well, on behalf of the CGH, I thank you for the service you've given."

I stared at him for a second and gave him a wry grin. "Couldn't have done it without you."

As it turned out, the CGH brought a new power core for the ship, and Crim had all but chased me out while it was being installed. The only beings allowed to help with the installation of the new power core were Ben, Jeshi, and Lanaya. I think the CGH engineering team might've been offended. However, when it came to my ship, I'd trust Crim's word over all others.

The CGH team transported the refugees to their ship that was waiting in orbit around the moon. I allowed Thing to stay aboard on a probationary basis. I told him to think of it as an ongoing job interview.

I saw Kaz speaking with my parents, and I couldn't imagine what they could be talking about.

Raylin walked over to me. The sun had dipped below the mountains. With the refugees and Darek gone, there were only a few of us left.

I arched an eyebrow toward her. "Crim's staying here for a while."

Raylin blinked, looking slightly amused. "I know. Did he make it official?"

"Mostly. He wants to help Ben."

Raylin stood next to me with her arms crossed. "What do you plan to do now that the danger has passed?"

I raised my chin toward T'Chura. He was speaking with Thing. They were across the valley, looking like the meeting of two titans.

"T'Chura has to return home. I told him I'd take him."

"And after that?"

I considered it for a few moments and then shrugged. "Something will come up."

She smiled. "You can be sure of that."

"Are you going to stick around?"

She gave me a sympathetic look. "My time on the ship hasn't come to an end yet."

I smiled. "Good. I think Kaz will stick around, too."

"Oh, he's not going anywhere."

My eyebrows raised. "No?"

She shook her head, looking confident.

Kaz joined us and tossed a wave back over his shoulders toward my parents.

"What did you talk about with them?"

"Oh, this and that. I like your parents, Nate."

I glanced at them and then looked at Kaz. "If you were Human, they might adopt you."

Kaz arched an eyebrow. "They asked me to keep an eye on

you."

I frowned. "They? You mean my mother."

He chuckled. "What can I say? Once she learned some of the trouble you'd gotten into, she just about insisted. How could I deny that kind of request?"

I stared at him for a few seconds. Once upon a time I'd been his prisoner. "What about your ship?"

"It's not going anywhere, and besides, I like the *Spacehog*."

"She's a good ship."

Kaz nodded. "Indeed."

I left them and walked over to my parents.

"It's almost time, isn't it, son?" my father said.

I nodded. "Getting that way."

My mother eyed me. "Have you spoken to Serena?"

I clenched my jaw a little. "She wanted space, so I'm giving her space." They both stared at me, and after a few seconds I decided to deflect. "Are you sure you're okay with Ben and Crim staying here for a while?"

"Of course," my father said. "They've already set up shop in the east storage shed." The storage shed on their property was akin to a warehouse that could double as a hangar. "Owen is making arrangements for a better facility," he continued.

"Yes, he said he'd have some options for Ben to consider. We'll help him however we can," my mother said. She eyed me for a few seconds. "Are you okay, Nate?"

I nodded. "Of course, I am."

She arched an eyebrow and glanced at my father.

"It won't be like before. You'll be able to contact me through the comlink Crim set you up with," I said.

"And you better answer when I call you," my mother warned.

I grinned. "Always, Mom," I said and gave her a hug.

My father came over and gave me a hug. As he started to

walk away, he stopped, eyeing me for a second. "You'll never know the answer if you don't ask."

I nodded. "Don't let Crim scare you off. He loves answering questions."

"That reminds me, there are a few things I wanted to pick his brain about," he said.

We walked over to the ship. A ring of lights blazed from the top as Crim and the others walked down the loading ramp.

"Looks like the power core is working," I said.

Crim nodded. "Passed all the checks. I've given Jeshi an extensive list of maintenance tasks."

"I can't believe you're leaving me in his hands. I thought you were my friend."

Crim frowned for a second and then laughed. "I'll miss you, too, Nate. Besides, this is temporary. It'll only be for a decade or two. Then, who knows?"

I blinked. "Decades?"

Crim nodded and gestured around the area. "This whole world is going to change."

I stared at him for a moment. "I'm going to miss the battlewagon."

His expression sobered. "As will I, but I can make some recommendations for a replacement vehicle."

"I'm sure you can," I said and glanced at Ben. He stood nearby, speaking with Kaz. "Take care of him."

Crim nodded. "I will."

"If you leave anything on the ship, I'll give you reasonable storage rates for keeping it there."

Crim rolled his eyes and chuckled, then went to speak with T'Chura.

Ben came over to me. "I'll have a proposal for you to review next week."

I frowned. "Next week?"

"Yeah, Nate. It's been years since I've seen a beach. I'm taking Lanaya on vacation while the facility that Owen is procuring is getting squared away."

I arched an eyebrow. "Only one week?"

Ben frowned. "Should it be longer?"

"How about a month, kid."

He grinned.

"Oh, I have a few recommendations. There are some great islands on the pacific that you'd like…"

After all the goodbyes were done, I walked up the loading ramp with T'Chura.

As the hangar bay doors closed, he eyed me. "You're pretty quiet all the sudden."

I bobbed my head once. "You know how it is. It's all changing. Some people are moving on while others are staying."

We left the hangar and walked down the corridor. The ship felt different, almost hollow.

"Others will come, and old friends will eventually return. That is the way of things," T'Chura said.

I arched an eyebrow toward him. "I promised to take you home. Maybe there will be someone there looking for work."

T'Chura narrowed his gaze. "What kind of work?"

I shrugged. "I don't know. It's a big galaxy out there. Who knows what we'll find?"

He nodded slowly and a comlink chimed from his omnitool. He raised his wrist and frowned. "Raylin needs me. I'll join you on the bridge later."

I nodded and walked down the corridor. I passed by the commons area and glanced inside. It was empty, so I continued on to the elevator and went to the bridge.

Kierenbot stood outside. He waved toward me.

"Where are you going?" I asked.

"I need to check on one of the maintenance hatches. It's throwing an error. Not to worry. I'll take care of it, Captain."

"I'll go with you."

"Not necessary. It won't take long," Kierenbot said and entered the elevator.

I continued to the bridge and went inside.

As I stood near the doorway, I looked around, remembering so many things that had happened there. I peered from the different workstations along the side to where the escape pod was hidden. A lot of memories swirled up in my mind all at once. I don't know what it was about the empty bridge that made me feel so nostalgic.

I walked toward the central workstation and brought up the navigation system. A holoscreen came on and I stared at the options. Kierenbot already had T'Chura's home world programmed in. We just needed to leave.

I brought up a map of the United States and my gaze settled on the west coast. As I set a course for Seattle where Serena was, I heard the door dematerialize behind me.

"Is the hatch fixed?" I asked as I turned around.

Serena stood there. She wore dark jeans and a cream-colored sweater. We stared at each other. Despite staying as busy as possible, I'd imagined what I was going to say to her, but it all fled my mind.

Serena glanced at the holoscreen and then at me. "Going somewhere?"

"Actually, I was just about to come find you."

A small smile teased the edges of her lips. "Really?"

I nodded and stepped toward her. "I've been doing that a lot lately."

She winced a little, her gaze lowering toward my chest. "Nate," she said quietly.

I lifted her chin and she looked at me. "I wanted to ask you something."

Her honey-brown eyes lured me in, and she pushed her long brown hair behind her ear. "I actually came back here to ask *you* something."

I chuckled and then smiled with half my mouth. "So, who goes first?"

She arched an eyebrow. "Typically, you'd let me go first."

"Well, I *am* a gentleman."

Serena grinned and shook her head. "No, you're not."

I shrugged. "Sometimes."

Her eyebrows gathered and she swallowed hard. "I'm sorry I left the way I did, Nate. I had to get away, but I should've told you first. That wasn't right."

I stared at her for a moment. "I wish you had. I've almost called you about a hundred times since you left."

She lowered her gaze and tilted her head a little, swallowing hard. "Me too." She inhaled a deep breath. "Nate, I'm sorry that you had to…that you almost died. And your family almost…"

"Kael Torsin hurt my family, you didn't."

She still wouldn't look at me. "I can't help thinking that this is my fault."

"It's not. It's not your fault. He was always going to come after them."

She closed her eyes. "But you almost died to save me, Nate." She lifted her gaze and stared into my eyes. "I should have…I should have waited like you asked me to."

I regarded her for a long moment. "I should've gone with you."

The edges of her lips lifted, and I felt heat rush to my face.

"Do you want to go for a ride?"

She smiled and clasped her hands behind my neck, lifting her mouth toward mine. "I thought you'd never ask."

# AUTHOR NOTE

Thank you so much for reading. I hope you enjoyed the book and the series. *Space Raiders Dark Menace* is the third book in the series. I enjoy writing the stories that I write and this book was no different. The characters and their interactions are what invest me in the story and what I look for when I read books.

I sincerely hope you enjoyed this book, and if you could help spread the word about it, I would be grateful. Reviews, ratings, and recommendations are ways to help.

Thanks again for reading my books. Please consider leaving a review for *Space Raiders - Dark Menace*

**If you're looking for another series to read check out one of the following:**

**First Colony Series:** The Ark – humanity's valiant effort to reach beyond the confines of our solar system to establish the first interstellar colony on a distant star. For three hundred thousand colonists, the new colony brings the promise of a fresh start…a second chance. Escaping wrongful imprisonment wasn't something Connor had in mind, but being put into stasis aboard Earth's first interstellar colony ship was something he couldn't have prepared for. Connor might be the wrong man for the colony, but he's the right man to see that it survives what's coming.

**Federation Chronicles:** First came the development of a Personality Matrix Construct—PMC, transferring human consciousness into a machine. It changed the galaxy and the way wars were fought. Then something went wrong with PMCs and the Federation Wars toppled the galactic order. PMCs became a menace to be hunted and exterminated. Long after the Federation Wars, the galaxy limps on. Spacers carve out an existence upon the bones of the old worlds, but things are about to change. . .something has begun broadcasting signals to reactivate PMCs that were stored in secret.

**Ascension Series:** Join the crew of the spaceship Athena on an epic journey. Kept secret for 60 years, the discovery of an alien signal forces a NASA pilot and computer hacker to team up to investigate an alien structure discovered in the furthest reaches of the solar system.

# ABOUT THE AUTHOR

I've written multiple science fiction and fantasy series. Books have been my way to escape everyday life since I was a teenager to my current ripe old(?) age. What started out as a love of stories has turned into a full-blown passion for writing them.

Overall, I'm just a fan of really good stories regardless of genre. I love the heroic tales, redemption stories, the last stand, or just a good old fashion adventure. Those are the types of stories I like to write. Stories with rich and interesting characters and then I put them into dangerous and sometimes morally gray situations.

My ultimate intent for writing stories is to provide fun escapism for readers. I write stories that I would like to read, and I hope you enjoy them as well.

If you have questions or comments about any of my works I would love to hear from you, even if it's only to drop by to say hello at KenLozito.com

Thanks again for reading *Space Raiders - Dark Menace*

Don't be shy about emails, I love getting them, and try to respond to everyone.

# ALSO BY KEN LOZITO

Acheron Salvation

Acheron Redemption

Acheron Rising (Prequel Novella)

**Ascension Series**

Star Shroud

Star Divide

Star Alliance

Infinity's Edge

Rising Force

Ascension

**Safanarion Order Series**

Road to Shandara

Echoes of a Gloried Past

Amidst the Rising Shadows

Heir of Shandara

If you would like to be notified when my next book is released visit kenlozito.com